BEST SERVED COLD

A Milt Kovak mystery

Susan Rogers Cooper

This first world edition published 2016
in Great Britain and the USA by
SEVERN HOUSE PUBLISHERS LTD of
19 Cedar Road, Sutton, Surrey, England, SM2 5DA

Trade paperback edition first published 2017
In Great Britain and the USA by
SEVERN HOUSE PUBLISHERS LTD
Eardley House, 4 Uxbridge Street, London W8 7SY

British Library Cataloguing in Publication Data
A CIP catalogue record for this title is available from the British Library.

ISBN-13: 978-0-7278-8669-9 (cased)
ISBN-13: 978-1-84751-772-2 (trade paper)
ISBN-13: 978-1-78010-839-1 (e-book)

BEST SERVED COLD

ONE

My name is Milt Kovak and I'm the sheriff of Prophesy County, Oklahoma, the county seat of which is Longbranch, Oklahoma. I was born and bred in Longbranch, and went to high school here, where I played an OK kind of football. I joined the Air Force when I was eighteen and somehow missed being sent to Vietnam. Which was OK by me. After my three-year stint, I came back to Longbranch, married my high-school sweetheart and went to work for her brother at his used-car lot. I was in my early thirties when it dawned on me that I didn't just hate trying to sell used cars: I hated my brother-in-law. That's when my daddy's friend, Sheriff Elberry Blankenship, suggested I try going to the police academy then come back home and be a deputy. Figuring that was a right fine idea, I did just that. The wife was belly-aching the whole time, saying I was leaving her brother in the lurch, I wouldn't be making squat as a deputy and how did I think I was gonna support her on that piddling salary. A few years later, with me not only a deputy but being promoted to chief deputy and the money raise that came with it (it too was a mite piddling, but a raise is a raise), I discovered just by accident that my wife had left me. It had been a couple of days, but she was a mostly quiet woman.

When Sheriff Blankenship retired, I was acting sheriff then ran for and won my first election. I've been running unopposed ever since. I doubt that has anything to do with the fact that the guy who ran against me in my first election was murdered. I didn't do it, of course.

Things went on, as things do, and I bought me a beautiful house on top of a mountain – or what we refer to as a mountain in Oklahoma – and then my sister, Jewel Anne, got in trouble down in Houston and I ended up bringing her and her three children back to Prophesy County to live with me in my beautiful house. The absolute longest year of my life.

Happenstance being what it is, Jewel Anne met up with an old boyfriend about the same time I met a lady, a Yankee from

Chicago – a psychiatrist named Jean McDonnell. And she just happened to be the love of my life. Still is, now that I mention it. We've got a son, Johnny Mac, who's twelve years old. Things were going great with me and Jean having to deal with my sister and her husband on about a monthly basis, which worked out well, until we had a tornado a couple of months back that blew Jewel's house away. Now her and Harmon, her husband, are *temporarily* living at my house.

Which leads me to the fact that I've got good news and bad news. That's a lie. I only have bad news. Billy Molini, the plumbing contractor from Oklahoma City who built the mountain chateau thingy down the road from me, died. That's not the bad news. Well, it's bad news for his fifth wife (or maybe not – he was pretty rich and she was pretty young). The mountain chateau thingy went on the market. That's not the bad news either. The bad news is that Jewel Anne and Harmon bought the damned thing. Now she's gonna live permanently less than an eighth of a mile from my house. An eighth of a frigging mile.

A while back, we had this big ass tornado up in Bishop, the north part of the county where the rich folk live, and Jewel Anne and Harmon's house flew off to Oz. Of course, they were insured down to her Jimmy Choos (those are shoes, my wife tells me), so Jewel Anne has been as happy as a pig in slop going on shopping trips to Tulsa, Oklahoma City, even Dallas.

And, meanwhile, they're staying at my house until she gets the damn chateau decorated. I've seen my sister's decorating skills and that could take a year or two (she tends to change her mind a lot). But even her decorating skills are better than her culinary ones. And for some reason she decided the only way to pay us back for our hospitality was to do all the cooking. And I mean *all* the cooking. So to say I wasn't happy when I pulled into the parking lot of the sheriff's department on Monday morning is, well, putting it mildly. She cooked breakfast. I didn't eat it. I was hungry and I was pissed.

Emmett Hopkins, my head deputy and second in command, met me as I walked in the side door. I didn't even get a chance to get to my office, which was only a few steps away from the door.

'What?' I demanded.

He grinned. 'What'd she fix you for breakfast?'

'Pumpkin pancakes with cranberry syrup.'

His grin got wider. 'Packaged or homemade?'

'Oh, no. Jewel Anne would never use a package. Then her food might be edible. No, no, she made this shit from scratch,' I said.

Unsuccessfully trying to suppress his grin, Emmett patted me on the shoulder and said, 'I'm really sorry.'

'Keep this up and I'll invite you over for dinner. Officially,' I said, frowning.

He handed me a piece of paper rather than responding.

'What's this?' I asked.

'You can still read, can't you? Or did the pumpkin pancakes blind you?'

'Actually it was the cranberry syrup.' My frown deepened as I looked at him. 'People usually put sugar in cranberries, don't they?' I asked.

He snorted in reply as I unfolded the paper. It was short and to the point. The writing said *I'm going to start by killing your entire family.*

I looked up at Emmett. 'Who's this addressed to?' I asked.

He shrugged. 'Didn't say. Holly found it taped to the front door when she went to unlock it a while ago. Brought it to me as you were still home enjoying breakfast.'

'Shut up,' I said, and bent back to the paper. It wasn't handwritten. It was typed, probably on a computer and printed on a printer. Sure wasn't a typewriter. Which was too bad. Used to be you could maybe find the typewriter somebody used by the smudges and hiccups and such. But printers are printers and they don't much vary. At least not in my experience. 'Did you check it for prints?' I asked.

Emmett gave me a raised eyebrow. 'How long have I been doing this, Milt? Of course I checked it for prints. There's just Holly's.'

I walked with the paper in my hand into the reception area. The way the department is set up, you come in the double glass doors in the front into the reception area and up to the front counter where Holly Humphries (now Pettigrew), our civilian clerk, sits. Behind her is the bullpen where the deputies hang out when they're not out catching speeders and other ne'er-do-wells. As you come in, off to the right is the hall that leads to Emmett's office, then my office, then the door to where department personnel park. Across from both Emmett's office and my office is a great big room where we keep evidence and the Xerox machine, office supplies and other stuff. To the left of the bullpen is the break room, the interrogation room and a door that leads to our two jail cells. I walked straight to the double doors that led to the public parking lot.

'Where was the note?' I asked.

Holly came up behind me. 'Right there,' she said, pointing to the center of one of the doors, about a foot above her head.

Turning to Emmett, I said, 'Don't get your panties in a twist, but did you—'

'Dust for prints? Yes,' he said.

'And?'

He shook his head.

I opened the door and used the door stopper on the bottom to keep it open. 'Show me again,' I said to Holly.

She pointed. Looking close, I could see a small smudge that might have come from Scotch tape. 'It was taped up there?'

'Yes, sir,' she said.

'Like Scotch tape, masking tape . . .'

She shrugged. 'Like Scotch tape,' she said.

I looked at the point where the little bit of adhesive residue still clung. It was about forehead height on me. 'Come here, Emmett,' I said, and he did. 'Stand there.' He did. The residue hit him at about chin level. 'If you were gonna tape a note so somebody would see it right away,' I asked Emmett, 'at what height would you tape it?'

He looked at me and frowned. Then he grinned. 'Eye level,' he said.

'Exactly,' I said. Turning to Holly, I asked, 'You got a measuring tape?'

She ran back to her desk and came back with one. 'How tall are you, Emmett?' I asked.

'Six foot one inch,' he said.

'Yeah, and I'm five foot ten,' I said. 'Which would make our note-writer . . .'

'About five eleven and a half,' Emmett said when we got through measuring.

We grinned at each other, then I sobered. 'How many five-eleven-and-a-half-foot people you think there are in Prophesy County?' I asked.

'We talking just men?' Emmett asked.

'I don't know why we would. My own wife's five eleven. Not that she wrote the note . . .'

'Of course not!' Holly said.

Emmett said, 'No way.'

'But that leaves us with men and women and anybody on the high-school basketball teams. Boys or girls,' I said.

'But who was the note to?' Holly asked.

And I thought, yeah, now that's the $64,000 question all right. Who's family's fixing to die?

We had to put the note on the backburner as we had a wreck in the northern part of the county and a fist fight at Buddy's pool hall. Well, not so much fists as pool cues, but nobody was dead, which was a good thing. Dalton, another deputy, took the pool hall as he's big enough to have a sobering effect on miscreants, while our newest deputy, Anna Alvarez, took the wreck.

We had an opening when my newest up till then deputy, Nita Skitteridge, had a second baby and decided to try out being a stay-at-home mom. Nita is one of my other deputies, Anthony Dobbins' cousin, so my second African-American hire, and I hated to lose her but, and don't tell anybody I said this, hiring Anna with her surname got me in good on statistics. That's just a fact, plain and simple.

Anna Alvarez is a seriously pretty young lady, but that had much less to do with the hire than some people might think. She had a real impressive résumé. She was a former sergeant with the Laredo, Texas PD, and had seen plenty of action down there on the border. She said she'd had enough of that kind of drama and wanted something a little more peaceful. Mostly I thought she was right in choosing Prophesy County.

I was a little taken aback, however, when I got a call asking for back-up at the wreck on the north end of Highway Five. The caller was a passer-by who said my deputy was throwing up on the side of the road. I thought for a minute that somebody who'd seen so much action on the Mexican border wouldn't be that prone to puking, but then found out the lone passenger in the Volkswagen-eighteen wheeler confab had been decapitated. I sent Anthony out to back her up.

Dalton came in a few minutes later with the yahoos from Buddy's pool hall. They were both cuffed but Dalton had 'em both by the shirt collars, one on each side as he dragged them in. I came out to meet him.

'Hey, fellas,' I said.

'I'm gonna kill him!' said the one on the right, a ginger straining against Dalton's pull on his collar, which got him to choking and coughing.

'Not if I kill you first!' the one on the left, a Choctaw, said, which got him to choking and coughing also.

'Dalton, why don't you take these boys into the interrogation room? See if you can't fix it so they can't get at each other.'

'Sure, Sheriff,' Dalton said, and dragged the two off.

We have a metal ring under the interrogation room table that we sometimes cuff rowdy guests to, but we only had the one. Dalton's not the brightest crayon in our box but I figured he'd find some way to detain the other.

I was right. When I walked into the interrogation room, one of 'em was cuffed to the metal ring but the other Dalton had cuffed to the handle of the door on the inside. Dalton himself was resting a hip on the table where he could keep an eye on both of 'em.

I got in there, started talking to 'em and found out what all the yelling was about. Not so unusual: it was a girl. Excuse me, woman. Seemed her name was Honey and she was the ginger's sister. And the ginger didn't much care for Honey to be dating a Choctaw – prejudices come in all shapes, colors and sizes. So the two met at Buddy's by accident, said a few words and pool cues were brought into it. I wrote it up and stuck 'em both in the cells to let 'em cool off. But since the cells were right next to each other – and we only have the two – I was afraid they might try choking each other through the bars. I sent Dalton in to watch 'em, and told 'em if they behaved themselves I might let them out before dark.

The long and the short of it was they did, so I did.

The next morning, after I got in my office, I realized I'd left the notes I'd taken the day before with the ginger and the Choctaw in the interrogation room. I buzzed Holly on the intercom and asked her to get 'em for me.

It wasn't but a few minutes later that I heard a bloodcurdling scream that brought me, Emmett and Dalton on the run. We stopped dead in our tracks when we saw into the interrogation room. Holly had stopped screaming but she was standing stock-still with her hands over her mouth, whimpering, her eyes glued to something above her head. Hanging from the overhead light was a dead baby. Not a real dead baby, but one of those nasty things they sell at Halloween – supposed to be a zombie baby, I think. Last year me and the wife took our son, Johnny Mac, to a Halloween store in Tulsa. He saw one of those and wanted to buy it but Jean said no, although I thought it was kinda cool. Seeing this one hanging there in my interrogation room, it no longer seemed that cool.

Dalton grabbed his wife and pulled her to him. 'Who did this?' he demanded, looking at me and Emmett. And I was just damn glad it wasn't either of us who'd done it. Dalton Pettigrew may be a little slow and he hasn't got a mean bone in his body – which can't be said for all cops – but, by the look on his face, I could tell Dalton was making plans to ensure the asshole who hung that zombie baby would be regretting it real fast.

'Holly, come on now. It's just one of those stupid Halloween zombie babies. You see 'em all the time,' I said. 'Let's get you out of here—'

'Dammit, Milt!' Dalton said, his voice kinda scary sounding. 'She's pregnant.'

'Dalton, no!' Holly said between sobs. 'We said we'd wait—'

'Come on, baby,' Dalton cooed. 'Let's go.'

I let Holly go for the day and Dalton drove her to his mama's house. Old Miz Pettigrew had totally gotten over the fact that Holly, with all her tattoos and piercings, wasn't the girl she'd dreamed of for her son. The pregnancy had totally changed that. Up until the zombie baby hanging, Miz Pettigrew was the only one – other than Holly, Dalton and the doctor – who knew. Now we all did. I couldn't very well *not* call my wife and tell her. Mostly – *mostly* – it was to see if she thought Holly should come in to see her because of the scare and all. My wife, Jean McDonnell, is the one and only – and best – psychiatrist in Prophesy County. OK, part of the reason I called her was just pure gossip. Women don't hold a monopoly on that. Some of the biggest gossips I've ever known have been men.

'She's with Dalton's mom?' Jean asked me on the phone.

'Yeah, that's where he said he was taking her.'

'I'll call over there. See if Holly wants me to drop by. Having her come to my office would seem too official. You know she's my friend, right?'

'Well, yeah, of course,' I said, back-pedaling. 'Makes sense.'

'Thanks for calling me, honey,' she said, and I could hear a smile in her voice.

'You are more than welcome. Wanna do lunch later?' I asked.

'Let me check my schedule and I'll call you back.'

And we left it at that. I have a great wife. She's smart, gorgeous, sexy and cooks a hell of a lot better than my sister. She walks with a brace on one leg and uses a crutch most of the time due to childhood polio. But that doesn't mean she can't move like lightning when she's in the mind to. I call our son Johnny Mac. His full name is John McDonnell Kovak but calling him Johnny Mac is funny, which makes him Johnny Mac Kovak and which the two of us (me and Johnny Mac) think is hysterical, but Jean calls him John. And gives the two of us dirty looks whenever we do the rhyming thing. Which we do a lot.

She called me back a half-hour later. 'I talked to Holly. I'm going by there around eleven. Meet you at the Longbranch at noon?'

I grinned. 'Sounds like a date.'

The Longbranch Inn was in the middle of the downtown square and had been there since just about statehood. It was a hotel with rooms on the second and third floors but mostly it was a restaurant, and one of the best in our part of the state. They make a chicken fried steak with peppered cream gravy that would make you wanna slap your mama. Unfortunately, due to the fact that I had a heart attack a few years back, the kitchen has strict orders not to serve it to me. There's even a new item on the menu called 'The Milt,' which is half a broiled chicken, mixed veggies and boiled new potatoes. No butter. No salt. Or I can have the turkey club, without bacon or mayo. Yeah, I don't go there as much as I used to. There's this Mexican place out on Highway Five where nobody knows my wife . . .

Me and Jean met up at our usual table a little after noon. I ordered 'The Milt,' palmed some salt for later and looked at my wife. 'So how's Holly?'

'She's OK,' Jean said, buttering a roll – right in front of me. She said I needed to be an adult about my restrictions. My response? Neener neener. 'It was a shock at first but she's handling it. With what Holly's been through most of her life, that wasn't as bad as it could have been.' Jean took a bite of the buttery, yeasty roll, chewed, swallowed and said, 'Mostly we talked about the pregnancy. She's seriously excited.'

'How far along?' I asked.

'Twelve weeks. And I understand why they wanted to wait to tell anyone. It's still early.'

'Yeah, but it's great news.'

She smiled and the food came. She'd gotten 'The Milt' too, in solidarity, I suppose (or she could have actually liked it, who knew), and while she was getting her napkin and utensils in line I shook the salt I'd palmed onto as much of my food as I could.

'She also told me about the note she found yesterday. You didn't mention it,' Jean said, finally looking up at me. My face was all innocence.

'Naw, didn't even think about it. But I guess, maybe the two jokes are related? You think?'

'Seems possible,' Jean said. 'Not very funny jokes.'

'No, not very.'

'How did they get in?' she asked me.

Well, she had me there. With all the Holly upset, I hadn't even thought about that. How *had* they gotten in? We don't have a night deputy anymore (county cutbacks several years ago saw to that), but we do have locks and an alarm system. The alarm system didn't go off. But then again, a lot of people in town had the code – me and all my deputies, Holly, and the once-a-month cleaning crew. Which meant a lot more people had access to that code just by knowing any of those people who might have written it down to remember it. I'll admit I've got the code written on a scrap of paper in my wallet. Maybe it was time to call the alarm company and change the damn thing. Hadn't been done since it got put in, over eight years ago. I had a feeling I was just about ready to embarrass myself – at least with my wife.

I sighed. 'Haven't changed the code in a while. Lots of people could have it.'

'About time to change it, I guess,' she said, keeping her eyes on her food.

'Yeah, probably.'

'Have you any idea who's doing this?'

I shook my head. 'Nary a one.' I shrugged. 'Maybe that's it. Whoever did it got a kick out of hearing Holly scream, you know, skulking outside the building, and that'll be the end of it.'

Jean looked at me and raised one eyebrow. I had to agree with her. What I'd just said was a crock.

'So who do you think would wanna kill one of our people's families?' I asked Emmett.

He shrugged. 'Can't think of anyone. I mean, we've put away a few scumbags over the years but offhand nobody comes to mind.'

'Maybe we should check the files to see who'd be pissed enough to do this. Seems like revenge, you think?' And then I had to broach the subject of the alarm code. 'And maybe we should check those files against anybody who might have access to the alarm code. I mean, it didn't go off, did it?'

'Hell, no, it didn't!' Emmett said. 'I never even thought of that.'

We'd been sitting in my office, me behind my desk, him in one of my two visitor chairs. He got up. 'Maybe we should go look at the system.'

'It's just sitting there on the wall, looking fine and dandy,' I said.

'I mean the outside one,' he said.

'What outside one?'

'Where the circuits are,' he said.

I followed as he walked out the door of my office, out the side door to the employee parking lot and around the back where the a/c unit, electrical meters and other maintenance crap was kept. On the back wall, behind the a/c unit, was an outdoor meter box. Emmett opened it up. There were loose wires hanging, their ends obviously cut.

'Well, that solves one mystery,' Emmett said.

'Maybe we should have Holly look into a whole new alarm system. You know, one that can't be hacked from the outside, for Christ's sake.'

'Works for me,' he said as we headed back to my office.

'OK,' Emmett said, 'so we got somebody who knows enough about antiquated alarm systems to hack ours, but why? What would be the gain? Revenge?'

'Blackmail? Extortion of some kind? "Pay me X amount of dollars and I won't kill your family"? That sort of thing?'

'Don't make sense.'

I had to agree. 'Then revenge. But for what?'

'For putting 'em away, probably. We put a lot of assholes away.'

'And we've killed a few, too,' I said, thinking about it. 'It may not be someone we put away but kinfolk of somebody killed in the line?'

'We need to look at the records,' Emmett said.

'They're on the computer,' I said.

We both stared at each other. 'When's Holly coming back?' Emmett asked.

'Sooner rather than later,' I said, picking up my phone to dial Dalton's mama's house. Holly was our computer person. As in practically the only one in the office who knew how to turn it on, much less find something on it. And while she was here, she could call a few alarm companies.

Turned out a new, updated alarm system was going to cost an arm and a leg, and I knew without asking that the county commissioners were going to say *nada, nein,* no way. Repairs to the existing one were steep enough but the alarm guy said our insurance should cover it. I asked if we could get the meter box moved inside the building rather than outside, but the guy said he doubted it. Then he suggested we get a state-of-the-art lock on the meter box, which he'd be happy to add to the final bill. I thought I'd have Holly look into the insurance aspect and see if we could add that state-of-the-art lock.

As far as the revenge scenario went, there were seventeen cases in the last five years where somebody could be pissed off enough. You know, sometimes it doesn't take much: 'You looked at my girlfriend crooked, prepare to die.' That kind of thing. Of those seventeen cases, two of the ones we'd sent up were dead of natural causes with no kin who'd care, one moved out of state, and four were still in prison. Which left ten. Who doesn't like a nice round number?

Of that ten, seven were dead either by the hand of law enforcement or due to circumstances surrounding the arrest. Of those seven, two were vagrants without known family, one was an idiot who'd blown up his own meth lab when we arrived to arrest him (there'd been a girlfriend there, but other than that, no family), and two were brothers who'd drowned when they jumped off the top of Mountain Falls in an attempt to evade capture. Which was a shame, since their crime had been more like a misdemeanor than anything serious. When I informed their father of their deaths he'd just shrugged and said, 'They both took after their mother. Stupid as a bag of rocks,' and closed the door in my face. The county had ended up footing the bill for their burial.

The last two were a little more serious – although I'm not saying the other deaths weren't serious; there's not much more serious than death. The first one was a guy beating his wife. Dalton handled that one. Domestics are always a bitch but this one was even more so. The girl'd been beaten pretty bad, lying in a pool of blood on the floor of their double-wide, and the husband was standing over her with a gun pointed at her head when Dalton walked up. Dalton drew his weapon, announced himself and the husband swung the gun up and out at Dalton. Dalton fired. End of story. Except his two brothers – even meaner than the husband – took umbrage and tried to come after Dalton. They ended up hospitalized and soon after became guests of the penal system. Those two went on my list. They'd been out for a while now.

Then there was Maudeen Sanders. Nice woman – Sunday-school teacher at the Methodist church. Husband was a long-haul trucker, died in a wreck up north some place, leaving her with a six-year-old child. Maudeen remarried when the girl was twelve to a guy named Wharton Jacobs, who was a pretty-boy who didn't do much of anything except live off his various and sundry wives. He'd had four by the time he married Maudeen, who, let's face it, should have known better, but, like they say, the heart wants what the heart wants.

Problem was Maudeen came home early from her shift at the Piggly Wiggly to find Wharton messing with her twelve-year-old daughter. So, being a reasonable woman, she shot him. Judge Norman, seeing that she'd spent the night in lock-up, gave her time served and sent her home. Unfortunately, old Wharton got out of the hospital and attempted to go back to the same house. Maudeen shot him in the head when he walked in the door. This time Judge Norman had to get serious and gave her ten years. Her daughter, Lynette, fought tooth and nail for her mom, with the help of her mom's brother and his wife. Could they all still be pissed at the sheriff's department? And, I had to wonder, did old Wharton have anybody left who cared that he'd got shot? But why would they come after us? We didn't shoot him.

That left three. There were those two rednecks who held up Smithy's gas station and pistol-whipped the attendant because he didn't have the key to the safe. One rolled on the other and got two years while his partner got fifteen for assault, battery and armed robbery. The one who got two years got out six months ago. I had to wonder what he'd been up to. Was he still in the county? But why would he be pissed enough to want revenge on the sheriff's office? I'd have to look into that.

Then we had two families, one with reason enough to seek revenge if they'd a mind to. There was this wreck on the highway that caused some serious road rage. One guy in an F150 pick-up and another in a Ford minivan. The guy in the F150 had his wife and two sons in the truck with him. The guy in the Ford minivan had his wife, two daughters, a son and a golden retriever in his. Both guys jumped out of their vehicles but the F150 guy had a revolver and shot the minivan guy before he could say boo. Minivan guy was dead at the scene and we had screaming wives and children on both sides, a dog barking its fool head off and the F150 guy being handcuffed by Anthony Dobbins. While Anthony was busy with the F150 guy, the two wives started in on each other, screaming, hair-pulling, eye-gouging, what have you. Anthony called for back-up. By the time Jasmine Hopkins and Dalton Pettigrew got there the F150 guy's two sons were beating up on the dead minivan guy's one son, while the dead minivan guy's two daughters were jumping on the backs of the F150 guy's sons. Everybody was screaming at everybody and the dog, for some reason, was trying to tear a hole in Anthony Dobbins' uniform. Eventually the F150 guy got fifteen years but unfortunately was killed in prison two years in. The wife of the F150 fella tried to sue the sheriff's department and the county but it didn't work. But both families still live in the county and I understand there's still bad feelings there – at each other and probably at us too, at least by the family of the F150 guy.

The other serious consideration was a home invasion robbery. John and Reba Connors – he was a bailiff for the county court and she was the county clerk. Reba was in the bedroom of their home when she heard a commotion in the living room. She peeked in and saw two guys holding a gun on John. She snuck back into the bedroom and called the sheriff's department. The invaders must've heard her on the phone because they found her and dragged her back into the living room, where they raped her in front of her husband. Anthony Dobbins, who was newly back to Prophesy County at that time, got lost and took too long to get to the Connors' home. The bad guys were gone before he got there. John had been pistol-whipped, mostly about the head, and Reba was in a pretty bad shape. They both quit their jobs and have been trying to sue the county and us ever since. It's not going well for them and I've had a few drunken late-night calls from John Connors. And we never found the bad guys. John Connors was definitely a possibility.

I set Holly up to dig deeper into those at the top of my list – the brothers of the dead wife-beater, Maudeen Sanders' relatives, the redneck who only got two years when he rolled on his partner, the families of the road-rage victims and John and Reba Connors. Holly was real good on computers and I knew if there was anything to find, she'd find it. Meanwhile, I had other things to consider: like filling out a hundred and eleven forms for the county, state and feds, getting the paperwork ready for Anthony Dobbins' review due the end of the month and finding a nice place to take my wife for our anniversary, which was coming up sooner than Anthony's review. I had my eye on this necklace with three little diamonds I'd found at Murray's Jewelry & More, which I thought nicely represented our little family of three. Now I had to come up with a good place to take her to dinner, and I'd be damned if it was gonna be the Longbranch Inn.

Later that evening, my sister, Jewel Anne, believe it or not, came to my rescue as far as a place to take my wife for our anniversary.

'I have an idea,' she said, sneaking into my little office off the kitchen.

'I'm not interested in dessert,' I said, a little terrified of what might be coming.

'No, not that, silly. Besides, there's homemade rhubarb ice cream in the freezer if you need something sweet. No, I'm talking about where to take Jean for y'alls anniversary.'

If I could, I would have raised an eyebrow. Instead, I just said, 'Oh, yeah?'

'Yeah. Your anniversary's on Saturday, so why don't you take Jean to Oklahoma City for the weekend? Harmon and I will keep an eye on John and the house. And,' she said, grinning wide, 'I have a fifty-percent-off coupon for that steakhouse downtown.'

'No shit?' I said, staring at her. 'You'd do that?'

She kissed me on the cheek. 'It's the least I can do for all y'all have done for us, big brother.' She whipped the fifty percent steakhouse coupon out of her pocket and handed it to me. 'I would suggest the Regents Hotel. It's very nice. And I hear they give an AARP discount, you old coot.' And with that last parting shot, she left. Being an old coot did have its advantages.

So it was all set. We would leave Friday after work for Oklahoma City. We had a suite at the Regents Hotel, with a nice AARP discount. We'd have room service for dinner, then spend Saturday shopping the antiques stores, with reservations for dinner at the Sooner Steakhouse that evening, which was within walking distance of the hotel.

For early March, the weather had been pretty good, and everything went according to plan. Our suite was a nice enough place, with a small living room leading into a small bedroom, and a small bathroom attached. The operative word here being small. But it was big enough for me and Jean. It had a large-screen TV and a small balcony that looked out over downtown Oklahoma City, which looks real good at night. We checked out the room-service menu and ordered a meal we agreed to share, a chocolate lava cake with vanilla ice cream (which my wife insisted we'd only get if we shared it too – sometimes this diet thing sucks), and a couple of alcoholic drinks. Me and Jean weren't big drinkers but it was our anniversary and we both figured a little booze was in order.

We were in a good mood all that Friday night, talking and watching an almost-new movie on the hotel's pay-per-view. After a little love making, we went to sleep and had room-service coffee and pastries the next morning. The weekend would have worked out great if I hadn't gotten a call from Emmett around noon on Saturday.

'Milt,' he said.

'Emmett,' I said.

'Got a problem.'

'I'm on vacation.'

'Anthony's wife Maryanne just had a wreck on Chapel Road. Brakes went out.'

'She OK? Was the baby with her?' I asked.

'Yeah, on both counts. But the thing is, Milt,' Emmett said, 'the guy at the repair shop says the brake lines were definitely cut.'

'What the hell?'

'I'm wondering if it might be Anthony's family that note was all about?'

TWO

I gave Jean the option of staying in the city and having our steakhouse dinner or going home. She opted for going home, which was mostly OK with me. I mean, I'd been looking forward to a good porterhouse with maybe some creamed spinach and the apple tart for dessert (I'd had Holly look up their menu for me online and figured I could get away with those things without Jean hollering too much about it), but being home to support Anthony and his family seemed like the right thing to do. Before we packed up to go, I sat Jean down on the little sofa in the little living room and handed her a black gift box with a big red ribbon and bow on it.

She gave me that raised eyebrow. 'What's this?'

'A present,' I said.

'I thought we weren't going to do that,' she said.

I shrugged. 'I forgot.'

She grinned at me. 'Like hell you did.'

I grinned back. 'Open it,' I said.

She tore off the ribbon and bow and opened the jewelry box. And there was the necklace – all three diamonds shimmering and shiny from the overhead light.

She looked up at me. 'It's beautiful,' she said.

'Let me put it on you,' I said, taking it out of the box. She turned so that I could put it around her neck and clasp it at the back. When she turned back around, I had to admit I'd done good. Real good.

She got up and moved to the little mirror over the little desk in our little living room. And for some reason or other we were a little later than we'd planned leaving that little hotel suite.

It was slow going getting back to Prophesy County. An eighteen-wheeler had jack-knifed across the highway, probably from a patch of ice still around in a shady spot, and, although nobody hit the truck, a couple of cars had ended up in the median and one in a ditch on the other side. I only saw this when I got out of my Jeep and walked half a mile to see what the hold-up was. Being a peace officer, it's kind of my job to check these things out. But the highway patrol was already there and everything seemed to be under control. It still took another half hour before we started moving again – slow as hell though because of everybody wanting to look at where the wreck *used* to be. Never could figure that out. Bad enough having rubberneckers checking out carnage moved to the side of the road – hoping, I guess, to see a little blood. But it seems there's a memory to a wreck, and somehow the site of one just stands out, whether there's blood or wreckage or not. Just one of those funny things.

But we finally got back on the road headed to Anthony's house. Him and Maryanne, his wife, had been trying for several years to have a baby, but she kept miscarrying around the third month. Even though she was three months along when she and my wife and most of the women I know got held hostage a while back, she was able to bring this one to term and it was a beautiful little baby girl. They named her Melinda Janell and she was a hoot and a half. But she was OK and her mama was OK, and that's all that really mattered.

Except finding out who the hell had it in for my staff. I mean, silly notes and zombie babies hanging from light fixtures is one thing but cutting the brake lines in a loved one's car was something else again. If it had been someone doing that to Jean, with or without Johnny Mac in the car, I'd want his head on a pike. I had a feeling Anthony's sentiments might be along those same lines.

I was right. We drove straight from Oklahoma City to the Dobbins' house on French Street, a nice eighties ranch with a well-kept yard with mature trees, the house white brick with green shutters and trim. Anthony's personal ride, a nineties Ram pick-up, was in the driveway, along with a couple of cars I didn't recognize and one I knew: Emmett's personal vehicle, a Toyota Land Cruiser. There was also a squad car which had the number of the one usually issued to Dalton Pettigrew. I had to wonder who was watching the shop.

Me and Jean got out of the car and went up the steps to the front door. I'd barely knocked before it was quickly opened. A black man stood in front of me, scowling. I held out my hand. 'Mr Carmichael,' I said, recognizing Maryanne Dobbins' daddy.

The scowl loosened and he took my hand and shook it. 'Sheriff. What you doing about this here?' he said.

'Gotta get me some details, Mr Carmichael,' I said. Turning, I indicated Jean. 'You remember my wife?'

He nodded. 'Doctor McDonnell. You might wanna look in on Maryanne. She's not doing too well.'

'Where is she?' Jean asked.

He pointed farther into the house. 'In the baby's room with her mama.'

Jean excused herself and followed his pointing finger. We both knew where the nursery was since we'd been there a couple of times to ogle little Miss Melinda. Jean was older than most first-time mothers when she had Johnny Mac and something had gone wrong, leading to her having to have a hysterectomy. So, both of us liking babies, we had to live vicariously through other people's infants now that Johnny Mac was getting on up there in age.

I followed Mr Carmichael into the house. It was crowded to the hilt. I recognized Anthony's mama in the kitchen with a couple of Anthony's sisters, and Anthony's father was in the living room on the couch next to Anthony, who had his head in his hands and his father's hand on his shoulder. My former deputy, Anthony's cousin, Nita Skitteridge, sat on the other side. I could see her husband across the room, an infant in his arms and a toddler holding on to his leg. My other deputy, Jasmine Bodine Hopkins,

Emmett's wife, stood next to Emmett, trying not to stare at Anthony. I'm thinking that was pretty hard not to do.

'Y'all got Holly holding down the fort?' I asked Emmett quietly.

'No. She's in the baby's room with Maryanne. Anna's at the shop.'

I nodded. We were a small shop – Anna was pretty new but this was necessary. This was family. I moved over in front of Anthony and put a hand on his shoulder. 'Can you tell me what happened?' I asked him.

He looked up at me and, though I was expecting red-rimmed and bloodshot eyes from an emotional day, all I saw was pure-dee mad. 'Some ass-wipe tried to kill my wife and daughter, that's the fuck what happened!'

'Anthony!' called his mama from the kitchen. 'Language!'

'Marguerite, leave the boy alone,' his father said back.

'But they're OK?' I said, squeezing his shoulder while holding out my other hand to Anthony's father. 'Mr Dobbins,' I said, and we shook hands, exchanging worried glances at each other and covert ones at Anthony.

Anthony stood up, moving me back a few steps. 'Yeah. They're alive, if that's what you're asking,' he said, heat in his voice. 'But Maryanne's a basket case and the baby's been crying for hours. The doctor looked at her, said she might have pulled something when Maryanne hit that curb but that he couldn't tell.' He glared at me. 'My three-month-old daughter is in pain, Sheriff, and there's not a goddamn thing I can do about it!'

'Sit back down and give me the details,' I said, putting my hand back on his shoulder. His daddy, standing next to him, did the same, and we encouraged him back onto the couch. Anthony looked a lot like his daddy, tall and thin with mocha-colored skin and no hair. I think it was natural on Mr Dobbins but I knew Anthony kept his shaved.

'She was on her way to the grocery store on Chapel Road, between our house and the Piggly Wiggly. She came to that stop sign on Signet Street, put on the brakes and nothing happened. Thank God there weren't any other cars at the intersection. She wasn't going much more than thirty, so she just ran the car up on the curb across Signet Street and got stopped by the mile post that's right there.'

'How'd you find out about the brake lines?' I asked.

'She called me at home on her cell and I took the Ram over there. We had Guy Bergen bring his tow-truck over and haul her car back to his shop. Didn't take him much more'n a minute to figure out the lines had been cut!'

'Definitely cut?' I asked. 'Maryanne's car's not all that new—'

'Yeah, Sheriff!' he said, standing again. 'The goddamn lines were cut! Deliberately!'

I nodded. 'So you got any suspects?' I asked him.

He sank back down on the couch. 'Nobody I can think of offhand,' he said.

'Well, me and Emmett came up with a possible list last week of people who mighta put that note on the door and that zombie baby in the interrogation room. You and me will go over it more thoroughly on Monday,' I said.

'To hell with Monday!' he said, standing up again. 'I'm ready to go right now!'

'Don't you think Maryanne might need you here?' I asked.

He looked around at the crowded house then down at the Berber carpet of the living room. 'She pretty much ain't speaking to me, Sheriff. She knows this was 'cause of sheriff's business, so it's my fault as far as she's concerned.'

'Now, boy, she never said that—' Anthony's daddy cut in.

'She didn't have to say it, Daddy,' Anthony said. 'I could see it in her eyes. And I know it's true. It's my fault she and Melinda almost got killed.'

I could see tears welling up and knew what I had to do. 'OK, fine,' I said. 'We go to the shop. You and me—'

'And me,' Emmett said.

'—and Emmett, we're going to go through those cases with a fine-tooth comb. We're gonna figure out who done this and we're gonna bury 'em under the jailhouse.'

'Now you're talking,' Anthony said, and headed for the door.

'You're not going anywhere, young man,' his mother said, catching him at the front door. 'Not until you eat something. You haven't had a bite all day.'

'Mama—' Anthony started but Miz Dobbins, a pint-sized woman, dragged him into the dining room.

'All right y'all,' she said, motioning to the rest of the room, 'get in here while everything's still hot.'

The dining table was loaded, buffet-style, with red beans and rice, pork chops, stewed apples, mashed potatoes, green beans with new potatoes and baby onions, a tomato and cucumber salad with blue cheese chunks in a creamy dressing, and corn bread.

Miz Dobbins loaded a plate and handed it to Anthony. 'You take this in to your wife, boy,' she said.

Anthony just stood there with that overflowing plate in his hands. Finally, Jasmine walked up and took it from him. 'I need to say hi to Maryanne and the baby anyhow,' she said. 'Let me take that, Anthony.'

We all filled our plates, me with more than my wife would think was my share, but I'd had Miz Dobbins' cooking before and I wasn't about to pass this up – semi-tragedy or not. Most of us moved into the living room, balancing our plates on our knees, glasses of sweet tea on the floor in front of us. It was quiet while we all stuffed our faces. All of us, except Anthony. I kept peeking at him, just like his daddy, and his mama, and all three of his sisters, and my deputies.

He picked at the food for about half an hour, then said, 'Sheriff, it's about time to go check out that stuff you were talking about?'

I looked at my plate. I hadn't touched the salad yet, but then again, why would I with everything else on my plate? I picked up my glass of sweet tea off the floor and met him and Emmett in the kitchen, where we cleaned off our plates like good boys and put them in the dishwasher. Then we headed out the door.

Holly had done a good job searching the Internet for stuff on our top suspects, so she came with us to the shop to print out what she'd found. John and Reba Connors were still living right outside of Longbranch in the same house that was in our jurisdiction. John got a DUI from the Longbranch police three months ago but he got off with community service. The records showed he missed four of the sixteen hours of community service he was assigned and got an overnight stay in a jail cell to make him rethink his tardy attitude. He finished up his service and, according to the records, hadn't had a problem since then.

'I was the first one on scene at that home invasion,' Anthony said. 'I got mixed up and went to the wrong house.' His voice was low. 'It was a real screw-up. Maybe if I'd gotten there earlier

Miz Connors might not have got raped. I don't know.' He shook his head. 'And I'm real sorry. But that's no reason to kill my wife and baby!'

'No, it's not,' I said, patting him on the arm. 'And we don't know that either of the Connors did this.'

'But I don't know if I was directly involved in any of these others,' Anthony said. 'If the Connors want to blame somebody for what happened, it would have to be me.'

'No, it wouldn't!' Emmett said. 'Who's to blame are the assholes that did it. Not you, not the county, not the department, just the assholes who broke in and did those terrible things!'

'Those assholes we never caught because I was too damned late,' Anthony said.

I had to think if somebody in the Dobbins family needed to talk to my wife it might be more Anthony than Maryanne. He was carrying some heavy guilt – both over what had happened to his wife and child and what had happened to John and Reba Connors. And now the two guilty feelings were warring with each other. I knew it was hard for most men, law enforcement in particular, to talk to an outsider about their problems (or really anybody, for that matter), but maybe a department-mandated couple of sessions might be an idea. It was something I'd discuss later with Jean.

'You were on the scene with that road-rage incident a couple of years ago,' I reminded Anthony.

He nodded. 'Yeah. What were their names?'

'The shooter was Danny Evans and the shootee was Tom Vaught,' Emmett said, reading from the reports Holly had printed out.

'Yeah,' Anthony said. 'I got to that one pretty quick. On the scene within minutes of the shooting.'

'How come so fast?' I asked.

'I was on the highway and saw the wreck. On my way to it I witnessed the shooting.'

'Oh, that's right, you testified at Evans' trial,' I said.

'Yeah. His whole family was there and one of his sons grabbed me on my way out. Said I was a dead man.'

Emmett and I looked at each other, then back at Anthony. 'And you didn't mention this?' I asked.

'Well, he called me a name and I figured he was just a redneck asshole with anger issues.'

'What'd he call you?' Emmett asked.

Anthony shot him a look. 'What do you think? He said, and I quote, "You're one dead nigger."'

'And you decided not to report this because . . .' I said.

'Hell, Sheriff, if I report every time someone calls me a nigger, all I'd be doing most days is paperwork.'

'Yeah, well, not when the word "dead" is in front of it,' I said. 'That's more than just a redneck being a redneck, that's threatening the life of a peace officer.'

Anthony shrugged. 'Yeah. Well. Maybe I should have at that.'

'You ever hear anything else from the Evans family?' I asked.

'Got some hang-up calls for a while after the trial but we changed our number and the calls stopped,' Anthony said.

'And you didn't report this either?' I asked.

'OK, no, I didn't. I screwed up, OK? But I don't think it was the kid.'

'Why not?' I asked.

'Well, I heard he's been working on an oil rig out in west Texas for the last couple of years. Making good money and sending it home to his mama.'

'Where'd you hear this?' I asked.

'Mama's got a friend, a white lady, who goes to church with Miz Evans. She's been keeping Mama up to date on what's been happening with that family.'

'OK,' I said, 'that's two out of our four top ones. The other one, Maudeen Sanders killing her husband, was before your time. Were you in on the interrogation of those two rednecks who held up the liquor store and pistol-whipped the attendant?'

Anthony thought for a minute. 'Jesse Trevino and Hank Witovec, right? Jesse got two years 'cause he rolled on Witovec, right?'

I looked at the printout Holly had given me. I didn't recall any names offhand but Anthony certainly did. 'Yeah. That's them. I was in on the interview, but isn't Witovec still in prison?' Anthony asked.

'He is, but Jesse Trevino got out a while back,' Emmett said.

'Why would he be pissed? I mean, he got off easy. Witovec's the one who'd want revenge,' Anthony said.

'Besides, if I remember right,' I said, 'you were just sitting in.

You'd only been on the job here a little while, right? I did most of the persuading.'

'Just moved back here from Tulsa,' Anthony said. 'I was just observing.'

'So no reason for Trevino to be pissed at you.'

'Or anyone, for that matter,' Emmett said.

'So maybe he got hurt in prison and blames us,' I suggested.

Emmett made a note of that on the pad in front of him. 'I'll have Holly call McAlester,' he said, mentioning the location of the state penitentiary, 'and talk to the warden. See if Trevino got in any bad trouble while he was a guest.'

'Anything else?' Anthony asked.

'Yeah, top of the list are the Permeter brothers. But Dalton was the deputy on that one.'

'The one where he killed the guy who was gonna shoot his wife?' Anthony asked and I nodded my head. 'Before my time.'

'Yeah, but we're gonna look into them just the same.'

'Shouldn't we be concentrating on the Connors' and the Evans' clan?' he said, showing more of the heat I'd seen at his house. 'I mean, Danny, Jr may be out in west Texas but there's another boy. And Miz Evans wasn't exactly nice about any of it.'

'What about Tom Vaught's family?' I asked. 'The guy Evans shot? They still around?'

Both Anthony and Emmett shrugged. 'Don't know,' Emmett said. Anthony followed up with, 'Me neither.'

Emmett wrote on his pad. 'I'll have Holly check that out, too.'

'What'd we ever do before Holly?' I asked the room in general.

'A lot more work,' Emmett said. We all three turned and stared at the young woman at the counter, busily pounding away on her keyboard. 'You know the best thing that ever happened to this department? Other than me joining, I mean.'

I ignored the last comment. 'Gladys retiring?' I said, mentioning the name of the mean old biddy that had been the sheriff's department's civilian clerk for almost thirty years.

'Exactly,' he said, and we both grinned.

Next couple of days we found out a few things, thanks to Holly's expertise with the computer and the telephone. Jesse Trevino, the redneck who held up the liquor store, rolled on his buddy and only got two years, did get hurt while serving his time. Seems he got shanked in the kidney, which necessitated an operation and the removal of said kidney, and which also got him out eight months earlier than his two years. He was living in Longbranch at his mama's house, and pissing in a bag, according to what the warden told Holly when she got a hold of him on Monday.

The younger Evans boy, son of the F150 driver, was named Tyler. He was living in the county and going to the community college in Bishop while working at his daddy's gas station in Longbranch. With the elder Evans dead, seemed the missus and Tyler were running the station. I thought maybe we could have a chat with both Jesse Trevino and Tyler Evans. I took Jesse and Emmett took Tyler.

Jesse's mama's house was a single-wide in a run-down trailer park just inside the city limits of Longbranch. I called the police chief and told him what I was up to, and he sent a uniform over to meet me. Jesse's mama's trailer was the neatest one in the trailer park. Recently painted blue and white, it had a nice little deck on the front with an awning. There was hardware on the awning where hanging baskets of flowers probably hung when it wasn't winter and empty pots for potted plants here and there. There was a bike sitting on the tiny bed of winter-dead grass in the front, with a Barbie hanging from the handle bars. The seat of the bike still had a little snow on it, and the once-bright colors seemed a little dimmed, probably due to sitting out all winter. I walked up the steps of the deck and knocked on the door. When it opened I found myself face-to-face with a girl of about three with thick black hair and the biggest, prettiest, brownest eyes I've ever seen. She stared at me, her mouth turning down at the corners.

'Your mama home?' I asked her.

She shook her head.

'Your daddy?'

She shook her head again.

'Anybody?' I asked.

'Nana,' she said. Looking over her shoulder, she yelled, 'Nana! Man!'

An older woman pushing a walker scurried toward the door. 'How many times I tell you not to open that door, *mija*? How many?'

'Lots,' the little girl said, and turned and walked further into the trailer.

The older woman looked at me. She was wearing something my mama used to call a house dress, something I hadn't seen on a woman in a lot of years. Her once-black hair was thin and graying and she wore heavy support hose on her legs. 'We don't want no trouble,' she said, her hand on the door, ready to close it. Then she saw the uniformed officer at the bottom of the steps. She frowned at me. 'What you want?'

'Jesse home, Miz Trevino?' I asked.

'You leave my Jesse alone!' she said. 'Bad enough he gotta pee-pee in a bag! Now you come 'round here accusing him of God only knows what!'

'Just need to talk to him a minute, ma'am,' I said.

'Get out of here with you—' she started but another voice was heard.

'It's OK, Mama,' Jesse Trevino said as he walked to the door. 'You go take care of Cara. I got this.'

Still glaring at me, his mother said, 'You leave my boy alone!'

'Mama!'

She turned with her walker and headed further into the trailer. Turning to me, Jesse said, 'Sheriff. Long time no see.'

'Been a while, Jesse. You gonna invite me in or you wanna sit out here on the deck?'

He stepped out and closed the trailer door behind him. Seeing him now brought back the incident, and I couldn't help thinking how much the boy had changed in the couple of years since I'd last seen him. His formerly olive complexion was wan, he had bags under his almost-black eyes and lines around his mouth. He was thinner – a lot thinner, like maybe thirty or forty pounds thinner – than he'd been when we'd arrested him. I was thinking prison food and a lost kidney hadn't been kind to the boy. 'Out here would be best,' he said. 'No need for my mama and my niece to hear any of your business.'

'Hear you got yourself hurt while up in McAlester,' I said as I took a seat on the top step of the deck stairs. It wasn't wet, but it was still cold enough for me to think about buying sturdier pants.

Jesse sat down beside me. 'Yeah. Lost a kidney. But that's OK. They tell me you can live with just one.'

'That piss you off?' I asked.

'Well, duh! What d'you think, Sheriff? I said, "Hey, guy, wanna try for the other one?" Yeah, it pissed me off, but I was in no shape to get back at the bastard. I was in the hospital for a couple of weeks. And then they decided to let me out early.' He grinned. 'Almost worth a kidney.'

'You hear anything from Hank Witovec?' I asked.

'Shit, no,' he said, shaking his head. 'He got transferred out of McAlester to some high-security place after he beat up a guard. Hell, that had to be, what? Third or fourth week we were both up there.' Again he shook his head. 'Ol' Hank, he's got a temper on him. Threatened me every time I saw him when he was still at McAlester, but we were in different units so we didn't see each other much, thank God. I think he got a few more years tacked onto his sentence for beating up that guard. God only knows what he's done since he got moved.'

'So you haven't heard from him? Or about him?' I asked.

Again with the shake of the head. 'Naw. And I don't care to. You know what folks always say when their kid gets in trouble? He was hanging with a bad crowd?'

'Yeah,' I said. 'I hear that a lot.'

'Well, in my case it was true. Hank Witovec was a bad crowd all by himself. I never done nothing illegal until that gas station and I ain't done nothing since I got out. So I don't exactly know why you're here, Sheriff.'

'Someone's been messing with my deputies,' I said. 'Silly pranks mostly, but it's been escalating.'

Jesse got wide-eyed, not unlike his little niece. He pointed a finger at his own chest. 'And you think I had something to do with that?' Again with the head shaking. 'No siree-bob. Ain't me. For one thing, I don't get out much, and for another, why would I mess with y'all? You done me a favor, giving me only two years for what me and Hank done. I got no beef with you or any of your deputies.'

I sorta believed him. Of course, he did lose a kidney because he went to prison, me and my staff were the ones who sent him there, and, even if that had been his first and only crime, you learn a lot of bad things in prison. Lying's just the tip of that iceberg.

I stood up. 'Good talking to you, Jesse,' I said. 'But do me a favor: don't leave town without notifying the Longbranch police, or me, or both. OK?'

He pulled himself up from the deck. 'I ain't going nowhere, Sheriff. And believe me, I ain't been messing with you and yours. But if I hear anything, I probably won't let you know.'

Then he grinned real big and went back inside his mama's trailer. I headed back to the shop.

THREE

E mmett wasn't happy. He didn't like any of this and wasn't sure why he and Milt were interviewing these two people. Seemed stupid to think Tyler Evans would want to harm the sheriff's department and even stupider to think Jesse Trevino would want to. But he didn't have any better leads than Milt did. All he knew was that whoever the hell it was better not go messing with him or his or there was gonna be hell to pay. He felt bad for Anthony, he really did, but secretly he was glad it was Anthony's family and not his own. Emmett felt bad for thinking that, but there it was. Truth he'd take to his grave.

It had turned cold overnight, and he was wearing a heavy coat as he got in his car and headed out. He decided to go by the Evans' gas station first, thinking mother or son or both would more than likely be there during the day than at home. It was your typical fifties Gulf station: six pumps, two bays, outside toilets and a small office. One pump was still serviced, the rest pump your own. The only pump in town, Emmett reckoned, where you'd still get service. He decided not to try it, thinking it was a good way to get a belt cut on a squad car if the Evans family was still holding a grudge. He pulled up to the side, trying not to block a pump or a bay, got out of his car and headed to the office. Once inside, it only took seconds before he began to sweat in his heavy coat. He took it off quickly as he approached the woman who sat behind the counter. He assumed it to be Mrs Evans, although he'd never met the woman.

There was a display case with cans of oil, windshield cleaner, extra wiper blades and little pine trees to make your car smell like a public toilet. A Coke machine was next to the door and advertised Cokes, Diet Cokes, Sprites and Dr Pepper. Emmett could hear hammering going on in one of the bays and thought maybe the son was out there working. The woman looked up when Emmett opened the door.

'Help you?' she said.

She was a pretty woman in her late forties, early fifties, with fluffy champagne-blonde hair, blue eyes enhanced with lots of make-up, buxom and showing more cleavage than she probably should have. But then, Emmett didn't mind that a bit.

'Miz Evans?' he asked.

'Yeah?' She looked from Emmett out the window to the squad car then stood up. 'What do *you* want?' she asked, her tone not exactly friendly.

'Wondering if either of your boys might be around?' Emmett asked.

'No,' she said.

'Who's that out in the bay there?' Emmett asked, pointing.

'A hired hand,' she said.

Emmett knew she was lying. The way she squared her shoulders and looked him straight in the eye was a dead giveaway. She was gutsy but she was still lying.

'Mind if I talk to him?' Emmett asked.

'Yes, I do, Deputy,' she said, with the word 'deputy' sounding a lot more like 'asshole' than it should have. 'He's hourly. I'm not paying him to be gabbing with you when he should be working.'

'Mind if I just stick my head in there and say hidy?' Emmett said as he walked toward the door to the bay.

'Yes, I do!' Mrs Evans said, rushing to said door. But Emmett got there first and opened it.

A young man, maybe nineteen, twenty years old, was working on a ten-year-old Buick up on the rack when Emmett opened the door. The boy turned when he heard the door open and saw Emmett and Mrs Evans standing there.

'Mama?' he said.

Emmett turned and looked at Mrs Evans. 'I do think you were mistaken, Miz Evans,' he said. 'Must be your hired hand's day off.'

'Fuck you,' the woman said. 'This is private property. Unless you got a warrant, get the hell out of here.'

'Now you really should watch your language in front of your boy, there, Miz Evans,' Emmett said.

'Mama, what's going on?' the boy asked.

'Nothing. Get back to work.' She turned to Emmett. 'Get out of here before I call my lawyer.'

'Ma'am, I need to talk to your son. I can do it here – it'll just take a minute. Or I can sit outside in my car with the lights and siren going and wait for your lawyer, then take your boy into the station. That could take the rest of the day. When's this Buick due back?'

'Mama, let him talk. I got nothing to worry about,' the boy said.

Mrs Evans leaned against the doorjamb, crossing her arms over her ample chest. 'You got five minutes,' she said.

'Or however long it takes,' Emmett corrected. He turned to the boy. 'You Tyler?'

'Yes, sir.'

'Seems to me you know your way around cars a bit, huh, Tyler?'

'Yes, sir.'

'You do brake jobs?' he asked.

'Your squad car got a problem?' the boy asked back.

'Answer my question,' Emmett said.

'Yes, sir, I do brake jobs.'

'Fix 'em and break 'em?' Emmett asked.

The boy frowned. 'What're you talking about? Yeah, I fix brakes.'

'I suppose you'd know how to cut a brake line, now wouldn't you?' Emmett asked.

'I didn't cut any brake line!' Tyler said.

'You and your brother seemed to have a problem with one of our deputies, Anthony Dobbins, who witnessed your daddy killing that man Vaught. You remember?'

'Of course I remember!' the boy said, getting heated. 'Worst day of my life! What's that got to do with anything?'

'Seems your brother said something pretty awful to Deputy Dobbins after your daddy got sentenced,' Emmett said.

'You need to leave!' Mrs Evans said, pushing away from the doorjamb, hands on her hips.

'What?' Tyler said.

'He said, and I quote, "You're one dead nigger." Unquote.'

Tyler shook his head. 'Yeah, well, that's just the way JR is,' he said. 'He's hot-headed. But that was a long time ago. What's it got to do with anything?'

'JR?' Emmett asked.

'Danny, Jr,' Mrs Evans said. 'We just call him JR for short. You can leave now that you know all our secrets.'

'So where's JR now?' Emmett asked.

'None of your damned business!' Mrs Evans said, moving closer to Emmett. 'You talked to my boy and now you can leave! Get your fat ass out of here!'

Emmett looked behind him. 'You shoulda seen it before my wife put me on a diet,' he said with a grin. Then he sobered. 'Where is JR?'

'Look, asshole—' the woman started but the boy broke in.

'Mama, stop.' To Emmett, he said, 'JR's in west Texas on a drilling rig. He comes home for Thanksgiving, Christmas and Mother's Day, and an occasional weekend. He's married, got a little girl and he's been born again. So whatever you think he's done, you best rethink it.'

Emmett took his leave, wondering if he could believe what Tyler said about his brother or anything else. Was Tyler just shining him on about not holding a grudge against his daddy? Did JR's born-again status make him want to turn the other cheek or decide an eye for an eye? He thought it might be a good idea to talk to Milt.

Me and Emmett met up at Manuel's on Highway Five. It was a Mexican place my wife didn't know about. I don't think Jasmine, Emmett's wife, was aware of the many times me and Emmett met there either. We both thought it wise to keep Manuel's a secret. They make a damn fine chili relleno, stuffed with fajita steak and cheese, then deep fried in panko breadcrumbs over a bed of rice and beans with a chicken taco on the side. Me and Emmett always split a salad, in case either wife asks what we had for lunch. We wouldn't tell a lie.

'What d'you think about your guy?' Emmett asked me.

'Jesse Trevino?' I shrugged. 'Lost a kidney 'cause he was in prison but that got him out of the joint eight months early.' I shrugged again. 'Didn't seem to harbor any resentment but then again . . .'

'Same with the Evanses. The missus is still mighty pissed, but the kid, Tyler, the younger one,' Emmett said, 'seems copacetic. Says his brother, JR, for Junior, is born again and not anywhere around anyway. Married, got a little girl. Life goes on?'

'So the mama?'

It was Emmett's turn to shrug. 'I could see the note and the zombie baby, but cutting the brake lines? She'd chip a nail.'

'My wife would say that was a sexist comment,' I said, shoving illegal refried beans into my mouth.

'I'd say she's more into advertising for a new husband than getting vengeful over a dead one. Lots of make-up, big hair, some real nice cleavage.'

'But she runs that gas station. Should know how to cut brake lines.'

Emmett shook his head. 'Naw. I doubt it. She's front desk. Doubt if she knows how to fill the gas tank.'

'There you go, being sexist again,' I said.

'Then go check her out yourself,' Emmett said, head down as he got serious with his enchilada platter.

'I think we should check out the Permeter brothers,' I said.

'Who?'

'The two brothers that went after Dalton after he shot their other brother in that domestic.'

'Oh, yeah. Them. They still in town?'

'I have Holly looking into them. We'll check when we get back to the shop,' I said.

'Sounds like a plan.'

My cell phone rang just as I was getting a good rhythm going with my chili relleno. 'What?' I said into it, seeing from the read-out thingy that it was the shop.

'Milt? It's me, Dalton.'

'Hey, Dalton. What's up?'

'I dunno. Something's going on at my mama's house. I gotta get over there. That OK?'

'You do what you gotta do,' I told him. 'Me and Emmett'll be at the shop in twenty. But you go ahead and take off.'

'Thanks, Milt.'

I said bye, hung up, and then me and Emmett got down to some serious calorie intake.

* * *

Dalton was worried about his mama. That was nothing new. He was worried about her a lot, which was one of the joys of Mrs Pettigrew's life. When she'd called just a few minutes back, she'd said, 'Dalton! Something funny's going on here! Get over here quick!' And then she'd hung up. Dalton had no idea what 'something funny' meant. He was pretty sure she didn't mean funny ha-ha, more like funny-weird.

He pulled up in front of his mama's house, his home up until six months ago when he and Holly had got married and moved into their own place. Although Dalton was considered not terribly bright by most, he *was* bright enough to know that Holly and his mama living in the same house would be a very bad idea indeed.

His mama's house was a post-WWII bungalow with some add-ons. It was painted white with yellow trim and, in the summertime, had big geranium plants on the small porch. Right now it just had a poinsettia that was giving up the ghost. But what worried him was the number of vehicles surrounding the house. Some of the cars he recognized as his mama's bridge cronies. It was the ambulance that worried him. He abandoned his squad car in the middle of the street and hightailed it up the porch steps and into the house.

Jasper Thorne, the African-American head EMT with Longbranch Memorial Hospital, and his new partner, Sylvia Bradshaw, were just putting someone on the gurney. Thank God, Dalton thought, it wasn't his mama.

'What's going on, Jasper?' Dalton asked the EMT.

'Got two down,' Jasper said. 'Miz Merkle here and Miz Jameson. She's already in the bus.'

'What is it?'

'Food poisoning?' Sylvia suggested and shrugged, then the two began to push Mrs Merkle out the door.

'Mama?' Dalton said, heading into the living room. His mother was sitting on the sofa, her face covered with her hands. Kneeling down in front of her, Dalton said, 'Mama? You all right? What happened?'

'It was the peach melba!' came a voice from behind him. Dalton turned to see the last of his mama's bridge cronies, Neva Keller, standing by the fireplace, her arms crossed over a skinny chest and staring daggers down at the two Pettigrews.

'It was not!' Mrs Pettigrew said, jumping up.

'Well, then, how do you explain it?' Mrs Keller said, hands on her hips. 'Me and you only drank the coffee. Enid and Doris had the peach melba and they're on their way to the hospital!' She sighed. 'I'm not saying you did this on purpose, Inez. But maybe you just got a little sloppy with your cooking, is all.'

'I am never sloppy! Never in my born days have I ever been sloppy!' Inez Pettigrew turned to her son. 'Have you ever known me to be sloppy?'

'No, Mama,' Dalton said.

'Well, maybe something was wrong with the peaches,' Mrs Keller said.

'There wasn't anything wrong with them peaches! Got 'em right out of the frozen section at the Piggly Wiggly!'

'Were they a name brand? You know, you buy those fly-by-night brands and you never know what you're getting.'

'Yes, they were a name brand! And we have no idea what Enid and Doris had to eat this morning. I mean, food poisoning takes a while to show up, right, Dalton?'

'Yeah, Mama, I think so.'

'He thinks so!' Mrs Keller scoffed. 'Like he'd know.'

'Don't you start on my boy!' Mrs Pettigrew said, advancing on Mrs Keller.

'Mama!' Dalton said, grabbing her arm. 'Why don't y'all grab your coats, get in my squad car and we'll all go to the hospital and see what's going on.'

'I'm not riding with her!' Mrs Pettigrew said, turning her back on her former friend and crossing her arms over her chest.

'Well, that's just fine! I'll drive my own self to the hospital,' Mrs Keller said and slammed out the front door.

'Come on, Mama. Let's go to the hospital.'

'The Permeter brothers,' Holly said, mentioning the two who'd tried to take on Dalton after Dalton had killed their brother in the line of duty. 'Nick and Joe. Nick is the older of the three, James is the one who got killed and Joe's the baby. Joe lives in Longbranch and works at Buddy's pool hall as a bartender. Nick lives out on Ranch Road two-forty, at the family farm. Still runs it but works part time at that tool and dye out on Highway Five.'

'Families?' I asked.

'Joe's single. I talked to my friend Carrie who waits tables at the pool hall part-time and she says he's a real player. Or at least he thinks he is. Most girls won't go out with him more than once, Carrie said.'

'He an abuser like his big brother?' Emmett asked.

'She didn't say anything about that. Just that he's mostly a jerk. She said she wouldn't go out with him if he was the last man on earth.'

'What about Nick? Married?' I asked.

Holly nodded. 'Wife and three kids. They kept the farm going while he was in prison. Oldest boy's nineteen and already been arrested for abusing his girlfriend.'

'We have him in here?' I asked, surprised.

'No. The girlfriend lives in Tulsa. He spent a night in the jail there but then the girl backed down and they let him off.'

'Any word on Nick abusing his wife?' I asked.

'No. But his mama lives with them and that might be a calming influence,' she said with a grin.

'I doubt it,' Emmett said.

'I do believe we need to interview these two,' I said, looking at Emmett.

'We go to them or bring 'em in?' he asked.

'Bring 'em in. But one at a time,' I said.

Joe Permeter certainly looked the part of the player Holly's friend Carrie had described. About six foot two inches tall, weighing in at a healthy one-eighty to two hundred pounds, he had dark, wavy hair, a little too long, big brown eyes, broad shoulders and a shit-eating grin, which he was using liberally on Holly as she walked him into the interrogation room. He sat down in the straight-legged chair across from me by turning it around backwards and strad-dling it in a manly fashion. I was sufficiently impressed by his masculinity.

He lost the shit-eating grin and frowned at me. 'I've done my time and I'm off probation, so I'm not sure what I'm doing here.'

'Just wanted to talk to you about what happened to your brother James,' I said.

'You guys killed him,' was Joe's reply.

'He was killed while attempting to shoot a peace officer.'

'Whatever,' Joe said, crossing his arms and leaning them on the back of the chair.

'You and your brother Nick tried to take down the deputy who was involved in that shooting.'

'Yeah. So what? He kills our brother and we took a swing at him. Your *deputy* damn near took out Nick's eye and he loosened one of my teeth. Not to mention my broken nose and collarbone. And Nick's still got back trouble. Then you assholes had the balls to send us to jail because of it. Man, that sucked.'

'So, the two of you, still sorta pissed off at the department?' I asked.

'Not my favorite place to be,' he said.

'Sure you haven't been hanging out here a little more than necessary?' I asked.

'Huh?' He was a bright one, that Joe.

'Like leaving notes taped to the front door, offing our alarm system and sneaking in to plant zombie babies—'

'Zombie what?' If the women of Longbranch could see the look of sheer stupid on Joe Permeter's face at that moment, he'd never get a *first* date, let alone a second.

'You know a lot about cars, Joe?'

'Huh?'

'Cars, Joe. You know a lot about them?'

'Like fixin' 'em and stuff?' he asked.

'Yeah, Joe, like fixin' 'em and stuff.'

'Yeah, I guess. I mean, I used to do all sorts of work on my daddy's ol' pick-up, but I'm not so good with anything after the catalytic converter.'

'What about brakes?'

'I never changed no brakes,' he said. His frown deepened. 'You got a problem with your brakes, Sheriff?'

'Joe, are you really as stupid as you're putting on?' I asked.

'Hey!' he said, standing up from the chair. 'Take that back!'

'Sit down,' I said. He kept standing. 'Sit down!' I said, real loud this time. He sat. 'See much of your brother Nick these days?'

'I don't know what you want, Sheriff. And I'm thinking I ain't gonna talk to you no more.' He folded his arms across his chest and turned his gaze to stare at the wall. I sorta felt dismissed.

*   *   *

I had Holly write up a paper saying Joe Permeter was a material witness and we needed to hold him in a cell for his own safe-keeping. She frowned when she typed it up, but she typed it up nonetheless. Then I had her take Joe to one of our holding cells. I could hear him alternatingly griping about getting locked up and hitting on Holly.

I'd sent Anthony to pick up Nick Permeter from his part-time job at the tool and dye company on Highway Five, and didn't have to wait too long for them to show up. I noticed when Anthony brought Nick in the side door that Nick was cuffed. Seeing me sitting in my office, Nick Permeter let loose.

'What the hell's going on here, Sheriff?' he yelled. 'Why'd you send this nigger to get me like I'm some sorta dog or something!'

'Watch who you're calling names, Mr Permeter. I'd hate to have to arrest you for being aggressive with a peace officer. With your record, you could get some real time,' I said.

Anthony nudged him forward with a knee to Nick's back. 'Keep walking,' Anthony said.

'I'm suing you!' Nick shouted. 'You, Sheriff, and this here *African-American gentleman*,' he said in a sing-song voice. 'And my mama's first cousin's ex-husband is a judge in Tejas County!'

'Gee,' I said, leaning back in my chair and putting my feet up on my desk, 'that should work out real well for you.'

Dalton called Milt from the hospital.

'What's up?' Milt asked after Dalton identified himself.

'Some of my mama's bridge ladies got sick,' he said, then, lowering his voice, whispered, 'maybe from something mama made. She's real upset.'

'Well, you stay as long as you have to,' Milt said. 'If anything major comes up, I'll call you. Otherwise, take care of your mama.'

'Tell Holly what's going on, OK?'

'Sure thing,' Milt said.

Dalton shut off his cell phone and turned back around. They were in the waiting room of the emergency department. His mama and Neva Keller were sitting opposite each other, both of them with their arms crossed and both of them staring at walls, but different walls, mind you. Dalton started to take the seat next to his mother when he saw Jasper Thorne and his female partner come out of the back. He hurried up to them.

'Any news?' he asked.

Dalton had gotten to know Jasper when the tornado hit nine months earlier. It was at the same time that Holly and her bachelorette party guests were being held hostage at the Longbranch Inn. Jasper had gotten promoted to head EMT after that. The only thing different now from then, Dalton reckoned, was that Jasper's hair was bigger – like an Afro from the sixties or something. He kind of liked it.

This was the first time Dalton had met Jasper's new partner. She was probably closer to forty than thirty but it was hard to tell with the burn scars. You could tell there'd been a lot of plastic surgery done but not enough to disguise the burns. Her hair was so obviously a wig that even Dalton could tell.

He held out his hand to her. 'Dalton Pettigrew, sheriff's deputy,' he said.

She smiled. It was a little lopsided but not unflattering. Actually, she looked a lot better when she smiled. She took his hand and he tried not to notice that it also had severe burn scars. 'Sylvia Bradshaw, EMT.'

'You from around here?' Dalton asked.

'Transferred in from Durant,' she said.

Jasper took Dalton's arm and led him away from the waiting room. 'Bad news,' he said, his voice low. 'Doris Jameson was DOA. And Miz Merkle ain't doing so great.'

'DOA? You mean dead?' Dalton whispered.

'That's what it means,' Jasper assured him.

'So what about Miz Merkle?'

'She's not responding to anything they're giving her. She's not conscious.'

'Damn,' Dalton said. 'You think it was my mama's cooking?'

'You need to find out what they ate and when they ate it,' Jasper said.

'They ate Mama's peach melba. It's usually real good.'

'Did they all eat it?' Jasper asked.

'No. Miz Keller said she and Mama just drank coffee.'

'So when did the other two eat the peach stuff?'

Dalton turned and looked at his mama. 'I don't know, but I reckon I'll find out.'

He left Jasper and went and sat down next to his mama. 'When did you serve the peach melba?' he asked.

'What do you mean when?' his mama responded.

'You know. What time?'

'I dunno! For God's sake, why would I know?' She sighed heavily. 'Neva, what time did I serve the peach melba?'

'I have no idea,' Neva Keller said, still staring at the wall.

Jasper came over. 'Ladies, I'm trying to find out how soon the ladies got sick after they ate that peach melba.'

'Right away!' Neva Keller said, looking at Jasper. 'Within minutes!'

Mrs Pettigrew sobbed. 'Yes, yes, it was. Oh, it was awful!'

Jasper turned and headed back into the emergency department.

FOUR

Nick Permeter was shorter and not nearly as good-looking as his younger brother. He had a beer gut and a mullet and wore a John Deer cap on his head turned backwards. And he was chewing a wad of tobacco. On seeing this, once I entered the interrogation room, I turned and asked Holly to get a plastic cup from the water cooler. She came back with one and I handed it to Nick. 'Spit,' I said. 'All of it. No tobacco products in the sheriff's department.'

'That's bullshit,' he said around the wad in his mouth.

'Either swallow it or spit the whole thing out. Now!'

He spat. I took the cup out and down the hall toward the cells where the bathrooms were. I wasn't about to ask Holly to deal with that. Women tend to be a bit squeamish about that kind of thing, and what with Holly being early pregnant and all, I felt it the prudent thing to do.

Since Anthony had handcuffed Nick to the metal ring under the table, he was still where I left him when I came back. Of course, he would have had a hard time getting past Anthony who was standing outside the door staring daggers at the asshole inside. I shut the door behind me and took the seat across from Nick.

'How's your family doing, Nick?' I asked.

'What the hell? What do you care? What is this? I did my time!'

'I hear your boy's taking up the family tradition of beating on women.'

'Fuck you,' he said.

'Well, that's Tulsa's problem, until Junior gets a girlfriend in Prophesy County, then I'll deal with it.'

Nick just glared at me.

'So, you still pissed about your brother? James, not Romeo Joe.'

'Of course I'm pissed! Y'all killed him!'

'He was gonna kill his wife and he turned the gun on a deputy. My deputy had no option but to shoot.'

'Bullshit! He wasn't gonna kill her! And your deputy just startled him. He wasn't gonna shoot!' Nick said.

'So, when you didn't get the satisfaction you wanted when Dalton took on you and Joe and beat the crap out of you both, did you decide to take revenge in a more subtle way?' I asked.

Nick frowned. 'Huh?'

I was quickly coming to the conclusion that there weren't a lot of rocket scientists in the Permeter family line.

'You been coming by the department here and doing jokes like putting notes on the door and stringing up toys in here?' I asked, pointing to the light fixture.

'Hell, no! I live on the other side of Longbranch. Why would I even come by here? That's just stupid!'

'You know anything about car brakes, Nick?' I asked.

'Of course. Car brakes, truck brakes, tractor brakes. Why?'

''Cause somebody cut the brake lines in one of my deputy's personal cars,' I said, watching his face close for any sign of guilt.

He laughed. 'Gee, Sheriff, I'm real sorry somebody's messing with y'all, but it ain't me. And don't even think about Joe. That boy don't know a brake line from a chorus line.'

'Stay here,' I said as I got up and left the room, heading for Emmett's office.

He was sitting at his desk, staring at the computer. I understood his pain. I waved for him to come in my office.

After we both sat down, I said, 'I don't think we're getting anywhere. I think those Permeter boys are too stupid to have even thought of doing this, much less be able to pull off silencing the alarm and getting anywhere near Anthony's personal ride.'

'Yeah, and the Evans kid and Trevino don't seem like likely suspects either,' Emmett said. 'Who's left?'

I looked at our list. 'The Connors and Maudeen Sanders' kin.'

'Well, hell. Maudeen Sanders had every right in the world to kill that asshole,' Emmett said, and since he was the father of a twelve-year-old girl, I perfectly understood. Hell, any human being could understand a woman killing a man who molested her child, whether they had kids or not. But when you have a daughter the same age Maudeen's was at the time, like Emmett and Jasmine did, it put a whole other spin on it. Like he might have helped her kill the bastard if he'd been around at the time.

'Doesn't mean her kin aren't taking revenge.'

'Her kin?' Emmett said, his voice skeptical. 'You mean her daughter and her brother? That the kin we're talking about?'

'Emmett, I'm not saying I like this one bit. They're just on the list.'

'We need to talk to the Connors. They're the most likely ones to have it in for Anthony. Him being late to get to their house and all.'

I sighed. 'Yeah, I guess I need to talk to them.'

'Want me to go with you?' Emmett asked.

I shook my head. 'Naw. Don't want to overwhelm them. Best do this one on my own.'

The Connors' house used to be a real nice two-story on about four to five acres outside the city limits. But it had seen better days. When I pulled up the long driveway I noticed tall grass and weeds choking the yard and paint chipping away on the house. A shutter on one of the upstairs windows was askew. I wondered if it was lack of income – since both had quit their jobs after the home invasion – or lack of interest. Probably both.

I rang the doorbell but, not hearing anything ringing inside, decided to knock as well. It took a while for someone to get to the door, but I stayed as I could hear someone moving around inside. When the door opened, I could only assume it was Reba Connors standing there. I barely recognized her. This woman was twice the size of the former Reba, her face swollen up and vein-riddled, wearing a muumuu kind of thing, obviously without a bra because her breasts appeared to be down around her waist. Her hair was short and matted and there was a crust of something around her mouth.

'What?' she said, slurring the word.

'Hey, Miz Connors,' I said, trying a smile. 'Sheriff Kovak here.'

'Yeah?'

'I wondered if I might have a word with you and Mr Connors.'

'Why?' she asked, her frown asking the same question.

'Is John home?' I asked.

'Yeah, I guess,' she said. She shrugged. 'I been asleep.' She turned and looked back into the house. 'Oh, yeah. There he is,' she said, backing away from the door. I moved inside the small foyer.

I could see John passed out on the couch in the living room. His head was on a throw pillow, his mouth open with harsh sounds coming out. One arm was flung on the floor, the other on the back of the couch. One leg was also on the floor, the other knee up. It was barely noon but it appeared these two were already plastered, or maybe just now getting up from the night before.

'Could you wake him up?' I asked Reba Connors.

'Why?' she asked and scratched her belly.

'I need to talk to y'all.'

She nodded, went to the couch and kicked it. 'Wake up!' she said, her voice loud. Then she put a hand to her head. 'Wow, that was loud,' she said, then giggled. When she did I saw teeth missing in her mouth.

I couldn't help remembering the woman I'd used to know, the county clerk who presided over the county with a gloved fist, always ready with a smile but never afraid to say no. She'd been a handsome woman, tall and big boned, but with her weight in check. Her husband John had been a court bailiff, good at his job, fast with a joke and a slap on the back. He hadn't been one of my favorite people but he'd been an upstanding man – not this balding, bloated heap I saw on the couch. It was hard to believe that only five years could do this much damage.

'You try,' Reba said, pointing at her husband.

I went to the couch and shook John's shoulder. It took everything

I had not to recoil from the smell. John had his very own noxious odor, not to be confused with the one emanating from the house, or the one that wafted off his wife. If I'd been the vomiting sort, the smells in this place might have done it to me. And I've been in houses with dead bodies that have been marinating for a while. That's how bad this place and these people smelled.

'Wake up!' I said, shaking him again.

His eyes finally fluttered open. 'Wha—'

'John, it's the sheriff,' Reba said. 'He wants to talk to us.'

John pushed himself up into a sitting position. 'Hey, Sheriff! Long time. How you doing?' he said, smiling at me.

'Just fine, John. Need to ask you and Reba some questions,' I said.

'Reba, honey, can we do that?' John asked his wife.

'Not hardly! We don't have to talk to you. And we don't want to talk to you! You owe us! We don't owe you squat.'

'Ma'am, if need be I can drive y'all to the station and you can call your lawyer—' I started.

Reba let out an unladylike snort. 'Lawyer? You think we can afford a stinking lawyer? With what, Sheriff? We spent all our savings on lawyers to sue y'all for what y'all did to us. But it's all gone now. Everything's all gone,' she said, and sank into an overstuffed chair.

'You talk to me now, Reba, or I haul you and John down to the station.' I grabbed John's arm and stood him upright, where he swayed a bit but kept smiling at me.

'Wait! Wait!' Reba said, holding up one hand in surrender. 'We'll talk to you here, OK?'

'Reba doesn't like to leave the house,' John said, and belched in my face. I let his arm go and he sank back down on the couch.

I stood above them for a minute, then pulled a straight-back chair in from the dining room and sat down. 'I'm real sorry about what happened to y'all, and real sorry we got here too late to stop what happened. But what happened was the fault of the two creeps who did this to you, not the fault of my deputy.'

'The two creeps y'all never found 'cause your deputy was so late. You know they raped me?' Reba said.

'Yes, ma'am,' I said.

'You know they tore me up and I can't have babies now?'

I cringed inside. 'No, ma'am, I didn't know. I'm so sorry.'

'You know they pistol-whipped John?'

'Yes, ma'am.'

'You know he's got brain damage from that? That's why he can't work? Did you know that?'

Again, I cringed. 'No, ma'am, I didn't know.'

'And I can't leave the house. At first I tried and tried, but I can't step outside. Used to have a real nice garden that I tended.' She stood and looked out the dirty front window. 'See it now? Just weeds. Just like our lives. We're just weeds,' she said, her voice low.

Damn, I wanted the county to pay them every damn penny they asked for. Maybe more. I wasn't blaming Anthony, but these people needed help.

'Is John getting disability?' I asked.

'Our finances are none of your business!' Reba said. I decided to let that go.

'We've been having some problems down at the sheriff's department,' I said, trying to stay on track. 'Mostly minor stuff, like notes and nasty toys. But the brake lines were cut on Anthony Dobbins' wife's car.'

'Anthony Dobbins?' Reba said, turning around. 'He's that black deputy who got here late, huh?'

'He was the deputy who arrived on the scene, yes, ma'am,' I said.

She frowned. 'Why would somebody want to hurt his wife?'

'We're thinking some kind of revenge, ma'am.'

'Oh!' she said, light finally dawning on her. 'You think John and I did stuff to y'all and messed with your deputy's car?'

'We're following up on all possibilities,' I said.

'Like everybody your deputies screwed over? Got to their place late or not at all? Ignored evidence and maybe broke a few laws themselves?' she said.

'Ma'am—' I started.

'I was the county clerk for Prophesy County for over ten years, Sheriff. You think I didn't read the reports? You think I didn't know all the screw-ups you and your deputies have done over the years? You *and* the police department? But it wasn't the police department I called when my husband and I were invaded by the hordes, Sheriff. It wasn't the police department that got confused and went to the wrong address. It wasn't the police department who got here so late my husband was barely alive and my body had been ravaged for life!'

'Ma'am—'

'Oh, shut up!' she said. She sighed. 'I haven't been out of this house in five years. I can't prove it, but it's true. John doesn't know how to cut his own meat, much less cut somebody's brake lines. Just go, Sheriff. Leave us alone.'

I looked over at the couch. John was fast asleep. I got up, put the chair back in the dining room and left the house, thinking maybe that DUI John Connors got a while back and the drunken phone calls he'd made to my house hadn't been due to alcohol at all. Just maybe a result of brain damage.

'It wasn't the Connors,' I told Emmett when I got back to the shop.

'What makes you say that?'

'Trust me. It wasn't them.' I had no desire to go into what Reba Connors had told me. I didn't want to check it out either, but I knew I had to get a search warrant to see the medical records on the two. I wondered if John was receiving Social Security disability? Reba hadn't answered my question about that – probably because it was none of my business. But he should be getting something. He was certainly entitled. And maybe Reba too. I'd check into that – my business or not.

'So it's on to Maudeen Sanders' kin,' I said.

'You know they had nothing to do with it!' Emmett said with a little heat in his voice.

'We don't know that,' I said as gently as I could. For Emmett, this was personal. He might not have known Maudeen or her brother and daughter, but it was still personal. And it had more to do with Emmett's daughter than Maudeen's.

'We should be following up on these others!' he said.

'And do what?' I asked.

'I don't know!' he said, the heat in his voice rising this time. 'Have Holly do something with the computer. Check their movements. Alibis, shit like that!'

'Well, we could do that—' I started, but Holly burst into the room.

'Dalton needs you at the hospital!' she said.

'His mama? What's going on?'

'One of those bridge ladies died,' she said.

'From his mama's cooking?'

Holly shook her head. 'Poison,' she said. 'And the Longbranch police just took Mama Pettigrew into custody.'

The delays and other problems that became apparent months back when the Longbranch Inn was taken over became a priority with the county commissioners when Milt and his whole department threatened to quit if something wasn't done about it. The fact that at that time they only had a coroner – a funeral director by trade – and not an actual ME was changed right away. And with the arrival of Dr Thurman, a modern young man who demanded equally modern equipment, came all the stuff needed to do various tests. One of those tests detected poisons and identified the kind, which was why the police were talking to Mrs Pettigrew.

'We just need to talk to her,' Charlie Smith, police chief of Longbranch, told Dalton.

'Y'all can do that right here!' Dalton said, standing squarely in front of his mama.

'It's all right, honey,' Mrs Pettigrew said. 'If I cooked something bad I need to know about it.'

'Ma'am,' Chief Smith said, 'the tox screen on Miz Jameson came back. It was arsenic poisoning.'

'Now wait just a damn minute!' Dalton said.

'Language, Dalton!' his mama said. To the chief, Mrs Pettigrew said, 'Arsenic's like a poison, right? How would that get in my peach melba?'

'That's just it, ma'am, someone would have had to put it in there,' Chief Smith said.

'On purpose?' she asked, wide-eyed.

'Are you trying to say Inez Pettigrew *intentionally* tried to kill Enid and Doris?' demanded Neva Keller. 'That's just crazy! Inez might be a lot of things but she's not crazy. She'd never hurt either one of them and that's the God's honest truth.'

Mrs Pettigrew reached behind her and took Neva's hand. Neva moved closer to her, putting her free hand on Mrs Pettigrew's shoulder.

'Dalton, it would be best if we went to the station—' the chief started.

'Not on your life!' Dalton said. 'I'm taking Mama home!'

'And I'm helping him!' Neva Keller said.

Just then the automatic doors to the emergency department opened and Milt and Holly came in. Holly ran up to her mother-in-law and embraced her. Milt walked up to Chief Smith.

'Hey, Charlie,' Milt said, holding out his hand to the chief. 'How you doing?'

'Fine, Milt. How're you?'

'Just great, except for some stuff we got going down at the shop.' And he proceeded to tell the chief of the pranks and the more serious cut brake lines.

'Hum,' the chief said. 'Miz Dobbins and that new baby OK?'

'Shook up mostly, but OK,' Milt said. 'I think that might put Miz Pettigrew's troubles in perspective.'

'You think this here has something to do with that?' Charlie asked.

'I'd bet on it. Somebody put poison in Miz Pettigrew's food, but instead of her getting it, somebody else did.'

Dalton grabbed Milt's arm. 'You mean this asshole was trying to kill my mama?'

Holly and Neva moved closer to Mrs Pettigrew, wrapping her in a cocoon of protection.

'That's what I'm thinking,' Milt said.

The chief was shaking his head. 'Well, don't that beat all. But, you know, Milt, I'm thinking I need to look into this a little more. I can't say Miz Pettigrew didn't have anything to do with this.'

'Well, I sure as shit can!' Dalton said.

'Dalton, language,' Mrs Pettigrew said automatically, her voice muffled by the bodies of her two protectors.

'I'm thinking the best thing we can do right now, Charlie, is let Dalton take his mama home. He's a deputy and he can keep an eye on her until we can rule out her having anything to do with it,' Milt said.

'Milt!' Dalton said. 'You know my mama—'

Milt patted Dalton on the arm. 'I know she didn't have anything to do with it, Dalton. But she needs to stay in one place while you and me prove it to the Chief, OK?'

Dalton nodded his head. 'Yeah, I guess.'

'But not her home,' Charlie said. 'Her home is a crime scene.'

'I'll take Mama to our house so Dalton can help you,' Holly said to Milt. 'If that's OK, Sheriff?'

Milt nodded.

'I'm going too,' Neva Keller said. 'Who's gonna call Enid's and Doris's families?'

'We'll take care of that,' the chief said. 'Y'all go ahead and take Miz Pettigrew home.'

Holly and Neva didn't wait for another dismissal. They were out the door quickly, practically carrying Inez Pettigrew between them.

Me and Dalton followed Charlie Smith to the Longbranch police station. The police station was located in the county courthouse. The sheriff's department used to be in the space across the hall from it, but we got moved to the 'new' location back in the mid-sixties and the police department took over both spaces. It was still too small. That's the thing about a growing town: the more people move in, the more problems you get. And more problems meant more police officers and more deputies to handle those problems. The city council had approved more police officers but the county commissioners were still being right stingy on the matter of more deputies.

The county courthouse was pretty damn old and smelled of mold and rotting wood. But it had high ceilings, dormer windows and wrought-iron stair rails. It was a pretty place if you held your nose. The inside of the police department didn't fare much better than the rest of the building. It had been painted that institutional green they used back in the sixties – the last time the place was painted – and it was flaking off in spots that revealed the yellow paint of a previous era. The wood railing of the counter was chipped and scarred, and the linoleum on the floor was buckled and stained. A nice reminder that moving to the cinder-block building outside of town had been a good idea for the sheriff's department. But I'm not sure a nicer building made up for the lack of deputies. The city and the county seemed to have opposing priorities.

We followed Charlie into his private office. I hadn't seen the place since it had been Emmett Hopkins' domain quite a while back – before politics had booted him out and he came over to the righteous side: i.e. the sheriff's department. The room hadn't changed that much over the last decade or so – same green paint, same regulation metal desk, maybe a new swivel chair. The only real difference was that Charlie had a nice-looking ivy plant on a bookshelf with tendrils running around the one window, and there were pictures on his desk. One, about ten years old, showing his wife and two sons, and newer ones – one of his wife, her hair lighter than it had been in the other photo, one of his oldest in his Marine uniform and one of his youngest in his football gear in the same stance I'd had my picture taken when I was his age. That picture of me had been on my mama's dresser until the day we buried her, when I put it in a drawer so as not to have to look at it any more. There were three more pictures on Charlie's desk – all of 'em of a little accident called Cherie. She was five years old and the apple of her daddy's eye.

'So,' Charlie said, settling into his chair behind his desk while me and Dalton took a couple of visitors' chairs. 'You got any suspects?'

'Lots,' I said. 'We've been concentrating on people who might hold a grudge against the department, or perhaps a specific deputy. Anthony Dobbins had a couple of cases that might blow back on him, but now, with Dalton's mama thrown into the mix, I just don't know.'

'I shot that Permeter fellow and his brothers got pretty mad,' Dalton said.

I nodded my head. 'I've got both of 'em at the shop now,' I said. 'I'm just not sure either one of 'em's bright enough to pull off any of this.'

'They may not be bright,' Dalton said, I thought a little defensively, 'but they're sly. Sly'll get you about as far as bright.'

He had me there. 'And they're going after relatives, not the actual deputy, right?' Charlie asked. I nodded again. 'So it makes sense they'd go after Dalton's mama.'

'Yeah,' Dalton said. 'They probably didn't know about me and Holly getting married.' I saw panic in his face. 'You don't think they'll go after Holly next, do you?'

I patted his shoulder. 'She's at home—' I started but Dalton interrupted.

'If they could get into Mama's house, they can sure get into ours!' Dalton said and jumped up. He didn't excuse himself, just shot out the door, presumably on his way to his house – or maybe, which didn't bode well for anybody, to the shop.

'Man, you got yourself some trouble there, Milt,' Charlie said.

'Tell me about it,' I said.

'You think Dalton's gonna go back to your shop and hurt those Permeter brothers?'

I shrugged. 'Maybe, maybe not.'

'You don't seem too concerned.'

I smiled. 'He won't kill 'em,' I said. 'Just make 'em pay attention.'

Charlie shook his head. 'You do run an informal shop, huh, Milt?'

'Well, we don't wear tuxes, I'll guaran-damn-tee you that.'

Emmett Hopkins sat at his desk thinking about Maudeen Sanders and her kin. If Holly ever came back from taking care of her mother-in-law, he'd ask her to run Maudeen's kid through the system, see what she could find. Her brother, Ralph Winchell, too. He knew Ralph from church, but only to nod to. He and his wife and kids all went there. He knew Ralph had taken in Maudeen's daughter after her mom's incarceration, and she'd been around the church a lot too. He tried to remember her name. Lisa, Lynne, Linda. Something like that. He looked at the computer screen in front of him. Hit the icon for Google and put in Maudeen Sanders' name. There were three. Who'd have thought there would be more than one? The first one lived in Oregon, the second in Vermont and the third in Georgia. Not one of them appeared to be *his* Maudeen Sanders. He sat back and stared at the screen some more.

The new deputy, Anna Alvarez, stuck her head round the door. 'You seen Milt?' she asked.

'He's over at the police chief's office. Can I help you?'

'I just wanted to remind him I gotta be in court tomorrow. That Hanson case.'

'Just leave a note on his desk,' Emmett said. Then, 'Hey, Anna. You know anything about computers?'

'Probably more'n you but not much,' she said with a grin on her face.

'I'm trying to look up Maudeen Sanders' kin. I tried Google but all I got was a bunch of Maudeen Sanders in other states.'

Anna walked around behind Emmett's desk. 'You gotta go into our database,' she said, hitting a couple of keys. A window opened up, asking for a password. 'What's your password?' she asked.

'Huh?'

'Never mind, I'll use mine,' Anna said and plugged in four numbers. The screen opened up with a menu. 'See that?' she said, pointing at an item that said 'Closed Cases.' She clicked on it, then typed Maudeen Sanders' name into the search area. *'Viola!'* she said when the woman's name came up. 'There you go.'

'Write all that down,' Emmett said, 'so maybe I can do it again.'

'OK. I'll do that and email it to you,' Anna said.

Emmett just looked at her. 'And when you gonna teach me how to get my email?' he asked.

'Oh, brother,' Anna said and left his office.

Emmett started reading the file on Maudeen. Her daughter's name was Lynette Sanders. He'd been close on the name, he thought. She would be twenty now. Her mother had two more years left on her sentence. He was surprised she hadn't gotten out early for good behavior. Lynette's address was listed as the same as her uncle's, Ralph Winchell. But this information had all been inputted from the file that was originally put together at the time of the killing. He would never call what happened to Wharton Jacobs murder. As far as Emmett was concerned, the man had it coming. Maudeen Sanders had put him down like you would a rabid dog. And good riddance was all Emmett had to say about it.

But still. Maudeen was doing time for it. Which pissed him off and he didn't even know the woman. He could only imagine how pissed off her daughter and her brother would be. But wouldn't they be pissed at the judge who gave her ten years rather than the sheriff's department? Maybe they were. Judge Norman had retired a couple of years ago. Emmett wondered how he was doing. He picked up the phone and dialed the county clerk's office.

After introducing himself to the lady who answered the phone, he said, 'I'm looking for Judge Norman. He retired a while back but I need to talk to him about an old case. It might be related to something we're working on.'

'I'm so sorry,' the woman said. 'Judge Norman passed away earlier this year.'

'What from?' Emmett asked.

'Well, I'm not sure. You want to talk to his former bailiff? I understand they stayed in touch,' she said.

'Yes, ma'am, thank you,' Emmett said and waited while the call was transferred.

'Bob Huntley,' said the man who answered the phone.

Emmett again introduced himself, gave his condolences about the judge, explained what he was calling about, then asked, 'I need to know how the judge passed.'

'Car accident. Brakes went out on a bad road and he crashed the car into a tree. He was in the hospital for about two weeks with broken everything, but then had a heart attack,' Huntley said.

'Anybody check the car's brake lines?' Emmett asked.

There was a moment of silence, then the bailiff said, 'No. Should they have?'

'You know where the car is?' Emmett asked.

'Probably at the junkyard over on Highway Five,' he said. 'But it's been a few months and the car was totaled. They may have already demolished it.'

'I think I'll find out,' Emmett said.

'So, Deputy, what's going on? You think somebody did something to Dave's car?'

Emmett was feeling bad about not being more circumspect when talking to the bailiff. With Huntley calling the judge by his first name, they were obviously pretty good friends. 'We're not sure,' Emmett said. 'But I'll keep you posted.'

'You do that. And if somebody did, you give me five minutes alone with the SOB, you got that?'

'I hear you,' Emmett said and rang off.

Dalton burst through the front doors of the sheriff's department like a rampaging bull. Anthony was still on the customer side of the bullpen counter – keeping an eye on Nick Permeter who remained in the interrogation room.

'Hey, Dalton,' Anthony said, stepping away from the counter where he'd been leaning an elbow. 'You OK?'

'Where are they?' Dalton demanded.

'Who?'

'The Permeter brothers!'

Anthony noted that Dalton's hands were fisted and his usually pale face was an unhealthy red. 'Milt's got 'em tucked away, Dalton,' Anthony said, warily walking up to his fellow deputy. He put both hands on Dalton's arms but Dalton shook him off.

He looked to the left, saw Nick Permeter in the interrogation room and headed in that direction. He threw the door open and stormed in, Anthony right behind him.

'Hey, Dalton,' Anthony said, trying to keep his voice even and soothing. 'Why don't we go talk to Emmett, huh? He's here. Milt'll be here in a minute. Why don't we talk to—'

'You try to kill my mama?' Dalton yelled, leaning his fists on the table and moving into Nick Permeter's space.

Permeter backed up as much as he could. 'What the hell? No, man! Who tried to kill your mama? Not me, man!'

'Then it was your goddam brother!' Dalton yelled. Turning to Anthony, he said, 'Where is he?'

Emmett, having heard the shouting clear across the department in his own office, came hurrying up. 'What's going on here?' he demanded.

'Ah, Emmett, Dalton here is a little upset—' Anthony started.

'You bet your ass I'm upset! One of these Permeter assholes tried to kill my mama and I'm damn well gonna find out which one did it! So where's the other asshole?'

'Joe's here?' Nick demanded. 'You got my brother here? What the hell! What are you people doing?'

Dalton swung back around to Nick, one arm raised. Emmett grabbed Dalton's fist and drew it behind his back. 'Not on my watch, Dalton,' he said, his voice soft. 'Let's go in my office.'

Dalton turned, tears in his eyes. 'Emmett, they tried to kill my mother, for God's sake!'

'Somebody did, sure, but we don't have any proof that says it was the Permeter brothers.'

'That's right, asshole!' Nick Permeter shouted. 'Don't go accusing people till you got some proof!'

Dalton swung back around and Emmett motioned for Anthony to take him out of the room. To Nick, Emmett said, 'You're lucky I don't let him at you. One more peep out of you and I will.' With that he left the interrogation room, locking the door behind him, and headed to his office, where Anthony had taken Dalton.

FIVE

When I got to the shop I noticed it wasn't a happy place. There was yelling coming from the wing where my office and Emmett's were housed and yelling coming from the interrogation room. I noted that the door to that room was locked, used my key and walked in. Nick Permeter shut up for a minute. 'What?' I said.

'That big asshole deputy of yours, the one that killed my brother – he just tried to kill me! And he ain't got any proof I done anything!' He tugged at the cuff on his wrist that was attached to the metal ring welded to the underside of the interrogation room table.

'Tell you what,' I said, coming around to his side of the table, my handcuff keys out. 'Let's get you out of here.'

I unlocked the cuff from the metal ring and Nick stood up, rubbing his wrist under the cuff. 'Good! I'd hate to have to sue your—' he started. But changed that to, 'What the hell?' as I cuffed both hands behind his back and led him out of the interrogation room.

'Thought you might wanna talk to your baby brother,' I said, unlocking the door to the cells. 'But you'll have to do it through the bars.' I opened the cell next to Joe's, took the cuffs off Nick and encouraged him inside.

'Hey! Get me out of here!' Joe yelled.

'You two are material witnesses,' I said.

'To what?' Nick demanded.

I shrugged. 'I'm not sure yet.' And with that I left the cells and headed down the hall to the other scream-fest.

I sorta thought on first hearing it that it was Dalton's voice, and sure enough I was right. Emmett was sitting behind his desk but Anthony and Dalton both were standing in front of it, Anthony with a hand on Dalton's arm, no doubt trying to calm him down.

'Hey, y'all,' I said from the doorway.

Dalton whirled around. 'They won't let me talk to them Permeter assholes!' he yelled.

'That's right,' I said. 'They're both in the cells now and neither one is going anywhere. We gotta be smart about this, Dalton. If we're gonna get them for this, we got to have all our i's dotted and our t's crossed. Right?'

Dalton grudgingly nodded his head.

'So, we need to gather evidence. I want you and Anthony to go over to your mama's house and use the crime-scene kits, see if you can find prints – anything that shouldn't be there. Your mama's a real neat lady, Dalton, so anything outta place was maybe put there by whoever did this. You with me?'

'Yeah,' Dalton said with a sigh.

'Anthony?' I said, looking at him.

'Got it, Sheriff.' To Dalton, he said, 'Let's go get the kits and head over there.'

Dalton nodded and followed Anthony out of the room. To Emmett, I said, 'My office.'

Once in my own chair I picked up the phone and called Charlie Smith. 'Got Dalton and Anthony going to Miz Pettigrew's house to dust and shit,' I said.

'We already did that, Milt,' Charlie said.

'Won't hurt to do it again,' I said. 'Besides, I need to keep Dalton busy, and he'd know if anything was out of place in his mama's house.'

Charlie sighed. 'Gotja,' he said. 'But I'll send Mike Reynolds over to keep 'em company.'

'You do what you gotta do,' I said and rang off.

'This is getting out of hand, Milt,' Emmett said when I'd hung up.

'You think?'

'No need to get snippy,' he said.

'You're the one getting snippy,' I countered.

We were silent for a while, both taking a couple of deep breaths.

'This sucks,' I finally said.

'Yeah,' he agreed.

'I'm sorry, man, I know how you feel about it but we gotta look at Maudeen Sanders' kin,' I said.

Another big sigh from Emmett. 'About that. I was looking at Miz Sanders' file on the computer—'

'How'd you figure out how to do that?' I asked, impressed.

'I didn't. Anna showed me how.'

'Makes sense.'

'Anyway, I was looking at Miz Sanders' file and saw that Judge Dave Norman's the one who sent her up—'

'No surprise there. He used to preside over most of our cases. He's retired, right?'

'And dead,' Emmett said.

'Dead? Jesus, when did that happen?'

'That's what I'm trying to tell you, if you'd hold your horses for a minute.'

I mimed locking my mouth shut and throwing away the key.

'At least we're being adult about this here,' Emmett said, sarcastically, I thought. But I could have been wrong. 'Anyhow, he got killed in a car accident. Brakes went out.'

I couldn't help it – I opened my mouth. 'Well, shit on a shingle,' I said.

'Yeah,' he agreed.

'You call the junkyard?'

'Didn't get a chance what with Dalton coming in and all.'

'Well, let's do that. Let me know what they say.'

'Right,' he said as he got up and left my office.

It was getting colder by the minute, and halfway to the junkyard a slurry of flakes began to fall. The trees were thick on this part of Highway Five, with drifts of snow under a lot of them. Traffic was light as Emmett headed for Sonny's Used Parts and Auto Shop, better known as the Longbranch junkyard. The call from his office had garnered the information that Judge Norman's car had not yet been demolished as it still had some salable parts Sonny hadn't yet scavenged. So Emmett was on his way there, Guy Bergen, the tow-truck driver who'd found the cut brake lines on Anthony's wife's car, riding shotgun, ready to check out the brake lines on the judge's car.

A dilapidated, almost-redwood fence surrounded the yard, and as Emmett pulled his car through the gate he noted the prerequisite junkyard dog barking its fool head off and jerking against its chain. This one was a pit bull mix, and Emmett parked as far away from him as he could. Sonny came out of the antique Airstream he'd been using as an office since Emmett was a kid trying to steal parts for his '46 Merc. Emmett hadn't seen Sonny since the day he got caught with the battery from a '49 Ford that he'd been told would fit his Merc. He never found out if it would or not. Sonny took back the battery but didn't press charges.

As far as Emmett could tell, Sonny hadn't changed much. He'd been older than God back then and still looked about the same. White hair in tufts around his head, a swollen, vein-riddled drinker's nose, a turkey neck and hands crooked from arthritis. The only thing different was he was now wearing a blue jumpsuit stained with oil rather than the army-green overalls stained with oil that he used to wear.

'You Emmett Hopkins?' Sonny said, his voice the only thing showing that he'd aged since the last time Emmett had seen him. It was thin and reedy, and quavered a bit.

'Yes, sir,' he said, sticking out his hand to shake.

Sonny shook his head. 'Don't shake hands no more cause of my arthritis. 'Sides, my hands are dirty.'

'Well, thanks for letting us come by and check out the judge's car,' Emmett said.

'You the mechanic?' he said, nodding his head toward Guy.

'Yes, sir. Been in here a couple of times getting parts,' Guy said.

Sonny nodded. 'Thought you looked familiar.' He turned and pointed toward the back of the yard. 'Well, come on then. Let's go check it out.' And he led them slowly through the mountain of wrecked Ford pick-ups, Chevy four-doors, Dodge Rams and the occasional Toyota, pointing out his more exotic treasures. 'Lookee here. It's a fifty-seven Studebaker. No call for parts but I keep it around out of nostalgia, I guess. And here's a Renault. Can you believe somebody around here actually bought a French fucking car?' He cackled. 'Don't that beat all?'

They finally came up on Judge Norman's 2010 Cadillac Seville. 'Really screwed it up,' Sonny said, shaking his head. 'But you should be able to check the line. If y'all won't need me, I'll head back to my office. Get cold real quick these days,' he said and shuffled off.

'Thanks, Sonny,' Emmett called to his retreating back. 'Well?' he said, looking at Guy.

'Gimme some room,' Guy said and, after scraping the

accumulating snow on the ground away with his foot, slid himself
under what was left of the Seville.

I thought I'd start checking out Maudeen Sanders' kin. I was
sympathetic to her situation, and her kin's situation, but if they
had anything to do with what was going on now, I needed to know.
And they had to stop before anybody else got hurt. So far we had
one dead – Dalton's mama's friend, Doris Jameson; one not doing
so well – her other friend, Enid Merkle; and possibly a dead judge.
Of course, Maudeen Sanders wasn't the only one of the bunch of
suspects to go before Judge Norman: he was the one who sent
both Permeter brothers to McAlester and agreed to the lighter
sentence for Jesse Trevino. So Jesse shouldn't be too pissed at the
judge. Or us. I really didn't see him as a viable suspect. Judge
Norman was also the one who presided over Danny Evans, Sr's
trial. The senior Evans had gone to McAlester too and had been
killed while he was there.

So I had seven possible suspects if it turned out the judge's
brake lines had also been cut: Maudeen Sanders' kin – her daughter
and her brother; both Permeter brothers; and Danny Evans' family,
which consisted of two sons and a wife. And that's only if I had
gotten all the assholes we'd arrested and/or killed over the years
who might – or family members who might – be holding a grudge.

But then there was old Wharton Jacobs, the man Maudeen
Sanders killed. Did he have kin? They could be upset with the
judge for only keeping Maudeen overnight in jail with the first
shooting and letting her go home to kill Jacobs when he tried to
come back. But I couldn't see what my deputies had to do with
that. Especially Anthony, as he'd still been in Tulsa when that
whole thing went down. Who handled that case? I wondered.
Maybe I needed to get Holly to check that out and see if Wharton
Jacobs had any kin around. Or maybe one of his other wives?
Maudeen was his fifth – that we knew of. Were the others from
around here? I knew two of them were but what about the other
two? And why would they care?

This whole thing was giving me a big old headache. I got
Maudeen Sanders' file off Emmett's desk, took it back to my office
and called the phone number listed for her brother, Ralph Winchell.
The number was out of service. Considering the file was near eight

years old, it wasn't a real big surprise. So I called information and got a new number, then dialed that.

A kid answered the phone. 'Winchell residence.' Couldn't tell if it was a boy or a girl.

'May I speak to Mr Winchell, please?' I asked.

'May I say who's calling?'

'Sheriff Kovak,' I said.

'Really?' said the kid with a high squeak of delight. 'You're a sheriff? You got a gun and a badge? You kill bad guys?'

'Is your daddy there, sweetheart?' I asked.

'Yeah. Daddy!' the kid yelled in my ear. I pulled the phone away from that ear and rubbed it to relieve the pain. 'Daddy! It's a sheriff!'

Winchell took the phone. 'Who is this?' he demanded.

'Hi, Mr Winchell. This is Milt Kovak, sheriff of Prophesy County—'

'What can I do you for, Sheriff?' he asked, the first of our suspects who didn't sound pissed at me.

'I was wondering if I could speak to you and to your niece, Lynette.'

'Why?' he asked, seeming genuinely puzzled.

'It's in regards to your sister, Mr Winchell.'

'Yeah? Why?' he said, and then came the pissed sound.

'There have been some developments I'd like to speak to you and your niece about,' I said.

'What kind of developments?' he asked.

'If you don't mind, I'd like to discuss that in person,' I said.

'Well, then, come on over and discuss it,' he said. But he didn't sound happy.

'Will your niece be there?' I asked.

'Probably not. She lives in Dallas now. Going to SMU. Doubt she could help you in any way,' he said in a way that seemed to put an end to the subject of his niece.

'Well, then, how about I head your way now?' I asked.

'Whatever,' he said and hung up in my ear.

'Yep,' Guy Berden said. 'Neat as can be. Whoever's doing this,' he said, pulling himself out from under Judge Norman's Cadillac Seville, 'sure knows his shit.'

'Damn,' Emmett said, leaning back against a vintage Dodge Charger resting on its rims with no trunk lid or hood. Or much of anything else. Emmett thought that didn't bode well for Maudeen Sanders' kin.

'Guess I need to get somebody out here and dust for prints,' he said, knowing that was a lose/lose situation. The Seville had been sitting in a junkyard for several months. It had been scavenged for parts, and whoever had cut the brake lines in Anthony's wife's car had left no fingerprints. Since Emmett was beginning to wholly believe that the two cut brake lines had been done by the same person, he was pretty sure that person would have used gloves on the judge's car, just as he did on Maryanne Dobbins' car.

He pulled his cell phone out of his pants' pocket and dialed Milt's cell. 'Hey,' Milt said on answering.

'The judge's brake lines were cut,' Emmett said. 'We can dust for prints but I don't think it'll do much good.'

'I'm on my way over to Ralph Winchell's house,' Milt told him. 'Wanna meet me there?'

'Yeah,' Emmett said, his voice dejected. 'I suppose we gotta.'

'Cheer up,' Milt said. 'Judge Norman presided over some of the other suspects, too.'

'Yeah?' Emmett said, brightening. 'The Permeters?'

'I'm happy to report that's an affirmative.'

'Gotta drop off Guy and I'll meet you there. Give me thirty.'

'Be careful. Snow's really beginning to come down here,' Milt said.

'Heard anything on the TV or radio about another cold front?'

'Don't think I need a weatherman to tell me it's cold out there,' Milt said, then laughed. 'Hey! I think I almost stole a line from Bob Dylan!'

'Bob who?' Emmett asked and hung up. He had one more call to make. He owed it to Bob Huntley, Judge Norman's bailiff, to let him know his friend had been murdered.

Huntley had given Emmett his direct line and answered on the second ring.

'Huntley,' he said.

'Hey, Mr Huntley, it's Emmett Hopkins from the sheriff's department.'

'Hey,' Huntley said.

'I got bad news. The judge's brake lines were definitely cut.'

'Goddamn,' Huntley said after a few seconds of silence. Then he said, 'You mentioned that there were some pranks played on y'all before the brake lines, right?'

'Yeah. Nasty note on the door, then somebody cut the alarm system to break in and string one of those ugly Halloween zombie babies up in our interrogation room.'

'Yeah, well, that got me to thinking. Dave told me he'd been getting crank calls at his house about a week before his accident. Well, I guess it wasn't exactly an accident.'

'How many, did he say?' Emmett asked.

'Yeah. Seemed to be a bunch. He said they were pretty nasty, and he said it sounded like they were using one of those voice things that change the sound?'

'I've seen that on TV,' Emmett said. 'Did the judge live alone?'

'Yeah. His wife died a couple of years ago and his kids are all grown and not living anywhere around.'

'So nobody else would have heard these crank calls?' Emmett asked.

'No,' Huntley said. 'I suggested he try to tape one of 'em but I don't know if he ever did.'

'Can you find out if one of his kids might have his answering machine or whatever he might have recorded it on?'

'Yeah, I can try,' Huntley said, 'but I doubt they would. They sold almost everything in a garage sale.'

'Well, we can at least try.'

'I'll do that. And get back to you. And Deputy,' Huntley said, 'thanks for keeping me posted on this. Let me know how things develop.'

'I'll sure do that,' Emmett said, noting how Huntley saying letting him know hadn't been in the form of a question. It sort of sounded, to Emmett's ear, like a demand.

Ralph Winchell and his family lived in a nice white-rock house on a couple of acres in a subdivision where all the houses had big, tree-lined lots and all the houses were at least three-to-four-thousand square feet. I'd say, looking at it, that Winchell's house went closer to the four thousand mark. I wasn't sure what he did for a living, but whatever it was it was doing him proud. The snow was beginning to pile up on the roof, making the house look like a Christmas card. There was a Jeep Cherokee, a lot newer than mine, in the driveway and another car could be seen through the windows of the garage. It dawned on me at that moment: what did Ralph Winchell do for a living that allowed him to be at home at two in the afternoon on a week day? Good work if you could get it.

I parked on the street and waited for Emmett to show up. He got there just a few minutes after me. We both got out of our cars and met on the sidewalk leading up to the house. There weren't curbs in the subdivision, just rich lawns sloping to the street to give it that country look. The sidewalk leading to Winchell's front door was made of paving stones looking a lot like the white rock of the house, but they were beginning to ice over and were slippery. There was a wide front porch and a double door with beveled glass windows on either side. I rang the bell and heard a few bars of *The Lone Ranger* theme. (I can hear my wife now – yes, I know it's the *William Tell* Overture but to me it'll always be the theme song to *The Lone Ranger*.)

A man opened the door. I didn't attend Maudeen Sanders' trial so I'd never met Ralph Winchell before, but I was pretty sure that's who was standing in front of me. He was a big man, well over Emmett's professed height of six foot one inch, with shoulders that would make a linebacker proud. He had a full sandy-blond beard and a buzz cut, with watery blue eyes behind wire-rimmed glasses. He was wearing baggy blue jeans and a plaid flannel shirt.

'Mr Winchell?' I said.

'Sheriff,' he said. Slowly he backed up and let me and Emmett in.

Me and Emmett dusted the snow off our shoulders and wiped our feet on the porch mat before entering the home. We were both raised right.

'This is my head deputy, Emmett Hopkins,' I said.

Winchell nodded at Emmett. 'Seen you around the church,' he said.

'Yes, sir. Seen you and your family there most Sundays,' Emmett said.

Just then a little boy of about six or seven came bounding down the stairs.

'This him? Daddy, is this the sheriff?' the little boy squealed.

'Yeah, Dustin, this is him,' Winchell said.

The little boy – Dustin – walked up to me shyly and held out his hand. 'Nice to meet you, sir,' he said.

I shook his hand. 'Nice to meet you too, Mr Winchell,' I said. 'This here is my deputy,' I said, indicating Emmett.

Dustin's eyes got big. 'Wow, a deputy!' he said. 'I watch *Gunsmoke*!'

Emmett held out his hand and the little boy shook it. 'You got a limp?' Dustin asked.

Emmett smiled. 'You mean like Chester on *Gunsmoke*?'

The little boy nodded.

Emmett shook his head. 'No, I'm lucky, I guess. No limp.'

'Didn't know you could still find *Gunsmoke* on TV,' I said to Winchell.

'We've got a dish,' he said by way of explanation.

I thought maybe I should get one of those.

Winchell indicated we follow him into the living room. 'Dusty, you go see Mama in the kitchen, OK?'

'Yes, sir,' Dustin said and scampered off. He was a real cutey that boy, blond like his daddy, with eyes a lot brighter blue and dimples in his cheeks – whether that was from his daddy or not was hard to tell, what with the elder's full beard covering everything up.

The living room was what my wife would call 'well-appointed.' Light brown leather furniture, dark wood floors with coffee and end tables the same color. Art on the walls that didn't distract, book shelves crammed full of books and knick-knacks and a few toys scattered about. It was a lived-in room of a well-off family.

'I gotta ask, Mr Winchell. What is it you do for a living?' I asked.

'I'm a commercial artist,' he said. 'I freelance but I got contracts with two New York ad agencies and a kids book publisher out of Chicago.'

'Huh,' I said. 'So you work out of your house?'

'I have a studio behind the garage. You come all this way to ask about that?'

'I'm real sorry to disturb you like this, Mr Winchell,' I said, 'but we've been having some problems at the sheriff's office.' I went on to describe the note and the zombie baby, leaving out the more serious problems.

'And you're here because . . .' Winchell said.

I sighed. 'We're trying to figure out who's been doing this and why. Went over some old cases—'

'And decided my niece or I looked good for it?' he said.

I shook my head. 'Not at all,' I said, but he could tell I was lying. 'Just following up on some outstanding cases.'

'How is my sister's case outstanding? She's in jail and has been for almost eight years. She goes before the parole board in a couple of weeks. She should get out. Are you trying to mess that up, Sheriff?' he asked, getting red in the face.

'No, sir, not at all. I'm glad to hear she should be getting out soon. We're just following up any leads we can.'

'For a couple of pranks?' he asked, arms crossed over his chest.

'Well, sir, it sorta escalated from there. Couple of cut brake lines, that sort of thing.'

Ralph Winchell shook his head. 'Look, I didn't cut anybody's brake lines. I don't know squat about cars. Ask my mechanic that I almost single-handedly keep in business. And my niece hasn't been back here since Christmas. She's on the dean's list at SMU so she doesn't have much time to be playing pranks all the way back up here. And I guaran-damn-tee you she knows less about cars than I do.'

'You got an address and phone number for Lynette?' I asked.

'Of course,' he said. 'But I'm not gonna give it to you. If you want it, you'll have to dig for it.' And with that, he stood up. 'I'll show you fellas to the door.'

And he did. As dismissals went, it was fairly abrupt.

Dalton left early to go check on his wife and mother. He was worried about both. What with Holly being pregnant and his mama having had such a bad day, he wanted to make sure everybody was OK. The weather was also taking a turn and he wanted to make sure he could get home while the streets were still passable.

Neva Keller met him at the front door. 'About time you got here, Dalton!' she said. 'Your mama's lying down but she's not doing too well. And Holly's trying but, well, what do you expect?'

'Excuse me?' Dalton said.

Neva Keller *tsk-tsked* a bit and shook her head. 'A girl like that, Dalton. What were you thinking?'

Dalton turned and opened the front door that he'd just closed behind him. 'Thanks for your help, Miz Keller,' he said, 'but you best be leaving.'

'Your mama may need me—'

'Holly and me are here. We'll take over. Thanks.'

Neva Keller seemed to finally notice the look on Dalton's face. 'Well, I never!' she said and headed out the door.

'Yeah, I bet you did,' Dalton said under his breath, but loud enough for his wife, who had come in from the kitchen, to hear.

Holly laughed. 'She's a treasure, that one,' she said, wrapping her arms around her husband's waist.

Dalton hugged her and kissed the top of her head. 'If you think a bag of snakes is a treasure then I guess you're right,' he said. 'How you doing? Baby OK?'

Holly let go of his waist and took his hand, leading him into the kitchen. 'Baby's fine, I'm fine. Even your mama's fine. Upset, but Jean came over and gave her some Valium and she's sleeping like an angel.'

'Sorry you got stuck with Miz Keller,' he said, sitting down at the kitchen table. 'Something smells good.'

'Since I had the time, I thought I'd make a pot roast – and I'm following your mama's gravy recipe.' She lifted the lid on the large pot on the stove. 'It's looking real good.'

'Smells good.'

'So, what's going on with the investigation?' Holly asked, sitting down at the table across from her husband. Since she was a department employee, even if not a deputy, she was most often in the loop on all cases.

'Me and Anthony went by Mama's house. You know Mike Reynolds, from the police department?'

Holly nodded her head.

'He met us there, but the police had already gone over everything so there wasn't much for me and Anthony to do. Since it was my mama's house, though, Milt thought I might notice if something was out of place.'

'And did you?'

'Yeah, I did. But I don't know if it was that big a deal,' Dalton said.

'What?'

'Mama keeps her brooms and mops in that closet right by the back door—'

'I know,' Holly said.

'Well, one of the brooms was missing and I found it in the kitchen, propped up against the wall.'

'Mama would never do that,' Holly said. 'A place for everything and everything in its place – that's Mama.'

'Exactly.'

'So did you tell Milt?'

'Well, it didn't seem like such a much—'

Holly stood up abruptly and grabbed the cordless phone. 'Call him, honey. It could be such a much.'

SIX

'So did y'all dust it for prints?' I asked Dalton.

'Anthony did, I think,' he said. 'Want me to call him and check?'

'No, you take care of your women. I'll call Anthony.'

With that I hung up on Dalton and punched the number on my phone that automatically called Anthony. Holly had set up the new phone system – each deputy and Holly had a one-digit number I could hit and call them directly. There was also a two-digit number I could punch in that would call all of 'em at the same time. That had come in real handy when we had that bad business at the Longbranch Inn.

Maryanne Dobbins answered the phone. 'Hey, Maryanne,' I said. 'How you doing?'

'Hi, Milt. I'm fine, thanks for asking.'

'And Melinda?'

'Sleeping like a baby.'

'Well, that's her job,' I said.

Maryanne laughed but her heart didn't seem to be in it. 'Anthony around?' I asked.

'Sure,' she said, and I heard her put the phone down and call out, 'Anthony! It's Milt.'

'Sheriff?' Anthony said when he picked up.

'Heard you and Dalton found a broom out of place at Miz Pettigrew's house.'

'Yes, sir.'

'Any prints?'

'Thing was wiped clean. Not even Miz Pettigrew's prints were on it.'

'Hum,' I said. 'I assumed the asshole was wearing gloves, but if he wiped the prints—'

'Then maybe not always?' Anthony supplied.

'Yeah. That.' I was quiet for a moment. 'Charlie or Mike say anything about the police finding prints?'

'No. Mike said they didn't find any in the house.'

'Any? Like the whole place had been wiped?'

'Hum. You know, I don't know. Want me to call him?' Anthony asked.

'No. You take care of your women,' I said. I seemed to be saying that a lot lately. 'I'll call Charlie.'

It was getting late and Charlie had already left for home – something I should be doing. But I did have his home number in my Rolodex, so I called it. He answered.

'Charlie, it's Milt.'

'Hey, Milt.'

'Did y'all get *any* prints at Miz Pettigrew's house?'

'Nary a one.'

'So the whole place was wiped down,' I said.

'Seems so.'

'So how would someone have had the time to do that?' I asked. 'I mean, Miz Pettigrew doesn't leave the house that much and wouldn't, what with her bridge group showing up. And you and your people were there pretty damn quick.'

'There was a little lag time, Milt,' Charlie said. 'The ambulance came and got the two ladies who were poisoned but everybody just thought it was food poisoning at that point. Dalton and that other woman went with Miz Pettigrew to the hospital. So the house was empty for at least an hour. Maybe more.'

'That's more than a little lag time,' I said.

'So I exaggerated. Shoot me.'

'Don't say that to me, I'm carrying.'

'Any ideas?'

'When you say y'all dusted everything, what does that mean exactly?'

'Oh, I don't know, maybe *everything*?' he said. I think he was being sarcastic. I can pick up on these nuances of speech.

'Somehow I doubt that,' I said. '*Everything*'s kinda hard to achieve.'

'Well, feel free to send your guys over there to re-dust,' he said.

'Did anybody tell you about the broom in the kitchen?'

'What broom in the kitchen?' Charlie asked, his voice indicating his impatience. Hell, what did he have to be impatient about? He was the one who was home, not like me, still sitting in the shop feeling sorry for myself.

'There was a broom in the kitchen that should have been in a closet by the back door. Miz Pettigrew doesn't leave shit like that lying around, Charlie. There's a good chance our perp put it there.'

'Why would he?' Charlie asked.

'I don't know! Maybe he dropped something and had to pick it up. Maybe he dragged in some dirt on his shoes and had to pick that up so we wouldn't know his shoe size. Hell if I know, but the thing is he did.'

'She coulda left it—' Charlie started.

But I interrupted him. 'No way, no how. Miz Pettigrew's as anal if not more so than my own mama. No way would she leave a broom leaning against the kitchen counter, especially with company coming over. It would be all over town in a New York minute that Inez Pettigrew was a sloppy housekeeper.'

'Bullshit,' he said.

'You obviously don't know that generation – at least, that generation in a small town. You're a city boy – what do you know? I'm telling you, the perp put that broom there.'

'OK, fine,' he said, obviously irritated. 'I'll have somebody swing by and pick the damn thing up. That work for you?'

'That works for me,' I said, grinning at the fact that he was getting pissed off. I'd obviously done my job well.

'Now if you don't have anything more you need me to do, can I get back to my supper before it's stone cold?' Charlie said.

'Sorry I inter—' But I was talking to a dead line.

I decided it was about time for me to head home. Then I thought about the fact that my sister would be fixing dinner and wondered if there wasn't something else I could do in the office. Then I chided myself for being a coward and headed to my Jeep, but I didn't get far. One foot shot out from underneath me on my first step out the door. Ice was everywhere. The snow storm had turned into an ice storm, which meant all hell was about to break loose.

Jean and John were alone in the house. Jewel Anne and Harmon had gone to Tulsa earlier in the day antiques shopping and had gotten stuck due to the weather. Then Milt called and said he'd best stay at the station because accidents were bound to happen. So Jean heated up a can of tomato soup, grilled some cheese sandwiches, and she and John had a picnic on the coffee table in front of the TV – something she usually didn't allow. They were halfway through a DVD of *The Lord of the Rings* – for the umpteenth time – when the lights went out. Suspecting that this might happen in an ice storm, Jean had set out a couple of flashlights.

She pulled herself up by her crutch and told John, 'I'd better get some candles. The lights might be out for a while and we don't want to run the batteries down on the flashlights. Could you please start a fire while I find the candles?'

'Sure, Mom,' John said, glad that she'd set him such a grown-up task. His father had taught him how to start a fire, but – until now – Mom had not seen fit to let him do it on his own. He was stacking two logs and looking for the kindling when he heard a sound at the window of the living room. He threw the flashlight beam in that direction and let out a scream.

Seeing as how I didn't have to eat my sister's cooking for dinner, and seeing as how Jean was nowhere around to tell me what I could or couldn't eat, I suggested – OK, ordered – Anna Alvarez to bear the storm and head to KFC. When she got back – the south

Texas girl half frozen from the storm – I indulged big time. Three pieces of fried chicken, two helpings of mashed potatoes and a corn on the cob.

Which may have been the reason I felt like throwing up an hour later. Before the heart attack, I could eat twice that much and have room for dessert, but after being on this stupid diet for almost two years, my belly couldn't handle it. Although I must admit my belly no longer hung over my belt. Which I suppose could be called a good thing.

The phone was ringing off the hook and I'd called in Emmett, Anthony and Dalton. Even Charlie Smith, police chief of Longbranch, dropped by to ask if we could back up each other on the wrecks, which I agreed to. Mostly they were fender-benders, cars slipping and sliding on the ice, but there was one bad one in downtown Longbranch that I sent Anthony to help with. Seemed old man Everett, the pharmacist at the Rexhall Drug Store, was coming out of his shop when a car slid on the ice and pinned him between that car and Mr Everett's own. Both his legs were at least broken, if not worse. It took the EMTs over thirty minutes to get there, with Anthony and a city cop trying to take care of the old man as he went into shock. By the time Anthony got back to the station, he said it wasn't looking good for Mr Everett.

The phones were ringing so much that I had to answer 'em a couple of times, which, in my vaulted position, I usually didn't have to do. The third time I answered it was my wife. All I heard before the line went dead was, 'Milt! Help!'

Jean heard John's scream and hurried back into the living room. 'What?' she demanded.

'Mom! There's a monster outside!' he said, his flashlight beam still focused on the front window.

'John, I don't see anything!'

'It's gone now! But Mom, I swear, there was somebody – or some*thing* out there!'

Jean sighed. 'It's the storm, honey,' she said. 'It may have knocked a branch down or blown something against the window—'

'No, Mom, I swear—'

'John, did you open the flue?' Jean asked, sniffing the air.

Johnny Mac turned to the fireplace, which seemed to be drawing fine. 'Yeah, Mom, I swear I did—'

Still Jean sniffed the air. 'Something's burning!' she said as she saw smoke coming from the area of the kitchen.

She hurried that way, telling John, 'Grab the extinguisher from under the sink! Hurry!'

She came into the kitchen to find the back door on fire.

My Jeep is a four-wheel drive, which works even better with chains and snow tires, but both those items were back in the garage at home, what with winter being mostly over and all. Who knew that March would start out with an ice storm? I jumped in my Jeep and headed home. Unfortunately my house is at the top of Mountain Falls Road and, as the name implies, it was steep going. I had to go off road most of the way, grabbing what traction I could in the frozen grass and weeds on the sides of the road. Even so, I beat the fire truck, which was about five minutes behind me.

I got to the house and bailed out of my Jeep, then slammed open the front door. Jean and Johnny Mac were in the living room on the sofa, cuddled up together with a blanket and a blazing fire in the fireplace.

'What the hell!' I demanded.

'Go check out the kitchen,' my wife said.

So I did. The back door was gone and the walls on either side were scorched, the windows busted out. By the time I got back in the kitchen, Jean was up and talking to one of the volunteer firefighters standing in our living room.

The volunteers decided to check it out anyway, to make sure there wasn't some residual sparks, or whatever, while I went up and took my wife and child in my arms. 'What happened?' I asked into Jean's hair.

She pulled away. 'We're not sure—' she started but Johnny Mac interrupted.

'There was somebody out there, Dad! I swear to God there was! I saw somebody at the window,' he said, pointing to the living-room window that looked out to the front of our property, 'and I yelled to Mom and then, before you know it, we started smelling smoke, and it wasn't coming from that!' he said, pointing at the fire in the fireplace. 'I built that!' he added, with pride in his voice.

I pulled him to me. 'You did good, son,' I said. Then, 'Did you get a good look at whoever was out there?'

'It looked like a monster to me.'

'Son—' I started, but again he interrupted. It was a new habit he was gonna have to break.

'I know there aren't monsters, Dad. I'm just saying that's what it *looked* like! Like maybe it was somebody wearing a mask or something.'

Thinking about the zombie baby someone had hung from the light fixture in our interrogation room at the station, I figured maybe our bad guy had picked up a few more tricks at that Halloween store.

'Sheriff,' one of the volunteers said as he came back in the living room, 'the fire's out but y'all can't stay here. We can put up some plastic until you can get repairs done but it's supposed to get down to the teens tonight.'

I nodded my head, thanked the volunteers who were already coming in the house with sheets of plastic and got on my cell phone to call the Longbranch Inn. Looked like we'd be spending the night there.

So I was tired the next day when I got to the shop. I was the last one in – except for Holly.

'She's staying with Mama,' Dalton explained. 'We didn't want to leave Mama alone just now.' He leaned in to speak softly in my ear. 'Miz Merkle died late last night,' he said.

So that was two dead from the arsenic someone had put in Miz Pettigrew's peach melba and one dead from cut brake lines. The fun and games part of this situation was definitely over.

But I was cranky, which may have had more to do with my over-indulgence with fried chicken than lack of sleep, so I said, 'I need Holly here to do some computer work!'

'I can help, Sheriff,' Anna Alvarez said as she came out of the bullpen.

'She's good, Milt,' Emmett said. 'Helped me a lot yesterday.'

'Yeah, whatever. Fine.' I turned and walked to my office. The ice storm was over but ice was still on the ground – and on the streets and sidewalks and driveways, and anywhere else that was level enough to catch it. The trees looked real pretty with the icicles hanging down like an old-fashioned Christmas tree but accidents were still bound to happen, and I was glad I had almost a full staff.

My breakfast was skimpy, just some coffee and part of half a grapefruit. And both of those were at war with what was left of my stomach.

'What's eating you?' Emmett asked as he followed me into my office.

I groaned. 'Don't say "eat",' I said.

'I told you not to have that fourth piece of chicken!' he said with a grin.

'It was a third, but who's counting?'

'Jean know what you did?' he asked.

'No, and she's not going to!' I said, giving him a look. 'Or Jasmine will find out about your penchant for the enchilada special!'

He held up his hands in surrender. 'Who? Me tell? Not on your life! Did you puke?' he asked.

'If only,' I said and groaned. I used to think not being prone to puking was a good thing, but my stomach was telling me that throwing up some of last night's indulgences would do me a hell of a lot of good. 'Got a Tums?'

He left for his office, coming back seconds later with a brand-new roll of Tums. 'Jasmine got me two at the store the other day. Haven't even started on the first one so you can have this.'

'Thanks,' I said, and popped two in my mouth, chewing slowly. The burp this produced moments later was awesome. If I coulda burped that loud as a kid I woulda been king of the playground.

'So what's happening?' I asked Emmett.

'Got Anna looking up Tom Vaught's family.'

I frowned.

'Tom Vaught. The guy Danny Evans shot in that road rage—'

'Oh, yeah. I guess we gotta look at them, huh?'

'They're the only ones left,' Emmett said.

'That we know of,' I said.

'What's that supposed to mean?' he said with an edge to his voice.

'Well, how the hell do we know the real perp is even in our list of suspects? I mean, it's not like there haven't been a slew of assholes we've put away – or killed, if it comes right down to it. And – *and*,' I said, getting hopped up a little, 'what's to really say this has anything to do with revenge? It could be something else entirely. It could be some stranger—'

Emmett sighed. 'Milt, I think we got enough. Any more suspects and we'd need to hire storage to keep 'em in.'

'Speaking of that, I think we should let the Permeter boys go.'

Emmett just stared at me for a moment and then said, 'You think that's wise? I mean, what's Dalton gonna have to say about that?'

'We've got no reason to keep 'em locked up,' I said, leaning back in my chair. 'I'll try to convey that to Dalton.'

'Better you than me,' Emmett said, stood up and left the office.

'Coward,' I called after his departing back.

Then I punched in Dalton's extension and asked him to come to my office. He came in, sat down in a chair and looked at me with those big doe eyes of his. I wished I could tell him I had one iota of evidence against anybody – especially the Permeters who nobody liked much anyway – but I didn't. And I couldn't legally keep the brothers locked up any more. Actually, I should never have done it in the first place. If they weren't too stupid to realize it had been illegal and called a lawyer, I could be in deep shit. But I was banking on the fact that knowledge was not a commodity the Permeter brothers had in stock.

So I just sighed, looked Dalton straight in the eye and said, 'I gotta let the Permeter brothers go.'

To my surprise, he nodded his head. 'Yeah, Holly told me you were holding them illegally.' He looked down at his hands. 'And I thank you for that, Sheriff. I've decided I'm gonna send my mama up to her sister's in Kansas. I'm trying to get Holly to go with her, but you know Holly.'

I smiled. 'Yeah, I know Holly. But she'll be here at the shop most days and with you at night. I'll make sure if you get stuck on a call after quitting time that she goes home with me or Emmett until you can pick her up. That work for you?'

Dalton smiled weakly. 'Yeah, it'll have to. I need this afternoon off. I have to drive Mama to Kansas and I'm taking Holly with me.'

I stood up and held out my hand. 'That'll be fine,' I said. 'Just be real careful. There's still a lot of ice out there.' He took my outstretched hand and shook it.

'Thanks, Milt,' he said, 'I'll be real careful.' And he left the office.

According to Anna Alvarez, Tom Vaught's family still lived in Prophesy County. They had a ranch not too far from the Tejas County line. Emmett decided to drive over there without calling first. Surprise can sometimes spook people into a confession. At least, that's what he'd heard. He took his personal car so as not to alert them as to who was driving up their road, and also because he'd procrastinated about changing out the snow tires which, in this instance, was a good thing.

The Vaught ranch was a real nice piece of property. According to the records Anna had found on the Internet, the Vaughts owned one-hundred-and-eighty-five acres and made their income off raising and selling Quarter Horses. The private road to the house was lined with white-washed fencing and lots of pin oaks dusted the grounds, icicles shining like diamonds in the sun that had decided to come out. He could see about ten horses far out in a field on the right and a couple in a corral on the left. He thought that while he was here, if he didn't piss anybody off too much, he might check and see how much a Quarter Horse cost these days. He thought his daughter would love that. Most girls did.

The house was a long, low ranch, well-kept with a cropped front lawn now brown from winter but shiny from the ice. A couple of drifts of snow rested against the north side of the trees. He stopped the car and noted that it had been surrounded by a pack of dogs. None of them were barking, just staring at him. Two were sitting on their haunches by his door, a couple on the other side and two more in front. He didn't like the odds.

Then the dogs looked up at the house and so did Emmett. A woman was standing on the front porch. She snapped her fingers and all six dogs rushed up the steps and sat down around her, all staring again at Emmett's car. He got out slowly, holding up his hands as if the woman had a gun pointed at him rather than a pack of dogs. Of course, he thought, a bullet could possibly miss him; six attacking dogs not so much.

'Miz Vaught?' he called up to the porch.

'Yes, sir?' she said, her demeanor friendly. She was a tall, rangy woman wearing old tight blue jeans and a Chambray work shirt, her gray hair cropped short. She wore no make-up but there were diamond studs in her ears that Emmett knew were over a karat each – he'd been looking at some just like them at a jewelry store, thinking of buying them for Jasmine for her birthday, but they were way too expensive.

'Emmett Hopkins, deputy with the sheriff's department.'

'Well, hey. What can I do you for?'

'Wondered if I could talk to you and your children?'

'Troy's out in the stables doing what needs to be done but Shelley's at school. She goes to OU up in Norman. Only one in the family ever to go to college,' she said proudly. 'Lorie lives in Oklahoma City now. Married with my first grandchild on the way.'

'Well, that's real nice, ma'am. Can I come up to the porch?'

'You afraid of the dogs?' she asked, grinning.

'Yes, ma'am,' Emmett said.

'Ah, hell, come on up and let's see what they do.'

Emmett gingerly walked up the porch steps and took each step slowly, keeping his hands out in front of him and his eyes on the dogs. Three had already sat down next to Mrs Vaught and three were standing, two with their tongues lolling out. He wondered if that meant they were hungry and maybe he smelled like lunch.

When he got to the top step one of the dogs moved forward and Emmett stood as still as possible. The dog smelled his outstretched hand, then licked it. One of the sitting dogs stood up and rubbed up against Emmett's pant leg.

Mrs Vaught laughed. 'They're not exactly watchdogs,' she said, opening the door behind her. 'Come on in.' To the dogs, she said, 'Y'all scat, now. Go on!'

The pack obediently hopped down the porch stairs and headed around the corner of the house. Emmett let out a sigh of relief.

'I was just messing with you. Have a seat,' she said, having led him into the living room. It was a big open room, a huge rock fireplace with a fire inside burning bright and warm, surrounded by bookshelves, a dining table at one end with an open kitchen next to it. It was the kind of room Emmett would love to have in his own home.

'You like something to drink? I always got coffee brewing and I got ice water but that's about it. Haven't made any iced tea yet.'

'Coffee sounds real good, ma'am,' Emmett said. 'Just a little milk, no sugar.'

'Be right back.'

Since the room was open, he could see Mrs Vaught in the kitchen, so he stood there in the living room until she came back with two cups of coffee.

'I grind my own beans,' she told him, setting his cup down on the coffee table in front of the sofa.

Emmett sat down on the fat, comfortable sofa while Mrs Vaught took an easy chair across from him. 'Now what's all this about, Deputy?'

Emmett took a sip of the coffee and nodded. 'Real good brew, ma'am.' Setting down his coffee cup, he said, 'We've been looking into some old cases, ma'am. There have been a few incidents involving our deputies that seem to have something to do with possible revenge.'

Mrs Vaught cocked her head. 'And you thought you'd come talk to me? Why would I want revenge against your deputies? I suppose this has something to do with my husband's murder,' she said. 'But that nice young black man who came to the scene did everything he could. I have no problem with him. If I wanted revenge, I'd go after Lou Anne Evans and her boys. But Lou Anne and her boys didn't kill my Tom – her husband did. And me and her might have gotten into it that day, pulling hair and what have you, but I hold no grudge against her. She might hold one against me since I testified against her husband at his trial, but I just told what happened. I mean, everybody there – including your deputy – saw Danny Evans shoot my Tom.'

'You hear anything from the Evans family?'

Mrs Vaught sighed. 'At first, right after Danny went to prison. His boys called up here and harassed my boy, even tried messing with Shelley, my youngest, but my boy taught them a lesson about that.'

'Oh, yeah?' Emmett asked.

She smiled. 'He didn't kill 'em, much as he might have liked to. Just beat on 'em a little, drove them across the Tejas County line and stripped 'em naked.' Her smile turned into a grin. 'I understand they spent some time in the Tejas County facilities.'

Emmett couldn't help but smile back. As far as he was concerned, Shelley's brother did exactly what any brother should do. 'So, no kickback from that?'

'No. Never heard from them again until Danny got killed up in McAlester. Then one of 'em called here, drunk as a skunk. I answered. Told him I was sorry he lost his father but if he ever called here again – drunk or sober – I'd have the sheriff arrest his ass.'

'And that was the end of that?'

She nodded her head. 'Been right quiet since then.'

Emmett stood up. 'Miz Vaught, thanks for your hospitality. Be OK if I went out to the stables to talk to your son?'

'All right by me.' She grinned at him. 'Now, don't you go minding them dogs, you hear?' Then she laughed outright.

'Yes, ma'am,' he said, for want of anything more appropriate to say.

She led him out of a side door and he could see the stable from there, about five hundred yards away. As she shut the door behind him, two of the dogs came up to him. One looked like it had a lot of Lab in him, the other possibly some kind of spaniel mix. Since he stood still looking at them, they both sat down on their haunches and looked up at him.

'OK, guys,' Emmett said to them, 'I'm going to the stables. Y'all can come if you want but no horsing around, OK?'

He decided to assume that they understood him perfectly and set off for the stable.

There were four Quarter Horses in stalls: a gray, a Rhone and two white ones. The Vaughts' only son was grooming the gray. He was tall and rangy, like his mother, with an unruly mop of bright red hair. When he turned, Emmett saw a heap of freckles on his face. An electric heater sat in the middle of the passageway between the stalls, giving out a poor excuse for warmth.

'You Troy?' Emmett asked.

'I'm Troy Vaught. Who're you?'

He took a glove off his right hand and held it out. Emmett shook the proffered hand and introduced himself.

'What can I do for you?' Troy Vaught asked.

'I was just talking to your mother. We've been having some problems at the sheriff's department. People threatening our deputies.'

'I'm sorry to hear about that, Deputy, but I don't see why you're here.'

'Your mother tells us you had a little trouble with the Evans boys.'

'That was a long time ago.' He took off his other glove and shut the gate to the gray's stall. 'You wanna go out in the sunshine, Deputy?' Troy asked. 'It gets kinda chilly in here and that damn heater doesn't do diddly-squat.'

Emmett nodded and he, Troy and now four dogs headed out of the stable. Troy went up to the fenced corral and leaned on the top post, one foot on the bottom rung. Emmett followed his lead.

'The Evans brothers tried to get Shelley in their car when she was about thirteen. She was right here at the driveway and just ran up. I saw her running and heard her screaming, then the assholes tearing out. Me and JR were in the same grade, so I knew that Camaro of his. Stupid piece of crap. Spoiler, lightning bolts on the sides. Dumb-looking ride.'

'So you dealt with 'em.'

'Yeah, I did,' he said, turning to look me in the eye. 'I had my daddy's unloaded forty-five since there were two of them and only one of me. They didn't ask any questions. I tied 'em up and swung at 'em a couple of times. No permanent damage, just a reminder not to mess with the Vaughts anymore. I figured their daddy killing our daddy was bad enough. And I told 'em so. Told 'em if I caught them even looking cross-eyed at Shelley again, I'd have to tear out their livers with a rusty spoon.'

'And they believed you?' Emmett asked.

Troy grinned. 'Well, I *did* have a rusty spoon in my hand at the time.'

'You and your sisters have any hard feelings against the sheriff's department?' Emmett asked out right.

Troy shook his head. 'Why would we? That black guy got Mr Evans trussed up real good, then your other deputies got there and pulled the Evans boys off me.' He grinned. 'Although my sisters were kicking some serious ass that day.' He sobered, shaking his head. 'That awful, awful day.' He looked Emmett in the eye. 'You ever meet my daddy?' he asked.

'No, not that I recall.'

'He was a good man,' Troy said. 'A good father. And I'm pretty sure a good husband. Mama seemed happy with him. This ranch has been in his family for four generations. The house is new – newish. Daddy built it for mama when she was pregnant with Lorie. The old house only had two bedrooms, and when Mama found out it was a girl, she said, "We gotta have a bigger house, Tom."' He sighed. 'At least that's the story he always told. The old house, the one my great-grandfather built, is on the other side of the property. I'm fixing it up to move into. Need my own space.'

'I'm sorry you lost your daddy, son,' Emmett said. 'Stupid way for him to go. He should be in there with you now, grooming those horses.'

Troy didn't say anything, just nodded.

'Well, then,' Emmett said, embarrassed a little from saying what he'd said. 'I'll be off.'

'Deputy, let us know if there's anything we can do to help out.'

'Thanks,' Emmett said, and headed to his car.

SEVEN

'**M**ama, you ain't gonna be gone that long. Two suitcases oughta do it,' Dalton said, watching his mother load a third suitcase.

'Hush. I need what I need and don't you go telling me what that is. 'Sides, I still haven't done the kitchen yet.'

'Mama, Aunt Mildred has a kitchen.'

'Well, you *know* she's not that great a cook. I need my own knives, and that colander of hers is rusty and it taints the food, but will she replace it? No, not Mildred. She thinks it's just fine.' She slammed down the lid of the third suitcase and turned to face her son, hands on her hips. 'Well, it's not fine with me. And if I'm gonna have to be there for whatever length of time you and your sheriff deem necessary, then I don't plan on getting myself poisoned.' Then she burst into tears and sank down on the bed.

Dalton looked from his mama to his wife, standing in the doorway of the bedroom. His eyes were pleading and Holly got the message. She motioned for him to leave, closed the door behind him and sat down next to her mother-in-law.

'Mama, I'm real sorry about Miz Jameson and Miz Merkle. I know y'all were close.'

Through her sobs, Mrs Pettigrew said, 'Me and Enid, we were in grammar school together. First grade all the way through our senior year. Then she married James Merkle and followed him for twenty years while he was in the Navy.' She grabbed a Kleenex from the box next to the bed and blew her nose. 'Didn't come back here until he died, about thirty-something years ago. It was good getting back in touch,' Mrs Pettigrew said, sniffing. She took a deep breath. 'Now, Doris, she didn't move here until sometime in the sixties. So she was fairly new. Her husband was the pharmacist over at the Rexhall on Main Street, right across from the courthouse. But then he started messing up prescriptions and killed an old lady who went to my church. They were gonna arrest him, but then they found out he had Alzheimer's and just sent him to a home. He's still there. Don't know if his children have told him about Doris. Not that he'd know who she was.' She sobbed, then said, 'But that Doris, she went to see him every day, even though he didn't know who she was. She'd say, "Malcolm, I'm your wife." And he'd say, "That's nice." And then the next day he still wouldn't know who she was.' Mrs Pettigrew grabbed another Kleenex and blew her nose, then shook her head. 'So sad. What she went through. I'm just glad my Elmer didn't make me go through any of that. No, sir. It was wham bam, thank you ma'am. Up on a ladder cleaning the gutters he has a heart attack, falls off and cracks his head open. But it didn't bleed much 'cause he was dead before he hit the ground.'

'Yes, ma'am, that's what Dalton told me,' Holly said.

'Real neat way for him to go,' Mrs Pettigrew said. 'I mean, it was a shock and all but it was quick. Bless him.'

'I think it's going to be good for you to spend some time with your sister,' Holly said.

Her mother-in-law snorted. 'Hardly. That woman gets on my last nerve.'

'Well, maybe this visit will be different.'

Mrs Pettigrew stood up. 'Don't see how. We haven't gotten along in eighty-two years. I don't expect this visit to be any different.'

She reached for one of her suitcases but Holly grabbed it. Mrs Pettigrew grabbed it back.

'Oh, no you don't, little lady!' she said. 'Pregnant women shouldn't be hauling heavy stuff around. Think that's what caused my miscarriage after Dalton. Speaking of him . . . Dalton!' she yelled. The door opened. 'Take these bags, will ya? And don't let your wife even think about carrying one.'

'Yes, Mama,' Dalton said.

I was having fits with my stomach. It was gurgling, making popping sounds, and my insides were doing a rumba. Twenty minutes in the men's room helped some but I figured I needed to pay a little more attention to this diet of mine. Cheating hadn't been all that much fun. And then finding my house part burned down didn't help with my digestion. Or my mood. Or my blood pressure. The thought that Jean and Johnny Mac had been alone in the house with someone creeping around, looking in the windows wearing a monster mask then setting fire to the back of my house was making me a mite crazy. I kept thinking of things I was gonna do to this guy when I found him. The Longbranch Inn is a nice enough place and all, but the bed's not as good as ours at home and, truth be told, I'd almost rather have my sister's cooking than stay away from home when it wasn't even my idea. I felt like I'd been kicked out of my house, which I had been, when you think about it. Which made me wonder if I should have someone guarding my house? Just in case this crazy asshole was going to go back, for whatever nefarious reason. But I didn't have the manpower to send someone out just to babysit my house.

I sighed and went out to the bullpen area. Only Anna Alvarez was there. 'So you're good with the computer?' I asked, trying to make up a little for my rudeness earlier. I suppose I could have apologized, but what would that have done to my position of authority? My old boss, Sheriff Blankenship, never apologized to anybody for anything. Of course, he died alone after his wife of forty years left him. Still and all, Anna was new – maybe not exactly an apology.

'Yes, sir,' she said.

'Holly's gonna be gone all day today so I might need your help with some research. You up for that?'

'Yes, sir!' she said, and actually looked happy about it. The only time I look happy around a computer is when I'm handing it over to someone else.

'OK, then. When Emmett comes in, send him to my office. Then we might have some stuff for you.'

'Yes, sir,' she said.

I nodded, then nodded again, thought better of doing it a third time and turned around and headed to my office. That's when a thought struck me and I turned around again and headed back to the bullpen.

'Anna, maybe you could look something up for me?' I asked.

'Yes, sir!' she said, seeming like she was anxious to get on the computer. Takes all kinds, I guess.

'Check out a guy named Wharton Jacobs. He's dead, but see about his kin and his ex-wives,' I said.

She looked at me with a questioning expression.

'He's the husband Maudeen Sanders shot. He'd been married a few times before her. Just wondering if any kin or an ex-wife or two might be pissed off.'

Anna nodded her head and grinned. 'Sounds like a good idea,' she said.

I couldn't say I agreed with her sentiments but at least it was an idea, good or not.

Twenty minutes later, Emmett walked in the side door. He stuck his head in my office doorway. 'Back,' he said.

'Go tell Anna then come in here,' I told him.

'Why do I have to tell Anna?'

'She's playing Holly today.'

'Gotcha.'

About a minute and a half later, he was sitting in a chair in front of my desk. 'So, the Vaughts?' I said.

He shook his head. 'Clean as a whistle. We knew going in they were a long shot. I mean, what would they have against the department? We helped 'em that day *and* at the trial. Miz Vaught's a real nice lady, makes a good cup of coffee. Kinda funny—'

'Funny ha-ha or funny weird?' I asked.

'Oh, definitely funny ha-ha. Met her son. Seems like a good sort. When Holly gets back—'

'Don't wait for Holly if it's computer work. Give it to Anna.'

'Right, forgot. OK, I'll have Anna run him through the system, see if there's anything outstanding on him but I doubt there will be. More likely, if somebody from that incident is doing this, it's one of Danny Evans' boys.'

'The one who's a born-again living in another state or the one that you interviewed? I thought you didn't like him for this?' I said.

Again, he was shaking his head. 'I didn't. And I still don't, but . . .' He shrugged, leaving the sentence open-ended.

'But we don't have anybody else,' I finished for him.

Just then my phone rang and I picked it up. 'Sheriff Ko—'

'Milt, it's Charlie. You know that second sweep you wanted us to do on Miz Pettigrew's house?'

'Yeah?'

'No prints, but . . . that broom Dalton found in the kitchen?'

'Yeah?'

'There was a tiny splinter on one side.'

'OK,' I said.

'And guess what was on the splinter!' Charlie said.

I sighed. 'Think you can drag this out much longer, Charlie? I really got nothing to do here today.'

'Blood,' he said.

I sat up straight. 'You're shitting me.'

'I shit you not, Sherlock.'

'What?' Emmett asked, sitting up straight himself, leaning on my desk.

Covering the mouthpiece of the phone, I told Emmett, 'They found blood on that broom of Miz Pettigrew's.'

'Halleluiah!' Emmett said.

'Y'all, now, don't you two start getting too excited,' Charlie said over the phone. 'We gotta send the blood off to Oklahoma City, to their DNA lab before we find out anything. But you might wanna start swabbing your suspects.'

'You'll make that DNA request a priority?' I asked.

'Priority plus,' Charlie said. 'If need be, me and you can take a trip to Oklahoma City and light a fire under their asses.'

'Sounds like a plan,' I said and hung up.

Then sat there for a minute, playing a scenario in my head of trying to get cheek swabs from our plethora of suspects. It wasn't gonna be pretty.

*   *   *

'You know, I'd really rather just stay with y'all,' Mrs Pettigrew said from the back seat of the car. Holly had tried to get her to ride in the front but her mother-in-law pulled the pregnancy card and told Holly she shouldn't be all squashed in the back seat. Instead, she complained of the lack of leg room so much that Holly's front passenger seat was now pulled up so close that, had she been any more pregnant, her belly would have touched the glove compartment.

The highway had been cleared of ice, even the bridges and overpasses, so it was smooth sailing all the way up I-35 to Kansas. They were headed for the Kansas state line, about an hour out of Prophesy County.

'Mama, we've been over this,' Dalton said from the driver's seat.

'I know, I know,' Mrs Pettigrew said, sighing. 'Y'all need your space. I understand.'

'Mama, you know it's not that—' Dalton started.

'Yes, I know,' she said. 'It's for my own protection.'

'Exactly,' Dalton said and sighed. Holly was the only one who heard the sarcasm in her mother-in-law's voice.

It was beginning to look like Kansas – a lot more flat land and fewer hills. They were on a stretch of highway without any trees, just prairie, with a filling station or two to break the monotony and more snow on the sides of the road as they headed north. The loud bang of a blown tire was heard and the car began to careen all over the highway, barely missing an eighteen-wheeler that was honking like mad. Dalton wasn't ready for it, and everything he'd learned at the advanced driving class he'd taken flew out the window, just like the shards of window glass that were freed by the impact of Mrs Pettigrew's head.

'So let's review,' I said.

'Let's don't,' Emmett said.

'Shut up,' I said.

'Bite me,' he said.

'Sheriff?' Anna Alvarez said from the doorway.

'Hey, Anna. You got anything?' Me and Emmett had given her some names to run through the computer, hopefully to find someone – anyone – who might stand out as our bad guy.

'Well, that Vaught guy, Troy?'

'Yeah?' I said while Emmett turned around in his seat in expectation.

'He got a ticket back in 2012 for running a red light but that's it. He's listed on the DMV records as unmarried, living at the address Emmett gave me with two vehicles registered in his name: a 2010 Chevy half-ton and a 1954 Jeep.' She looked up with a frown. 'They made Jeeps that far back?'

'Yeah,' I said and sighed at her youth. 'Even way back then.'

'Jeez, who knew?' she said.

'Anything else?'

'I checked out that guy, Wharton Jacobs, like you asked me to. Jacobs isn't even his real name, Sheriff!' she said, all excited like. 'His real name is Jacob Wharton – can you believe it?'

'So why'd he change it?' I asked.

'Probably because he was wanted in Alabama for fraud,' she said.

'Well, I do declare!' Emmett said, playing with a Southern accent even worse than his own.

'Hum, so did Jacob Wharton have any kin?' I asked.

'No, sir. He was a product of the Alabama foster care system, with a detour to a juvie center when he was fourteen, and it appears he was a guest at a correctional facility as an adult. Did eighteen months,' she said.

'What about the ex-wives?' I asked.

'Two of them are living here in the county but I doubt either one would want to take revenge for his death. Seems more than likely they'd want to help Miz Sanders kill the SOB,' Anna said, a slight indication that maybe she felt the same way about Mr Wharton Jacobs née Jacob Wharton as everybody else in our small world did.

'The other two?' I asked, just because it was expected of me in my vaulted position as sheriff of Prophesy County, Oklahoma.

'One died of cancer shortly after her short marriage to Wharton broke up and the other remarried, has three children with her new husband and is living back east in, I think . . .' she checked the notes in her hand, 'Baltimore, Maryland.'

'OK, let's forget about old Wharton, whatever his name is. Anything else?' I asked.

'Yes, sir. I dug deeper into all the others like you asked and the only thing I got was that John Connors was married before his current wife, Reba, and had a son from that marriage.'

'No kidding?' I said. Now this was a new wrinkle. A son. Was he close to his daddy? Did he want revenge on the deputy who was too late to the house to keep his daddy from becoming brain damaged? And did that revenge just lap over to the rest of us? 'What's his name?'

'John, like he was a junior maybe, but he was adopted by his mother's new husband when he was still a baby, so his last name's not Connors. It's Brewer. John Brewer.'

'Age?'

'Twenty-seven. Lives in Oklahoma City. Unmarried. No children. Drives a truck for Walmart.'

I held out my hand for her notes on John (Connors) Brewer. 'Thanks, Anna. Anything else?'

She shook her head. 'No, sir. Want me to keep trying?'

'No, you done good. Go get some lunch.'

'Yes, sir,' she said and left.

I was beginning to like her. She was the only one in the department who said 'yes, sir' and 'no, sir.' There was something to be said for a little respect for authority. When the rest of her paperwork showed up from Laredo, I might just put her in for a raise.

'So, you wanna go check this guy out? This son?' Emmett asked.

'It's a longer shot than any of the others we've been looking at,' I said. 'Don't see how I can justify a trip to the city to the county commissioners.'

'Yeah? So how long you gonna wait to go light a fire under those DNA guys? Two birds, one stone,' Emmett said, wiggling his eyebrows.

'You got something you want to do in Oklahoma City?' I asked.

'You still got that coupon for that steakhouse?' he asked.

A plan was coming together.

The car rolled over three times, going off the highway and stopping upside down in a ditch. Dalton was screaming Holly's name, even though their hands had found each other, even as he undid his seat belt and got himself upright. 'Baby? You OK?' he asked, holding on to her shoulders.

'Yes, yes, I'm fine. Mama?' Holly yelled into the back seat.

Dalton unclipped Holly's seat belt and turned her to an upright position, then flung himself between the two front seats to look in the back.

His mama hadn't answered. His first look told him she was dead. 'Mama!' he shouted. 'Oh, my God, Mama!'

'Move!' Holly said, clawing at her husband's back. 'Let me see her!'

Holly was small enough to climb into the back seat. There was blood everywhere but she was able to find its source – a gash on Mrs Pettigrew's head. Feeling her neck, Holly found a strong pulse. 'She's alive, Dalton! She's alive! Call an ambulance!'

Dalton grabbed his cell phone and dialed. Nothing happened. 'It's broken!' Dalton said with a sob.

Holly grabbed the phone and looked at it. No service. They were definitely out in the boondocks.

'Get me that box of Kleenex up there!' she said. When Dalton handed it to her, Holly grabbed a handful of tissues and made them into a bandage of sorts. 'String? Tape? Anything to keep this in place?' she demanded.

'Ah, I dunno! I dunno!' Dalton cried.

'Damnit, honey! Get a hold of yourself. I need you! Check the glovebox! See if there's anything in there.'

Two seconds later Dalton handed her a box of dental floss. 'This work?' he asked.

'Perfect,' she said, smiling at her husband, then turned to Mrs Pettigrew to try to staunch the bleeding.

It stopped after a few minutes, then she felt again for a pulse, which was still strong. Holly rubbed the inside of her mother-in-law's wrists and slapped her face.

'Oh, jeez, Holly, whatja doing?' Dalton demanded.

'Honey, I'm trying to wake her up,' she replied.

'Maybe you shouldn't oughta slap her,' Dalton said. 'She'd be real mad.'

'You wanna do this?' Holly said, almost – but not quite – snapping at her husband.

'Oh, hell no,' Dalton answered.

'Then do something useful and walk back to that gas station we saw a few miles back. And keep looking at your cell phone to see if you got service.'

When he gave her the look she usually found charming, she

sighed and grabbed the phone. Holding it out to him, she pointed at the bars in the corner. 'See this? When you get two or more bars that means you're in the service area and can use the phone. Call nine-one-one. Get an ambulance for Mama.'

'Right, right.' Dalton stared at the phone. 'Two bars. Call nine-one-one. Gotcha.' He kissed her deeply and said, 'I'll be back quick as can be.'

She touched his face with her fingers and smiled. 'I know that, honey. Just be careful. Watch for ice.'

'Is an ambulance on the way?' I asked Dalton, my hand tight on the phone receiver.

'Oh, yeah. Mama's already in the hospital. Me and Holly got a ride with a state trooper. But Milt, I gotta tell you something bad.'

'Your mama's OK, right?' I asked, beginning to sweat.

'Oh, yeah, mostly. She's still asleep and all and she's got concussion. They wanna keep her here, at least overnight. No, the thing is, Milt, that blown tire?'

'Yeah?'

'It was brand new, so I had 'em check it out. Somebody shot out the tire, Milt. Somebody did this on purpose.'

'This is insane,' Emmett said.

'That's one word for it,' I said.

'That's two hits on Dalton. It's gotta be the Permeter brothers.'

'Yeah, you're right. What they got in the way of alibis?' I asked.

Emmett leaned back in his chair, the front two legs off the floor and yelled out the door, 'Anna! Get me that file on the Permeter brothers, please.'

'Yes, sir,' she called back, and Emmett grinned at me.

'She called me sir,' he said.

'Did Jasmine finally stop calling you that?' I teased.

Anna was in quick with the files – two of 'em, not as thick as one might wish for.

'OK, so we don't have a definite time for the note or the zombie baby, or when somebody messed with Maryanne's brakes, or the judge's brakes, or when somebody broke into Miz Pettigrew—' I started.

'Yeah, we do, with Dalton's mama. Remember? The house was

empty when they took those ladies to the hospital,' Emmett said.

'Well, yeah, Emmett,' I said, somewhere between snippy and sarcastic, 'but the poison had already been put in the food by then!'

'Yeah your own self!' Emmett said. 'But somebody went in her house and cleaned up, remember? The broom? The blood?'

'Oh,' I said. I don't do sheepish, but if I did . . .

'So maybe we should bring in them Permeter boys and see where they were during that hour.'

'Call Charlie and find out our window,' I said. 'And call Jasmine and Anthony. I want those boys picked up now.'

Jasmine was scared. She and Emmett were the only ones who hadn't been harassed by this guy yet. She was waiting for the other shoe to drop. They had talked the night before about having Petal, their daughter, go stay with Jasmine's sister Daisy in Little Rock, but Emmett was worried about Petal missing school.

'Better to miss school than end up in a car accident or whatever!' Jasmine had countered.

'You're being paranoid,' Emmett had said. 'If this asshole was after you or me he'd have done something by now, don't you think? He seems to be concentrating on Anthony and Dalton.'

And now Milt, she thought. Who was to say she and Emmett weren't next? With them it would be two birds with one stone. But, after the phone call from Dalton, Jasmine was relaxing a little bit. Two attempts on Dalton's family meant, maybe, that her family was in the clear. Obviously someone was after Dalton. She was really sorry about what happened to Dalton's mother but secretly she was just damned glad it wasn't her family. She still wanted to send Petal to her sister's, though.

She was supposed to be going after Nick Permeter. She'd never met any of the Permeters and wasn't looking forward to meeting one of them now. Jasmine was beginning to wonder if it was time for her to retire. She was getting less and less interested in getting shot at or beaten up by a perp and more and more interested in being a stay-at-home mom with all the perks of the PTA, being a room mother and occasionally sleeping in. Maybe she'd take a cooking class, get better at it. She was pretty sure Emmett was tired of chicken nuggets. She needed to expand her horizons. Maybe read a book. It had been a while since she'd had time for that. She was so wrapped up in her reverie that she barely felt the bullet that blew out the glass of her side window. She slumped over the steering wheel and her foot slid off the gas pedal as the squad car she was driving ran over the side of the road and into a ditch.

EIGHT

Anthony got back to the shop with Joe Permeter shortly after noon.

'I didn't get to eat my lunch!' Joe said. 'You can't take me in when I'm hungry!'

'Never heard of that one,' Anthony said, pulling him along by the arm. 'And quit your belly-aching. I've heard enough from you and your brother to last me a lifetime.'

'Yeah, well, you ain't heard from our lawyer yet! That's the next voice you're gonna hear!' Joe said, trying to pull away from Anthony. But, with his hands cuffed behind his back, resistance, as they say, was futile.

Anthony had come in the front door and could see Anna Alvarez in the bullpen. 'Hey, Anna, tell Milt I got me a Permeter,' he said. 'I'm taking him to interrogation.'

'Got it,' she said and headed down the hall to the sheriff's office.

Anthony took Joe Permeter into the interrogation room and sat him down on the side of the table that faced the two-way mirror into the break room, the side of the table that also held the iron ring to which he cuffed his prisoner. He knew he should have just cuffed one of Permeter's arms to the ring, but not being in a real friendly frame of mind, Anthony cuffed both of his hands under the table, which made Joe have to bend over. Anthony went to the door, his back to it, his arms crossed over his chest and a grin on his face.

'You enjoying this, Deputy?' Joe asked, sneering at him.

'Oh, yeah,' Anthony said, his grin getting wider.

'Well, enjoy it while you can because my lawyer's gonna sue the department and you personally!'

'Which lawyer is this? Your mama's first cousin's ex-husband who's a judge in another county?'

'Fuck you!' Joe said and looked away, his mouth grim.

Anthony didn't laugh out loud, only because, deep down, there was nothing funny about anything right now. Not with his wife still acting like what happened was all his fault, his baby girl still crying a lot – from pain or her mama's tension, he wasn't sure – and with Dalton's mama in the hospital and two women dead. No, not much funny about this. And if he wasn't the good cop he was, Anthony thought, he'd uncuff this bastard and beat the living hell out of him. But, and in his head it was kind of a mantra, he was a good cop.

There was a knock on the door he was leaning against and he turned to see the sheriff standing there. Anthony opened the door and Milt came in. The two took seats across from Joe Permeter.

'So, Joe, what you been up to?' Milt asked.

'I'm not talking,' Joe said.

'I'd sorta like to know your whereabouts this morning. From say eight o'clock to ten o'clock.'

'I was asleep! I work nights, ya know!'

'Anybody vouch for that?' Milt asked.

'No, I sleep alone,' Joe said, still not looking at anybody.

'Really?' Milt said, a surprised look on his face. 'I keep hearing you're such a player. Women coming out of your ass. Yet you sleep alone?'

Joe turned and looked Milt in the eye. 'I don't like to wake up to a skank. I send 'em home early.' He smiled.

Milt shook his head. 'Joe, you must be the poster boy for the feminist movement, huh?'

Joe shrugged and returned to staring at the wall.

'So, no alibi,' Milt said, turning to Anthony.

'Looks that way,' Anthony said. 'Want me to swab him?'

'Sounds like a good idea. Then lock his ass up.' Milt stood up and left the room.

Anthony brought a swab out of his pocket and told Joe, 'Open your mouth.'

'Make me!' Joe said, clenching his mouth shut.

'OK,' Anthony said, and pinched Joe's nose shut.

I went back to my office, a little worried that I still had no evidence worthy of locking up the Permeter brothers, but here I was, doing it again. I wondered if I could get a law passed saying it was OK to lock up assholes. Of course, we didn't have enough room to do a thorough job of that.

Nick Permeter should be here in a minute, I thought, so I set about getting ready for him. I knew Nick probably didn't sleep alone, being married and all, but what wife wouldn't give their husband an alibi? Unless she was pissed at him. And if I was married to the likes of Nick Permeter, I'd be pissed all the time.

I got started on some paperwork and didn't realize that time was passing until Emmett stuck his head in the door. 'Jasmine back yet with Nick Permeter?'

I looked at the clock. It was after two. I got up and walked out to the bullpen. No Jasmine.

'Ah, I already looked,' Emmett said.

'Anna, get on the radio and find out Jasmine's ETA,' I said.

Which Anna did. There was no reply from Jasmine.

'Her radio working OK?' I asked the room in general.

'She never said it wasn't,' Emmett said.

'Try her again,' I said to Anna.

She did. No reply.

'Milt,' Emmett said with a touch of fear in his voice.

'OK, she was headed to Nick Permeter's house. Out on Ranch Road two-forty. We'll head that way. Come on.'

Emmett and I hurried out to a squad car, jumped in, turned on the siren and floored it out of town. Ranch Road 240 hadn't been deiced and I had to slow the squad down as it skidded and swerved. It was a rarely traveled road that led to only two farms before it circled back to Highway Five. Halfway down we saw the squad car tail up in a ditch.

'Jasmine!' Emmett yelled, bailing from the car before I'd even stopped completely.

I got on the radio. 'Anna, get an ambulance to my GPS location.'

'Yes, sir,' she said as I too bailed from the car.

Emmett was in the ditch on the driver's side, his hands inside the busted window. 'She's alive!' he yelled at me.

'Gotta bus coming!' I yelled back as I hurried down the steep wall of the ditch. 'Is she conscious?'

Emmett shook his head. I could hear him cooing to his wife. 'You're OK, baby. I'm gonna get you outta here. You're OK.'

I nudged Emmett away from the broken window. 'Let me look,' I said. I figured she'd skidded on the ice, just like I had, but when I leaned in I saw her head was lolling to the right, blood seeping from several cuts on her head. The window was broken but I couldn't figure out why skidding on the ice would do that. There was a deep gully carved out of Jasmine's neck, in a location that couldn't have been from the broken glass of the window. That's when I looked at the passenger seat and saw the bullet hole in the side of it. Looking at the road where she would have been driving, I saw only the skid marks from my own hasty stop. Nothing else. Jasmine didn't slam on her brakes. 'She's been shot,' I told Emmett.

'It's bad,' Anthony said to Anna as he put on his vest.

'But she's alive?' Anna asked.

'Yeah, I guess,' Anthony said and sighed. 'This is getting way out of hand.'

'Where are you going?'

'To check out Jasmine's squad car and then pick up Nick Permeter.'

'I'm confused,' Anna said. 'I thought the Permeter brothers were Dalton's problem.'

'Yeah, me, too,' Anthony said and sighed again. 'I don't know what the hell's going on.'

He headed for the side door and his squad car. Seeing that it was gone – probably taken by Milt and Emmett – he headed to his pick-up truck, figuring he could just handcuff Nick Permeter to the passenger-side door handle. Not perfect but it would have to do.

Anthony knew what he'd said to Anna was a vast understatement. 'Getting out of hand' didn't really sum up what was going on in Prophesy County. Somebody, and he had no idea anymore who that might be, was out to get all of them. Not just him, not just Dalton and not just Jasmine and Emmett. All of them. Even Milt, because the fire marshal had already said that gasoline had been used to start the fire at Milt's house's back door. It was only pure luck that Jean and Johnny Mac hadn't gone to bed yet.

Who was doing this? And how were they all connected? Anthony held himself totally responsible for what happened to John and Reba Connors and was present at the car wreck and murder on

Highway Five with the Evans family and the Vaught family, but he had nothing to do with the Permeter brothers or anybody else. There was one person they hadn't talked to yet. One person who could be holding a big old grudge against Anthony, and that was John Connors' son from a previous marriage. What was his name now? Brewer. John Brewer. Truck driver for Walmart in Oklahoma City. Maybe he should be heading there instead of going after Nick Permeter once again. But somebody shot at Dalton's car and somebody shot Jasmine in the head. And he didn't see how that could be any concern of John, formerly Connors, Brewer.

Anthony sighed deep in his soul and turned on the county road leading to Nick Permeter's house and Jasmine's wrecked car. Nothing to it but to do it, he told himself.

My wife found me in the ER waiting room. 'How is she?' Jean asked, slightly breathless from her rush down from the fourth floor where her office was.

'She's alive,' I said, taking her in my arms.

Jean and Jasmine had gotten tight over the years, with our kids being in the same class more often than not and me and Emmett being best friends and all. It got to the point where they either had to like each other or somebody needed to get a divorce. Luckily they liked each other fine. But that didn't help my wife's composure at the moment.

'What happened?' she asked, pushing away to look me in the eye.

'We don't really know,' I said, 'except she was shot and lost control of the car. That's how she ended up in the ditch. Knocked her head about some, glass cuts in her scalp, nose busted probably by the airbag and a pretty deep gash on her neck where the bullet grazed her.'

'Grazed? You call that a graze?'

'Yeah, honey, I do. No hole, just a gash. The bullet's probably still in the passenger seat. I got Anthony checking that out now.'

Jean sank down on one of the chairs in the waiting room, tucking her crutch between the chairs. 'Have you heard from Dalton?' she asked as I sat down next to her.

'Yeah, I called him to tell him about Jasmine. He's leaving Holly with his mother and heading home. I'm pretty short on deputies.'

'How's Anthony holding up?'

I shrugged. 'Who knows? Probably better now that this asshole is concentrating on the other deputies.'

Jean took my hand and squeezed. 'And you,' she said. 'Should I be thinking about taking John and heading to my parents' house?'

I sighed. 'Yeah, maybe.'

'And talk to Emmett about taking Petal with me,' she said.

'Yeah. That'd probably be a good idea.'

My cell phone rang and I picked it up, seeing Charlie Smith's name on the read-out. I took the call. 'Yeah, Charlie?'

'I just heard,' he said. 'You're down to a skeleton staff. I got officers I can lend you.'

'Thanks,' I said. 'Let me see how this plays out. Dalton's on his way here and I still have Anthony and Anna, although Anna's pretty much doing administrative stuff right now.'

'Which just leaves you Anthony till Dalton gets back. Let me send Mike over there.'

I nodded my head, then said, 'OK. Thanks. I'll call Anna and let her know he's on the way.'

'No problem.'

'Any word about the DNA on that blood?' I asked.

'No. I keep calling them, though. I figure squeaky wheel gets the grease.'

'Yeah. Another day then you and me are going to the city to bust some ass. 'Sides, I've got another possible suspect up there I'd like to chat with.' Me and Emmett's plan about the steakhouse was moot now, what with him stuck like glue to his wife's bedside.

'Oh?' he said. 'Who's that?'

'Seems John Connors has a son from a previous marriage. Grown up now. Might have a problem about his daddy.'

'Kinda farfetched, huh?'

'Hey, man,' I said, a little more heat in my voice than I'd intended, 'I'm doing all I can.'

'I know, I know,' he said and sighed. 'Gotta hit all the bases.'

'Exactly,' I said and hung up.

Jasper Thorne was getting concerned about the county deputies and their kin he kept hauling off to the ER. He'd been hearing some scuddle-butt that somebody was out to get the sheriff's department and he wondered if he and his partner Sylvia should start wearing vests.

He broached the subject with his partner.

'Why?' she asked.

'Well, you know, just in case,' he said.

'Just in case what?' she said and laughed. 'You think he's coming after us next? We don't have anything to do with the sheriff's department.'

'No, but we could be carrying another one of the deputies to the ER, like we did with Jasmine Hopkins, and if he wanted to finish the job—'

'He'd start blasting away at the ambulance?' she said, grinning at her partner.

'You ain't taking this very seriously!' Jasper said.

'Oh, come on! What's to take seriously? If he starts shooting at the ambulance bulletproof vests aren't gonna help us that much! We'd just end up hugging a tree or upside down in a ditch.' She pointed at the scars on her face. 'See this? A bullet didn't do this. A car wreck did this. And with me in the back of this thing? With no seat belt? I'd be a goner for sure.'

'Yeah, but I'd have my seat belt on,' Jasper said.

Sylvia shook her head. 'Then you go get you a vest,' she said. 'Be my guest.'

'To Chicago?' Emmett said, rubbing his face like he was scrubbing it at the sink. We were in Jasmine's hospital room, Emmett sitting by her side, Jasmine still unconscious. I'd just broached Jean's suggestion that she take Johnny Mac and Petal to her parents' home in Chicago.

'Yeah, they'll all be safe there,' I said.

'That's a long way away. And besides, Chicago? That's kind of a rough town, right? How're they gonna be any safer there?' He shook his head. 'I don't want Petal that far from her mama. In case—'

'Stop it. In case nothing. She's got a concussion is all. She's gonna snap out of this in a New York minute,' I said. 'Besides, the McDonnells live in an upscale suburb with its own police department. The kids couldn't be safer if we stuck 'em in our jail.'

Emmett looked up at me. 'Maybe that's what we should do.
Bring in a lot of toys—'

'Remember this asshole got in the shop once before,' I said.

'So why did you mention it?' he said, glaring at me.

'Sorry,' I said. 'I wasn't thinking.'

Emmett sighed. 'I know Petal would be safer with Jean somewhere else than here in town. Jasmine had mentioned sending her
to her sister's in Little Rock. I *do* want her out of town, but
Chicago?' He shook his head. 'Man, that's just too far away.'

'Like Little Rock's not?' I countered.

Emmett looked at his wife, silent except for the drip of the bags
going in her veins and the occasional beep of the monitors. 'Hell,
I don't know what to do,' he said. 'We need to protect them, but
Chicago?'

I nodded. I had to agree. I wasn't sure I wanted Jean and Johnny
Mac that far away either, but they needed to be out of town. 'You
still got that fishing cabin on Lake Blue?' I asked.

He turned and looked at me, a slight glimmer of hope in his
eyes. 'Yeah. I do. I most certainly do.'

'Who all knows about it?'

'Me, you, Jasmine's sisters, Dalton, maybe Anthony, although
I don't think he's ever been there.'

'Mostly people we can trust?' I asked.

'Only people we can trust,' he said.

'I'll take 'em up there myself.'

'Remember how to get there?'

'Does the pope shit in the woods?'

He didn't laugh. 'Stop by the school and get assignments for
Petal, OK?'

I wouldn't have thought of that. Although I'm pretty sure my
wife would have.

Since I was already at the hospital, I took the elevator up to the
fourth floor to see if I could catch my wife between patients.

'Hey, Brenda,' I said to the woman who sat at a desk outside
my wife's office.

'Hey, Sheriff! How you doing?'

'Fine,' I said. 'You?'

'Fine. You looking for Doctor McDonnell?'

'Good guess,' I said, smiling at her.

She smiled back. 'She's got a patient but he should be leaving in less than five minutes.' She nodded to a couple of easy chairs against a wall. 'You wanna have a seat while you wait?'

'I could take a load off,' I said, and headed in that direction.

It was less than five minutes when Brenda said, 'She's free. You can go in.'

I wasn't surprised that I hadn't seen her patient leave. There was a back door to Jean's office that led to another elevator. Patients came in the front entrance by Brenda and out the back. That way patients didn't see each other. Which, in a small town like ours, wouldn't be wise. Everybody knew everybody and rumors would be flying.

Once inside, I kissed my wife, settled down on an easy chair across from her desk and explained about the idea me and Emmett had come up with.

'A fishing cabin?' Jean said, raising one eyebrow. I hate it when she does that. It's a definite sign of disapproval.

'It's a nice fishing cabin,' I said. 'Two whole rooms!'

The eyebrow did not go down.

'And a kitchen. And an indoor bathroom!'

The eyebrow went down, only because she needed it to so she could roll her lovely brown eyes. 'My parents' house has indoor plumbing, too,' she said. And yes, I can interpret sarcasm. 'Plus central heating, comfortable furniture and nine rooms rather than two.'

'Oh, nine rooms,' I said, shaking my head. 'The kids could get lost!'

'Milton!'

Personally I disapprove of her using my full name like that. She knew it reminded me of my mother scolding me. I was beginning to wonder if we knew each other's buttons a little too well.

'Jean!' I shot back. 'Look,' I said and sighed. 'Emmett doesn't want Petal that far away from him and, truth be told, I don't want you and Johnny Mac that far away either. We don't know what this guy's gonna do next. I want to be able to get to you when I need to.'

'And what makes you think he can't find us even better at a

fishing cabin on Lake Blue than at my parents' house in Chicago?' she demanded.

'Nobody knows about the fishing cabin,' I said.

'Nobody?' That damned eyebrow again.

'Well, me and Jasmine's sisters, and Dalton and probably Anthony—'

'Now I'm feeling *really* secure!'

'OK, how about a compromise? They're moving Dalton's mama to a hospital in Oklahoma City tomorrow. What about we get the county to pay for a couple of rooms for you and the kids and Holly? We'll keep it on the down-low. Nobody but you, me, Emmett and Dalton will know about it.'

Jean sighed. 'I guess,' she said grudgingly.

'Were you really looking forward to seeing your folks?' I asked, my voice gentle.

'It's been a while,' she said.

'After this is all over, I swear we'll take all of spring break and go to Chicago. Deal?'

Jean's father had been sick lately and, as both he and her mother were getting on in years, I knew she wanted to get up there as soon as she could.

She gave me the eyebrow, then lowered it and held out her hand. 'Deal,' she said and we shook on it.

I could only pray that this thing would be over before spring break.

I'd barely gotten in my office from the hospital before Anna called me on the intercom and said that there was somebody on the line who wanted to speak to Emmett. 'Well, tell them he's not here and take a message,' I said.

'I tried that,' she said, 'but he insisted he speak to someone. Said he's Bob Huntley, the bailiff for Judge Norman?'

Hell, I thought. Another complication. 'Put him through,' I said and sighed. I didn't need this right now. There was enough going on to keep my mind occupied. When the phone rang, I picked it up and said, 'Sheriff Kovak.'

'Sheriff, I need to speak to Emmett Hopkins.'

'He's not available right now, Mr Huntley.'

'That's what your girl told me, but he called me a little while ago and said that Dave Norman was murdered. Is that right?'

'Well, his brake lines were cut, yes, sir,' I said.

'What more can you tell me?' Huntley asked.

'That's about all—'

'Bullshit!' he said. 'What made y'all start looking into his wreck in the first place? I know there's more going on here!'

'We've been having some trouble here,' I said, not wanting to get into it all. 'It may be connected.'

'How so?' he asked.

'Mr Huntley,' I said, 'this is an ongoing investigation and I can't really get into the particulars, but—'

'Again, I say bullshit, Sheriff! I'm an officer of the court. I know about confidentiality. Maybe I can help.'

I thought about what this guy might know about the judge's cases that corresponded with ours. I thought maybe he might have a point.

'OK,' I finally said. 'Let me tell you what's been going on.'

NINE

Jasmine's squad car wasn't hard to miss. The butt end of it was blocking half of the eastbound lane. Luckily – for the squad car, not so much for Jasmine earlier – this wasn't a well-traveled road. Anthony pulled as far off the road as he could get without landing in the ditch himself, parked and got out. He stumbled down the icy embankment and opened the driver's-side door. The window on that side was gone and blood soaked the cheap fabric seats. He saw the hole Milt had mentioned, in the top half of the side of the passenger seat, in a straight line from the broken window. He pulled on gloves and got some tweezers out of the crime-scene kit he'd carried with him. It didn't take long to find the spent bullet. It was the same caliber as the one found in Dalton's tire. The police department had the wherewithal to check if the two bullets came from the same rifle. Anthony was pretty damn sure that answer was gonna be yes, indeed.

He put the bullet in an evidence bag, put the bag in the crime-scene kit and put the crime-scene kit in the back of his pickup.

Then he drove on to Nick Permeter's house. Three dogs and four men seemed to be waiting for him in the front yard. On closer inspection, only two of the humans were actually men – the other two weren't much more than boys. But the one in the middle he recognized as Nick Permeter and the one next to him, standing a couple of inches taller than his daddy, Anthony reckoned to be the oldest son, the one who like to beat up on women.

Anthony stopped his pickup and got out, pulling his uniform Stetson onto his head, his gun holstered and his badge riding his belt. 'Mr Permeter?' he said, looking at Nick.

'What?' Nick asked.

'I need you to come with me back to the sheriff's department.'

'What the hell for?'

'Got a few more questions,' Anthony said.

'Go ahead and ask 'em,' Nick responded.

'No, sir. That'll be up to the sheriff. I need you to come with me peaceful.'

'Or what?'

'We do it the hard way,' Anthony said, his hand resting on the butt of his gun.

Nick laughed. 'You gonna shoot me?'

'No, don't think so. But I might shoot one of your dogs.'

'Hey, fuck you!' yelled one of the younger boys.

'Great language you're teaching your children,' Anthony said.

'I'm teaching 'em not to take any shit off the likes of you!' Nick said, then spat on the ground in front of Anthony.

Anthony was rethinking his answer to the question: 'You gonna shoot me?' He sorta wished he could.

'I need you to get in the truck, Mr Permeter,' Anthony said, his voice almost stuck on the 'mister'.

'You don't even have a squad car. How do I know you're planning on taking me to the sheriff's department? How do I know you're not gonna take me out in the woods and shoot my ass?'

Anthony smiled. 'I guess you don't. But you have my word I'm taking you to the sheriff.'

'Don't take that nigger's word for nothin', Daddy!' the big one next to Nick said.

'Don't get him any more riled up, son,' Nick said. Then to Anthony, 'How 'bout one of my boys follows us in one of my cars?'

Anthony nodded. 'Sensible compromise. Shall we?' he said, ushering Nick Permeter to his pickup while all three of the boys ran to an old Dodge Charger with the fading paint job of a Confederate flag – just like the Dukes of Hazard. No surprises here, Anthony thought.

'I hate running out on you and Mama,' Dalton said as he stood in the doorway of his mother's hospital room.

'You're not running out,' Holly said, stroking Dalton's cheek. 'You're important to the department. They need you. Mama and I are safe here. Safer than going back to Longbranch.'

'Yeah, I guess,' Dalton said.

'Besides, Milt said Jean's on her way up here with Johnny Mac and Petal and we'll all be staying in some motel rooms that the county's paying for.' She grinned at her husband. 'And as soon as possible, I'll move Mama there and we'll have a grand old time!'

'You think?' Dalton said.

'I know!' Holly said, lifting herself up on her tiptoes to kiss Dalton on the lips. 'Go, baby. They need you.'

'Tell Mama—'

'I know,' she said and gently shoved him out the door, closing it behind him. She didn't know how much good he was going to do the sheriff, what with worrying about Mama and the baby. Dalton was a worrier, that was sure, and there was very little she could do about that. But she'd call him every couple of hours to assure him that all was well. That's about all she could do.

She walked into the room and looked at her mother-in-law. Her face was pale except for the bruises, which stood out something awful on her wan face. Holly sat down in the chair next to the bed and took Mama Pettigrew's hand in hers. 'You're gonna be OK, Mama. Dalton needs you and this baby needs you, so you gotta be OK. Because I don't know much about babies, and I'm gonna need you too. You're the only mama I got.' And with that she burst into tears.

Having grown up in the foster care system, it was true that Dalton's family was the first she'd ever known. And, although Mama Pettigrew could sometimes be a pain in the ass, she knew that, in her own way, the woman loved her. And now that she was going to bear her first grandchild, that love was more evident than ever. This baby was going to need a grandma. All babies did. Holly didn't have grandparents to give her baby. There would only be Mama Pettigrew. And that would be more than enough. If she made it through this hell.

'Holly?' came a small voice from the bed.

Holly quickly wiped her tears away. 'Mama! You're awake!'

Mrs Pettigrew squeezed her hand. 'You're OK? The baby's OK?'

'Yes, Mama. Everybody's fine. Dalton had to get back to the shop but he's fine too. You cracked your head on the window.'

Mrs Pettigrew reached up and touched her head. 'It's all bandaged up?' she asked and Holly nodded. Then Mrs Pettigrew got that look on her face, the one Holly knew could definitely mean trouble. 'They didn't touch my hair, did they? If they cut my hair, I'm gonna sue—'

Holly rubbed the older woman's hand. 'Your hair's fine, Mama. They didn't have to cut anything.'

'Well, they better not! I pay eleven dollars and fifty cents every week to get Rosalie Barber to fix my hair and I'm not gonna have some nurse come by and mess with it willy-nilly.'

'Don't worry, Mama. I won't let 'em,' Holly said and smiled.

'See that you don't, young lady.'

'Yes, Mama.'

'And Holly . . .' Mrs Pettigrew started, her eyes getting droopy.

'Yes, Mama?'

'No more tattoos, OK? Not while you're pregnant,' the old lady said.

'Definitely not, Mama.'

'Good girl,' Mrs Pettigrew said, closed her eyes and began to snore softly.

Petal Hopkins looked a lot like her mother: dark brown hair, pale freckled skin and blue eyes rimmed with long black lashes. Unlike her mother's sensible short cut, Petal's hair was long, almost to her waist, and thick with waves. Johnny Mac Kovak thought she had the prettiest hair of any girl at Will Rogers Middle School. In fact, lately, he'd been thinking she was possibly just about the prettiest girl in the whole school. Even prettier than Miss Swan, who was his art teacher last year and who he had a pretty big crush on. But that was over. Miss Swan got engaged and Johnny

Mac realized the futility of a May/December romance. But Petal. Hell, he'd known her his whole life. How come he was crushing on her now? She was like a sister – sorta. But not really.

The two sat in the back seat of his mother's SUV playing MadLibs. They were whispering and giggling because they were using bad words to fill in the blanks. Neither wanted his mother to hear that. He liked it when Petal giggled. It made his head spin a little.

He even forgave her for the dumb name. It wasn't her fault, after all. Her parents named her. There was this thing in her mama's family. Jasmine, her mama, was one of five sisters. The others were named Rose, Lily, Daisy and Violet. Aunt Jasmine told his mother in front of him that she thought the next generation should carry on the tradition but Johnny Mac knew one of Miss Rose's boys and his name was Trent. Shouldn't it have been Tree, or Branch, or Bark, or something? Didn't seem fair that Petal got stuck with her name.

'How much longer, Aunt Jean?' Petal asked from the back seat.

'Look out the window. You can see the city coming up,' Jean answered.

Both kids stretched out their seat belts to look out of the front window.

'Wow,' Petal said.

'Oh, that's nothing,' Johnny Mac said. 'Houston's bigger.'

'Really?'

'Oh, yeah. Lots. We went to Houston when we went on that cruise ship.'

'I'd like to take a cruise one of these days,' Petal said with a sigh.

'Well, if you do, I hope it's calmer than the one we went on.'

His mother glanced at him through the rear-view mirror, thinking she couldn't agree more. What with a plethora of murders and Milt's heart attack, that cruise had been anything but calm.

'So where we staying?' Johnny Mac asked his mother.

'The county okayed three rooms at the Holiday Inn but I'm upgrading us to a suite at the Regents Hotel, the hotel your dad and I stayed at on our anniversary.'

'How many bedrooms does a suite have?' Petal asked.

'This one has a large living room with a fold-out sofa for John, a bedroom with a king-sized bed for you and me and a connecting room with two queen-sized beds for Holly and Mrs Pettigrew.'

'Cool,' Johnny Mac said, but could feel himself blush even as he said it. He turned his head to stare out of his side window.

They got to the hotel and Jean drove the car up to the front and parked it under the portico. Johnny Mac and Petal looked at each and mouthed 'wow.' Then a guy in a red jacket came out with a shiny gold cart and began unloading the stuff out of the back of the SUV. Petal grabbed Johnny Mac's hand and squeezed. Getting close to his ear, she whispered, 'That's a bellhop! I've seen one on TV.'

'Yeah, me too,' he whispered back, reminding himself to tell her later about the steward on the cruise ship that would leave them towels shaped like little animals. She'd like that.

With her crutch under one arm and the other around Petal's shoulders, Jean ushered the children into the hotel, smiling to herself as they oohed and awed over the chandeliers and other over-the-top accoutrements. Jean knew they'd be talking about this at school for weeks. Poor little country bumpkins, she thought with a smile.

The room was even better than his mother had described, Johnny Mac thought. It had a kitchen with a small fridge loaded with all sorts of nuts and chocolates. There was also booze, but he knew better than to try to grab any of that. His mother was quicker than he thought she could be, though, coming up behind him and closing the fridge door.

'Everything in there, even the tiniest piece of chocolate, costs an arm and a leg. If you want something we'll go to the store and get it. We eat nothing out of this fridge that we don't put in there ourselves. Got it?' she asked, eyeing both children.

'Yes, ma'am,' Petal said while Johnny Mac just nodded his head in mute agreement. He wondered how they'd know if he took just one tiny piece of candy but, as his dad said, he'd been treading on thin ice lately so he'd better watch his P's and Q's. He didn't know what P's and Q's were but he knew what would happen if that thin ice broke.

He and Petal wandered into the bedroom to look around, then found the bathroom with its huge sunken tub. 'Wow! It's like a swimming pool!' Johnny Mac said.

'More like a sauna,' Petal said. Her parents had a hot tub so she knew about that.

Johnny Mac looked at her and felt himself blushing again. Jeez, he wished he'd stop doing that. It was the height of dorkdom.

'But there's no reason we can't wear our swimsuits and get in!' Petal said, grinning at him.

Johnny Mac could feel himself falling in love.

Inez Pettigrew woke up again and felt her hand being held. She looked over and smiled at Holly, that silly little girl who'd won her boy's heart. And maybe a little bit of hers, too. But she felt something – or somebody – squeeze her other hand. Carefully she turned her head, hoping to see her son. Unfortunately for her, it wasn't Dalton. Instead it was her sister Mildred, sitting there all high and mighty, looking like the cat who ate the canary, staring down at Inez like she thought her being in that hospital bed was somehow her fault.

Inez pulled her hand away from Mildred's. 'What are you doing here?' she asked.

'Well, Dalton called me to say you got hurt, and I couldn't let my big sister be lying in some hospital bed without me coming to check on her.'

'I'm not your big sister, Mildred Maxine! I'm two years younger than you, even though you've been trying to forget that fact for nigh on eighty-some-odd years!'

'I said you were my "big" sister, Inez Dolores! Not older. I mean, you been outweighing me by some big numbers since you was thirty years old.'

Inez Pettigrew turned quickly to her daughter-in-law. 'Can you get this she-devil out of here? I can*not* believe you and Dalton were trying to send me to spend time with the likes of her! What *were* you thinking?'

Holly had no answer for that. This was her first time meeting Dalton's Aunt Mildred as she hadn't – as Mama Pettigrew said – seen fit to show up for her only nephew's wedding. And she was beginning to see Mama's point. The woman was – well, Holly didn't like to speak ill of people in general but, hey, she thought, you gotta call a spade a spade and a bitch a bitch. Aunt Mildred sure fit the latter category.

'I'm not going anywhere, Inez! I'm here to take care of you and bring you back to Topeka with me. We'll have a grand old time with me pushing you around in your wheelchair,' Mildred said. Mrs Pettigrew turned on her daughter-in-law. 'Wheelchair? You didn't say anything about a wheelchair! I thought it was my head that got hurt!'

'Yes, Mama,' Holly said, stroking the old lady's shoulder. 'That's all that got hurt.' Turning her eyes like daggers on Mama's sister, she said, 'Mama doesn't need a wheelchair and I don't think she's going to be going home with you.'

Mildred rolled her eyes. 'Inez isn't in her right mind now, what with the head injury and all, and I'm sure not listening to the likes of you! My boy John William saw you at the sheriff's department last year and he told me all about you! You and your tattoos and your pierced this and that! At least you got your hair a natural color now! My boy John William said that when he saw it, it was purple or pink or something awful like that!'

Mrs Pettigrew pulled herself up in the bed. 'So that's why you didn't come to the wedding! You know, I never did tell you this but Daddy always said you were a prissy-like brat!'

'Well, you did too tell me that! Whenever we had a fight! And no, Daddy never said that! Not ever! See?' she said, looking at Holly. 'She's not in her right head!'

'I'm right enough in my head to tell you that your boy John William is gay! Bet you didn't know that!' Inez Pettigrew all but shouted.

Mildred stood up. 'That's an awful thing to say! How dare you?' She held her hands up and wiped them against each other. 'That's it! I wipe my hands of you! I don't care if you get in a hundred hospital beds, I'll not be coming by to check! I no longer have a sister.'

'That's true enough,' Mrs Pettigrew said with a grin, 'but you still got your gay son!'

Mildred was out of the door in a flash. Holly had been looking from one sister to the other for a while. Now she came to face her mother-in-law. 'Is it true? Is John William really gay?'

'Oh, hell, honey,' Inez said, patting Holly on the arm. 'I got no earthly idea.'

*   *   *

Considering the fact that Nick Permeter was coming along peacefully, Anthony decided not to handcuff him to the inside of his truck. He did check his rear-view mirror frequently to see if the next generation of Permeter brothers were still following, and not getting so close they could ram him. He wouldn't put a hijacking beyond the Permeters. But they got through Longbranch and out the other side to the sheriff's department with no problems. Anthony parked in front so that they could all go in through the public front doors.

Anna Alvarez saw them coming and met Anthony on the public side of the bullpen.

'Need some help?' she asked, checking out the three younger men.

'You might want to keep an eye on these guys while I talk to their dad. That OK with you boys?' he asked.

The elder brother leered at Anna and said, 'No problemo.'

Anna rolled her eyes and indicated the two benches in the waiting area. 'Sit,' she said, and waited while they did so. Anthony was already on his way back to the interrogation room with Nick Permeter.

'So,' said the still-leering elder brother, 'what's a hot babe like you doing in this line of work?'

'I enjoy arresting guys that piss me off. And you're about an inch away from it,' she said, turning her back on the trio and going to the bullpen.

'Hey, spunky broad. I like spunky broads.'

'Likes to cut 'em down to size anyway!' said one of his younger brothers and the other laughed.

'Fuck you!' the elder said.

'It's against the law to use obscenities in the sheriff's department,' Anna said, having no idea if it really was or not.

The elder crossed his arms over his chest and stared out of the glass front doors.

Inside the interrogation room, Anthony said, 'So we've been having a bit more excitement around here.'

'Like I give a shit?' Nick said.

'Just need to know where you were at certain times.'

'Where's my lawyer?' Nick said.

'I have no idea. Where *is* your lawyer?' Anthony asked with a grin. 'This that same ex-cousin-in-law?'

'Fuck you,' Nick said.

'Nick, you have a very stunted vocabulary. Has anyone ever told you that? Like your last teacher? Fifth grade, right?'

'OK, I don't have to sit here and take this shit from the likes of you! I'm outta here!' Nick said and stood up.

Anthony stood up, too. 'You're making me arrest your ass. I don't want to do that, Nick. But you're a material witness so—'

'Material witness to what?' Nick yelled. 'Y'all keep saying that but I ain't seen nothing! I ain't witness to nothing!'

'Sit down!' Anthony said, his hand on the revolver at his hip. Nick sat down.

'Now, where were you at ten yesterday morning?' Anthony asked.

'What the hell happened yesterday morning? I was doing what I do. Milking cows and slopping hogs. The usual shit.'

'Got any witnesses?'

'Yeah. You think I milk them cows and slop them hogs my own self? I see myself in a mostly supervisory role. The boys do the work and I tell 'em how bad they're doing it.'

'Man, you are a role model, aren't you, Nick?' Anthony said.

'I do what I can,' Nick said.

'So those three out there are your alibis?'

'Jason and Tim. Not Randy. Randy's still in school. He helps in the afternoons.'

'Jason and Tim. They're the two older ones?'

'Yeah, genius. You figured that out all on your own?'

'I can still arrest you, you know,' Anthony said.

'For what?'

'Smartin' off to a deputy. There's a law.'

'Show me!'

'In a minute. Now, where were you at noon today?'

'Same damn place, asshole! What's your problem?'

'So you were at your farm around noon?'

'Didn't I just say that?'

'So you heard the shots?'

'What shots?' Nick asked, frowning.

'The shots that took out a deputy's car less than half a mile from your place.'

'I didn't hear no shots.'

'Maybe that's because you're the one who was doing the shooting!' Anthony said.

Nick Permeter laughed. 'If I was doing any shooting, I'd have heard the shots, dumbass!'

'What I was implying is that you're lying.'

'At noon I was having lunch with my wife, my mother and my two older boys. Ask them.'

'You saying that your family wouldn't lie for you?'

'I'm not saying another word,' Nick Permeter said.

'Fine. You're a material witness. Gonna put you back in the cells with your brother,' Anthony said, standing up.

'Like hell you are! And you got Joe in there *again*? What the hell is this? Are you people stupid or something?'

'Guess I'm gonna have to cuff you, Nick. You don't seem to be cooperating.'

'I'm gonna sue your asses off! Hide and watch if I don't!'

'That's nice,' Anthony said, cuffed him and hauled him out of the interrogation room, headed for the cells.

'Jason!' Nick yelled to his eldest. 'Go home and get your gramma to call Cousin Sarah! Me and Joe both need a lawyer! Go!'

The three boys hightailed it out of the sheriff's department.

Dalton got back to Prophesy County in record time, but instead of going straight to the sheriff's office he detoured to the county hospital. When he found Jasmine's room, he also found Emmett and Milt.

'Hey,' Dalton said from the open door to her room. Both men's heads turned toward the sound.

'Hey, Dalton,' Milt said, going up to him and shaking his hand. 'How's your mama?'

'OK, I guess. Still out. How's Jasmine?'

Emmett walked up and shook Dalton's hand also. ''Bout the same,' he said. 'They got her in one of those induced comas while they do some medical crap.' He shrugged. 'You know.'

'Yeah.' Turning to Milt, Dalton asked, 'So who's doing this?'

'We don't know, but we're gonna find out. I'm glad you're back.' Milt turned to Emmett and said, 'If you don't need me any more, I'm gonna go with Dalton back to the shop. We need to start doing something about this.'

Emmett nodded, patted both men on the back and went to sit with his wife.

TEN

I was so mad I could spit nails. Who was doing this shit? And why? I wasn't much closer to this than when I first read that message taped to the front door of the shop: *I'm going to start by killing your entire family.* That's what it said. But so far the only people killed have been outsiders. Except maybe Judge Norman. Somehow he was involved in all this, and since he was one of only three judges that served Prophesy County, it was a pretty sure bet that he'd presided over some of the cases we'd been dealing with.

I found Anna, told her to call the bailiff, Bob Huntley, at the county courthouse and see if we could get into Judge Norman's files. I wanted to see if there was a crossover. Then I went to my office to study on all this.

My studying came to naught, and when Anna came to my office door I was thrilled for the interruption.

'Whatja got?' I asked.

'Mr Huntley really wants to help,' she said. 'He seemed pretty upset at the thought that the judge had been murdered.'

'Yeah,' I said. 'I kinda got that when I talked to him.'

'He said we couldn't get access to the judge's files from this computer but I can come over there and look at theirs. Is it OK if I bring up our files on their computer?' Anna asked.

'If you do will they be able to see our stuff?' I asked.

'Yes, sir,' she said.

'Is that a good or a bad thing?' I asked.

'Well, they'll only be able to see it the little bit of time I have ours up on their computers. As soon as I get through a comparison, I'll delete our stuff.'

That sounded reasonable to me. 'OK, then let's do it. Want me to come along?'

'I think you're needed here more,' she said. 'Besides, Mr

Huntley seemed real eager to help out. Also, he wants you to call him.'

I was sure he was eager to help out. And Anna was right in a way about me being needed more here, but as my studying the situation was getting me nowhere I thought I'd be more help looking over her shoulder and wondering what the hell she was doing. But I sighed and agreed and she left for the courthouse. And I wondered why the hell Huntley wanted me to call him. I'd only met the man a couple of times and talked to him that one time on the phone. As far as I was concerned, that was enough interaction for me. But I called him anyway.

'Bob, Milt Kovak,' I said when he answered the phone.

'Sheriff, glad you called. Gotta ask you a question.'

'Shoot – and call me Milt.'

'OK, Milt. Here it is: your girl Anna better at computers than she is at testifying?' he asked.

Well, he had me there. 'What's that supposed to mean?' I asked.

'She was in court the other day, testifying on the Hanson case – that guy that hit that kid in the crosswalk?'

'Yeah, right. How'd that turn out anyway? She never said.'

'Well, I know why she didn't say. She blew it big time.'

'How so?' I asked, getting a little pissed off at where this guy was going. Who was he to say crap about my deputies?

'She was on the scene, wrote the guy a ticket, got the kid an ambulance and all but she wrote down the wrong date on the ticket and the wrong street address, and when she was testifying the biggest words to come out of her mouth were "ah" and "huh,"' he said.

Uh oh. 'Let me check into that—' I started, but he interrupted me.

'Nothing to check into, Sheriff. The girl screwed up big time. The case got thrown out. The asshole walked. And it was all her fault! What you teaching your people over there anyway?'

OK, so now I was getting huffy my own self. 'The girl's from out of state. Probably just got nervous her first time in our court. But to answer your first question, she's *real* good at computers. Better than anybody you got over there! So I'd be nice if I were you.'

'I'm being nice, Sheriff,' he said, and I noticed he'd given up on calling me by my first name. I thought I'd still call him by his, though. Hoping maybe it would piss him off.

'Bob, all I can tell you is this: it is what it is and if you want to help us find out what happened to Judge Norman, let Anna Alvarez check out his cases to see if they connect to any of the ones we got. Is that clear enough for you?'

'Well, I hope she's as good at the computer as you say she is 'cause she's a piss-poor witness, I can tell you that.' And he hung up.

I slammed the phone down, madder than I'd been in a while. Asshole, I thought. I took a couple of deep breaths, trying that yoga breathing my wife had taught me, and calmed myself down. Too much was going on around the county to let myself be sidetracked by an uptight bailiff.

I always did better thinking when I had Emmett to bounce ideas off, but he was pretty much occupied, waiting for his wife to come out of a coma. I thought of bouncing things off Dalton but they'd pretty much just hit him and get stuck. Anthony could work, I thought.

I wandered out to the bullpen and found Anthony at his desk, looking at the computer.

'Got anything?' I asked.

He shook his head. 'No. Just verifying that both of the Permeter brothers' alibis are solid as a rock.' He sighed. 'Hell, Milt, I really wanted to send those boys up for this.'

'I thought Joe was asleep, alone?' I said.

'You're gonna love this. He may have slept alone but Loretta, your favorite waitress at the Longbranch Inn, says he was sitting at one of her tables yesterday morning barely after ten a.m., eating biscuits and gravy when Dalton got shot at, and he was with the Budweiser guy bringing in cases of beer to the pool hall when Jasmine got shot. No way he could be that far up north when Dalton's tire got shot out and get back to the Longbranch Inn that quick.'

I sighed my own sigh. 'Well, damnation. I really wanted to stick it to them boys, too. Wanna come in my office and we can throw this stuff around, see if anything sticks?' I asked.

'Beats staring at the computer,' Anthony said and followed me to my office.

'Well, shit,' I said once we'd both sat down. 'So what about the Evanses? JR may be off in Texas somewhere being born-again but the younger one's right here in town. Has he got an alibi? And the mama! I wouldn't put anything past that woman.'

'Tyler was talking to Will Freznoe about his Prius today from like eleven until after noon, which covers the time for Jasmine, and as for yesterday he was working all day, had a bunch of cars and had to call him some part-time help. And both those guys – and his mama, of course – vouched for him.'

'And the mama?' I asked, still hoping for something – anything.

'The part-time boys say they saw her off and on all day yesterday but the only one to vouch for her today is her son. Will said he didn't notice if she was there or not.'

I sighed. 'Well, thank you, Anthony. You did a real good job making sure none of our suspects are guilty.'

Anthony shrugged. 'Just doing what I can for justice, sir.'

'And the American way?'

'Something like that.'

'Mind if I yell and start throwing things at the walls?' I asked.

'Only if you won't let me help.'

Again, I sighed. 'I suppose we need to be grown-up about this.'

'Do we have to?' Anthony asked, a decided whine in his voice.

'OK,' I said, sitting up and straightening my shoulders. 'We've got the Connors left. We've pretty much excluded both John and Reba—'

'Wait, now. Reba says she's got agoraphobia but how do we know that's true? Anybody can say they're scared to leave the house, or scared of heights, or whatever, but that doesn't make it true.'

'Yeah, you got a point,' I conceded. Half to myself, I asked, 'I wonder if she ever tried to get help?' And picked up the phone, knowing the only help for this kind of thing in a fifty-mile radius was my wife.

I called Jean's cell phone since she was in the city and asked her if she'd ever had Reba Connors as a patient.

But I might as well have saved the minutes. Jean said, 'You know I can't answer that.' She sighed. 'How many times do we have to go through this?'

'Maybe a hundred and eleven more times?' I said, smiling big enough that she should be able to hear it.

'Not funny,' she said and hung up on me. I told myself that was because she had somewhere to be and not because she thought I was an irritating asshole.

I thought of ways to double-check Reba Connors' agoraphobia. Set fire to the house and see if she runs out? Not a good idea. Do a Noriega and blast loud rock and roll outside their house until she came out? Probably would accomplish just the opposite. Set someone on the house to watch her twenty-four-seven to see if she left? I didn't have the time or manpower for that.

Which basically just left me with John Connors' son from that former marriage. And the DNA on the blood found at Miz Pettigrew's house. Neither of those things could be dealt with unless I was in Oklahoma City.

I called up Charlie Smith and said only two words: 'Road trip!'

Anthony Dobbins had nowhere to go but home. He wasn't much of a drinking man, so going to sit in a bar for a while didn't seem like his idea of fun, although nothing much seemed like fun nowadays. He drove home like he was supposed to but just sat there in his truck, looking at his house. He had to park in the street due to all the cars in the driveway. His mama's Lincoln, his mother-in-law's Ford Escort and one of his sister's cars. All the women converging because he wasn't man enough to take care of his wife and child.

Anthony steeled himself. It was time. He got out of the truck and walked up to the front door, opening it boldly like it wasn't something he did every day. So many pairs of brown eyes stared at him as he walked in. Finally, his mother stood up and came to him.

'Hey, boy,' she said, kissing him on the cheek and giving him a hug. 'Was wondering when you'd be getting home.'

''Bout the same time every night,' Anthony said, which used to be true, before his mistake had almost killed his wife and child.

His mama looked at him with a skeptical eye, knowing his statement hadn't been all that truthful.

With his hand on his mama's shoulder and his eyes on the rest of the room, he said, 'Ladies, if you don't mind, me and Maryanne need some time alone. Y'all can come back tomorrow if you've a mind to.'

The women looked at each other. Anthony's mother looked at him, then at the women. 'So y'all come on,' she said. 'We need to be fixing dinners at our own homes.'

She walked to the front door and opened it, standing there like a doorman, waiting for the others to vacate the premises. Still looking at each other, then covertly at Maryanne and then Anthony, the others, his sisters and his mother-in-law, slowly stood up and headed for the door.

'Maryanne, honey,' his mother-in-law started, but Mrs Dobbins took her by the arm.

'Let 'em be, Marvella, just let 'em be,' and ushered the last of them out.

Then Anthony just stood there, looking at his wife of twelve years, holding their three-month-old daughter asleep in her arms.

Finally, he said, 'We gotta talk.'

Maryanne said, 'OK.'

Anthony sighed and moved to the sofa, sitting down beside her and taking his sleeping baby in his arms. He looked into her beautiful face, then up at his wife. 'I've got something to tell you. Something I've never told you.'

She cocked her head, a frightened look in her eye. And he began, starting with getting lost on his way to the Connors' home.

When he finished, Maryanne took the baby from his arms and laid her gently in the cradle she kept in the living room. Then she sat back down and took her husband in her arms.

'Oh, baby,' she whispered.

'So, you see, it's all my fault. You and Melinda getting hurt. It's all my fault.' And for the first time since he broke his knee in freshman football, Anthony Dobbins cried.

I got sorta lonely that night, all alone in my house, with the wind blowing the plastic sheets at the back of the house and the cold seeping in. I started a fire and sat close to it, thinking I might just sleep on the sofa that night.

I used to live in that house all by myself for a couple of years, then my sister and her kids moved in, and right after Jewel Anne married Harmon and the bunch of 'em moved out, Jean and I got married and, well, I'll admit it, six months later we had Johnny Mac. But now it was lonely, and the wind had picked up, it being

March and all, and it wasn't just blowing the plastic sheeting but seeping through some of the windows, making a howling sound that made me even lonelier. I thought maybe I'd have whoever we hired to fix the back door check for cracks and stuff, what with the long summer coming up and the cost of electricity when the a/c was going full blast. That thought didn't take long, and my loneliness just came crawling back.

My kid is my best pal, although don't tell him that, it would just embarrass him. I'd given up hunting and fishing years ago but me and Johnny Mac had taken it up recently, this past deer season. We never got anything but enjoyed walking around in the woods carrying our shotguns and acting like big shots. And we'd borrowed a boat a couple of times to go out on Lake Blue with newly bought fishing gear. We didn't catch anything but we had fun. If lots of laughing and dirty looks from other fishermen could constitute fun – which Johnny Mac and I deemed righteous. And on a daily basis, it was just great to come home and see him – whether he was shooting hoops in the yard or working on math problems with his tongue sticking halfway out and his hair all messed up from scratching his head over a problem. I'd always wanted to have a kid – my first wife and I could never conceive – but even though I'd wanted one, I'd never known just how plain great it could be.

Not that he wasn't a pain in the ass half the time. You could tell him to clean his room a hundred times a day and threaten all sorts of recriminations – including bodily harm – and it would still be a mess the next day. You could make him a superior lunch and come home to find the lunch box still on the table because he forgot it – or pick him up from school only to find he didn't have on his coat – or gloves, or hat, or once even his shoes – because he forgot them and left them in the classroom. He could talk a mile a minute about anything but then be real closed-mouthed when it came to something you deemed important. But, after talking to other parents – and my wife who knows this stuff because she's a psychiatrist – I've come to realize that's just the way kids are. And, to tell you the truth – and again, don't tell him because it would give him the upper hand – I wouldn't have it any other way.

And my wife. Well, let me tell you about my wife. We've been married twelve years now and I love her more than I did when we first got married. Of course, then we'd only known each other for a little while and we sorta rushed into the marriage because she was pregnant and we both wanted that baby real bad but, still and all, she's the light of my life. The woman's beautiful, sexy, smarter than anybody I know, funny, caring and kind. Sometimes she thinks I'm an idiot, but reading Ann Landers and Dear Abby and the like, I figure most women think that about their husbands.

So I sat in my living room, TV turned on, trying to stay warm and concentrate on *NCIS*, and missed my family. To say I was looking forward to the next day's trip to the city was putting it mildly.

It took a while, but Anthony composed himself. 'Milt's going to Oklahoma City tomorrow to interview Mr Connors' son by his first marriage. Maybe he's the one that did that to you.'

'But all the others?' Maryanne asked. 'Why would he be bothering everybody else?'

Anthony sighed. 'I don't know, honey. I just don't know.' He was quiet for a moment, then said, 'All I do know is I'll never forgive myself for what happened to you, or for what happened to the Connors.'

Maryanne took her husband's face in her hands, turning him to look at her. 'You're not to blame for what happened to me and the baby. And you're not to blame for what happened to those people. The only thing you could have done even if you had gotten there on time was maybe – and I mean maybe – catch whoever did it. What happened to them would have happened no matter what. And what happened to me and the baby probably had nothing to do with those people. Everybody in the sheriff's office has had something bad happen. You're not special in that way,' she said, smiling at Anthony and letting go of his face. 'But you're special in so many others.'

She took him in her arms and he rested his head on her shoulder, feeling that, finally, he really had come home.

Wednesday dawned gray and cloudy and colder than it had been since the ice storm. I put on a red flannel shirt over a George Straight T-shirt, blue jeans and cowboy boots, and finished off the look with my sheepskin jacket. I was ready to take on the city. I called into the department, told Anna Alvarez where I was headed and that I'd be on my cell phone, then loaded the Jeep with a duffel bag stuffed to the gills since I planned to spend the night with my wife and child. I had no idea what Charlie Smith's plan was and I didn't really care.

I got to Charlie's house a little after seven in the morning and, while sitting at the kitchen table drinking coffee with Charlie and his wife Maxine, told him about my intention on spending the night. Maxine said, 'Go ahead, honey. You could use a little time off. The police station won't collapse and me and the kids are more than likely gonna be here when you get back.'

'More than likely?' Charlie asked.

Maxine grinned. 'Well, I wouldn't take it to the bank but the odds are in your favor.'

Charlie shook his head and went into the back of the house, I presumed to pack a bag. My presumption proved correct when he came out five minutes later with a duffel bag similar to mine in all but color. We country he-men like to keep our macho up at all times. A rolling suitcase just wouldn't be manly enough.

The drive to Oklahoma City was uneventful. Even our conversation was uneventful. We both went over and over what we had on the case and nothing new came up.

'So you're hanging this all on John Connors' kid?' Charlie asked me.

'He's all I got left.'

Charlie shook his head. 'Did you question John about him?'

'Naw. John's not exactly compos mentis these days.'

'Reba?'

I didn't answer. I should have questioned Reba about her stepson, if she even knew she had one. Holly had had to do a lot of digging on the computer to find the kid. But I should have questioned Reba Connors. Should have questioned John, too, but my heart just wasn't into going back to that depressing house and those beaten, depressing people. Especially knowing that I – through my deputy – had a hand in what had led to it all.

When we finally got to Oklahoma City we went straight to the crime-scene lab to put a bee under their butts about our DNA evidence. We lucked out. We introduced ourselves to the guy at the reception desk only to have a woman walking down the hall stop and say, 'Hey! I just tried to call y'all! You Chief Smith?'

Charlie identified himself then me. 'You've got something?' I asked, sorta breathless.

'Yeah, come on back. Let me get my notes.'

We followed her into a lab with all sorts of machines and a desk or two. She sat down at one of the desks while simultaneously pulling the chair from the other desk over to hers. 'Sit,' she ordered. Charlie sat and I pulled up a stool from one of the lab tables and perched.

'OK, here we go. Longbranch, Oklahoma. Bloody splinter. Blood type O positive, female.' She shook her head. 'We know it's a woman with the most common blood type around and that's all we know.'

'A woman,' I said, looking at Charlie.

He looked back at me, his brows knitted. 'Yeah. A woman?'

'Don't that beat all,' I said.

'Shit, I reckon,' he answered.

'Oh, are we playing country bumpkins today?' the lab tech asked.

I smiled weakly at her. 'Sometimes it just comes out. Especially when we're totally stink-bombed from out of the blue.'

'No female suspects?' the woman asked with a raised brow.

'Not so you'd notice,' I said, thanked her and headed out, Charlie behind me.

A woman, I thought. Damn, a woman. And a big woman at that, I thought, remembering the tape on the front door indicating somebody standing about five foot eleven inches. Reba Connors was a big woman. Big boned, but how tall?

The first thing I did when I got in the car was call the shop. I got hold of Anthony and said, 'Go out to the Connors' place. Get some DNA from Reba. Toothbrush, hairbrush, a used Kleenex, whatever. And try to figure out how tall she is. Also, ask her what she knows about John's kid – John, Jr, now John Brewer.'

'Milt, I can't. I just can't go out there, knowing what I did to them—' Anthony started.

'Man, you're all I got. I can't send Dalton to do this, you know that. He's there for wrecks on the highway and that's about it. You're all I got. You gotta man up.'

'Shit, Milt.' Anthony sighed and said, 'Yeah. You're right. You're right.' And he hung up in my ear. I only hoped he intended to call me back at some point.

Then I called Emmett on his cell phone.

'Yeah?' he said, his voice low.

'How's she doing?' I asked.

'Still out,' he said.

'Listen. The DNA came back as a female—'

'No kidding?' he said.

'I got Anthony checking out Reba Connors. But I got to thinking – what about that Evans woman? Lou Anne, right? At the gas station.'

'Yeah, what about her?' Emmett asked.

'How tall you think she is?'

'Hell if I know.'

'Didn't you see her standing?'

'Well, yeah, but I was down in the bay and she was standing up a step in the doorway of the office.'

'Would you say she was tall?' I insisted.

He thought for a minute, then said, 'Tallish.'

'That's good enough,' I said.

The last thing in the world Anthony Dobbins wanted to do was talk to either John or Reba Connors, and definitely not both. He'd never really gotten over what happened at the Connors' house but he'd thought he'd put it out of his mind. Now it was back, full-blown guilt eating at his stomach lining. He was barely dealing with the guilt over his wife and daughter being in danger because he was a deputy; now he had to deal with the people who were the end result of his biggest failure. He was glad he'd talked to Maryanne. Her knowing his guilt helped him some, being able to share it, even though she seemed to think it wasn't his fault – what happened to the Connors and, he guessed, what happened to her and the baby, too.

Everybody said what happened to the Connors was just a mistake. That he'd been away from the county and didn't remember the roads as well as someone else might have. There were even those who said it was the sheriff's fault for sending him in the first place rather than a more experienced deputy. But it wasn't experience that was the problem. He was experienced. He'd been a cop in Tulsa. No. It wasn't lack of experience: he simply got lost. But he knew his way to the Connors' house now. It was etched in his brain. He could get there blindfolded, even though he'd only been there that one time. That one time when he was late and Reba Connors was raped on account of that, and John Connors was hit on the head so hard he couldn't function any more. That was on him, Anthony thought. All on him. No matter what anybody said.

He got to the house and just stared at it. It had been a pretty place the first and only time he ever saw it. Flowers in borders, a well-tended lawn and freshly painted trim on the house. That picture, like the path to get there, was etched in his brain. It had been a nice place. Not any more. He turned off the engine and just sat there in his squad car, looking at the house, feeling his gut heave, thinking he might vomit, but he pushed it down and felt the burn. He knew he deserved that ulcer he was getting, had been getting since that day. He'd never gone to the doctor so he didn't know if he already had one or not. He just lived with the pain. The pain he thought he deserved.

Then the front door of the house opened and John Connors stuck his head out. 'Whatja want?' he called from the door.

Anthony opened his car door and got out, walking up to the porch. 'Mr Connors, it's Deputy Dobbins with the sheriff's department.'

'Oh, yeah! I remember you!' John Connors said and smiled.

OK, Anthony thought, the man really was out of his head if he felt he could smile at Anthony. 'Yes, sir. Can I come in a minute? Talk to you and the missus?'

'Sure! Come on in!' Turning and walking further into the house, he called, 'Hey, Reba, honey, we got company.'

Mrs Connors walked in from the kitchen, saw Anthony and stood stock-still, just staring at him. Finally she said, 'Get out.'

'Ma'am, the sheriff asked me—'

'Get the hell out of my house!' she screamed.

'Ma'am, I gotta talk to you. It's either here or at the station. If y'all wanna get in my squad car—'

'You have the audacity to come in here and demand to talk to me? After what you did?'

'Ma'am, I'll never forgive myself for being late to get here. Not until the day I die, I can promise you that. But people are getting killed now and I gotta talk to you.'

Reba Connors moved slowly into the living room and took a seat on the sofa next to her husband, who'd been following the exchange between his wife and the deputy like a fan at a tennis match.

'Who got killed?' she asked.

'Enid Merkle and Doris Jameson, and possibly Judge Norman.'

'I heard Dave Norman died, but you think he was murdered?' she asked.

'Yes, ma'am,' Anthony answered.

'Who's that, honey?' her husband asked.

'Dave Norman. From the courthouse. You remember him, John.'

'Do I?'

'Yes, baby, you do.'

'OK,' he said and grinned at her, then turned the grin back at Anthony.

Reba said, 'You kill 'em? Be your style.'

'No, ma'am.'

'The two women, Enid and Doris. I knew Enid from church, back when I went. Doris who?'

'Jameson.'

She shook her head. 'Doesn't ring a bell.' She sighed. 'I used to know just about everybody who lived in this county. If I didn't know 'em by sight, at least I knew the name. I kept the records for the county, you know,' she said, looking up at Anthony. 'Sit down, for crying out loud. I'm getting a crick in my neck.'

'Yes, ma'am,' Anthony said and sat.

'So what do these killings have to do with me and John?'

'The sheriff wanted me to ask y'all about John, Jr.'

John, Sr smiled really big. 'That's my boy. John, Jr. How old is he, honey? Three now?'

Reba patted his hand. 'That's right, sweetheart.' She leaned down to the coffee table in front of the sofa and grabbed the TV remote. 'Here, John. It's time for your stories.' She switched the TV on, found the right channel and put the remote back on the table.

'In here,' she said to Anthony, indicating the kitchen.

He followed her in there and took a seat at the kitchen table.

'You want coffee?' she asked.

'No, thank you, ma'am.'

'You're overdoing the polite crap, Deputy.'

'I'm always polite, ma'am,' Anthony said.

She laughed mirthlessly. 'Well, polite's nice and all, but being on time would be even better.'

Anthony sighed. 'Yes, ma'am.'

'Why you asking about John, Jr?'

'Need to know if y'all keep in touch. How upset he was about his dad getting . . .' Anthony faltered, not knowing how to continue.

'About his dad getting knocked stupid?' she said, raising her eyebrows. 'Wouldn't know. The reason John thinks junior is three years old is because he hasn't even seen a picture of him since then. John was a drinker when his first wife divorced him and she got full custody without any visitation from John. Not that that meant we couldn't keep paying child support until he was eighteen, which we did, every month like clockwork. But did we ever get a thank you or even an invite to his graduation? No, we did not.' She stared hard at Anthony. 'John quit drinking when we met. Hasn't had a drop in almost twenty years. Except now, thanks to you, he acts drunk every waking minute of every day.'

'Ma'am, I need to get a DNA swab from you and your husband,' he said, adding John to keep Reba from knowing he was after her DNA only.

'You're not touching me,' she said. 'Or John. I need you to leave our house.'

'Then I'll be back with a warrant for that swab, ma'am.'

'Oh, for crying out loud,' she said and opened her mouth.

Anthony hastily got the swab out of the carrier in his pocket and swabbed the inside of her cheek. 'How tall are you, ma'am?' he asked.

She just stared at him. 'Why you want to know? You got a measuring tape in your other pocket?'

'No ma'am. The sheriff just wanted me to ask.'

'I'm five-seven and maybe a half. Unless I've shrunk.'

With that, Reba stood up and walked into the living room.

'John, need you to open up. This man's gonna stick a Q-tip in your mouth.'

John smiled. 'OK,' he said and opened his mouth wide.

When Anthony had finished, Reba Connors pointed to the front door of her house. 'Now get out. And don't even think of ever coming back.'

Anthony left.

ELEVEN

The doctors had told Emmett that Jasmine could be out for days. And he remembered the thought he'd had when Dalton had his troubles – secretly glad it hadn't been him or his. Well, that sure came back to bite him in the butt. He should never have thought such a thing – being glad it was Dalton's mama who got hurt and not his own wife or daughter. Emmett wasn't a religious man, not really, just went to church to please his wife. But he was pretty sure, if there was a God, he wouldn't have done this to Jasmine just to get him back for bad thoughts. No, Emmett decided. It was the cosmos. What you put out there often comes back to bite you. And he'd been bitten big time. Here she was, his Jasmine, her face so still, breathing tube in her nose, all sorts of tubes stuck in her arms. He wasn't sure how much more he could take.

He needed to think about something else. Get his mind off his own troubles. Which made him think about Lou Anne Evans. The perp was a woman – DNA proved that. The tape on the front door – if it had really been at eye level – showed someone five foot eleven. But what if it hadn't been at actual eye level? What if the perp stood on her tiptoes just to throw them off, or even just lifted her arms up a bit? She could be just about any size.

He knew Reba Connors definitely blamed them for what happened to her, and maybe rightly so, but she was a shut-in. She didn't leave her home. Lou Anne Evans seemed to be pissed as hell when he talked to her, though. And she wasn't a shut-in. She was up and about and it was just Emmett's own prejudices, he decided, that had declared her unfit to be messing with the brakes on the judge's or Maryanne's cars. She owned a gas station. Had been married for twenty years to a man who was a mechanic and her son was a mechanic. Why the hell wouldn't she know some of it? Osmosis, if nothing else.

He looked at his wife again, still unconscious. Maybe he could take a few minutes to run by the Evans' gas station. Just have a quick talk with bosomy Lou Anne.

We had an address on John Brewer, formerly John Connors, Jr, and Charlie, who knew about these things, put the address into his phone and got directions there. Some woman told us where to turn and how many yards we had to go. I need to get one of those. My phone doesn't have it.

I wasn't sure exactly why I was continuing with checking out John, Jr, now I knew it was a woman doing all this, but there was always the possibility John, Jr was working with somebody else. A sister we didn't know about, a girlfriend, maybe even his mother? I had no idea, but we were here in the city and I was damned if I wasn't going to see this through.

Brewer's address proved to be a duplex that had seen better days, in a neighborhood of duplexes that had seen better days. The grass was more than early March brown – it was mostly weeds and dirt. The siding was a pinkish orange brick that they haven't used since the sixties, to my knowledge (and why would they? It was ugly then). The trim had been painted white, but when was obviously a very long time ago. We got out of my Jeep and went to the door. The doorbell had a piece of tape across it so I knocked on the door instead. No answer. I went to a window to peek in. The mini-blinds that covered the front window were in bad shape and a black-and-white cat had his paw on one slat, bending it down to look out. I had a feeling he did a lot of that and might be the architect of the mini-blinds' new look. I walked up close to the cat and he backed down, so I peered through the opening into what appeared to be a living room.

Obviously John Brewer wasn't married. There was a brand-new lounge chair, the only chair in the whole room, in front of the largest TV I'd ever seen, a TV tray next to the chair with a lamp sitting on it and an ashtray filled with butts. The cord of the lamp stretched tight from the TV tray to a plug in the wall. I had to assume that neither Brewer nor any guest ever went that direction, unless he went through a lot of lamps. Although where the guest would sit wasn't obvious. The lamp wasn't on, the TV wasn't on, I didn't hear any music and could see no other lights. I was beginning to think no one was home.

'Can I help you?' a voice said to my right, almost causing me to fall into the dead shrubs under the window.

I whirled around, as did Charlie, who'd been standing next to me, to find a frail-looking old lady standing there. Frail except for the revolver she held in a two-handed stance, aimed vaguely between me and Charlie.

We both stuck our hands in the air. 'Ma'am, put the gun down,' Charlie said.

'We're law enforcement, ma'am,' I said and started to reach for my badge in my back pocket.

'Move and you'll lose your nuts,' she said in a conversational tone of voice.

'I was just gonna show you my badge, ma'am,' I said.

'Real slow,' she said.

I did. I pulled my badge out of my back pocket slower than I've ever done anything. There was no doubt in my mind that this lady would shoot both of us dead if we even looked at her cross-eyed. I kept both my eyes open wide.

'Toss it over,' she said.

I did.

'Now you,' she said to Charlie.

He was as slow as me getting his out of his jacket pocket. He tossed it too.

'Now sit down with your hands on your heads.'

We did.

She slowly leaned down and picked up one badge, looked at it, threw it back in the dirt, picked up the other, looked at it, and threw that one back in the dirt too.

'So maybe you guys are real, or maybe you got these badges out of a Cracker Jack box. I dunno. And I don't care. Why you snooping around here looking in Jackie's window?'

Charlie and I looked at each other. 'Who's Jackie?' I finally asked.

'Jackie Brewer. The young man who rents that half of my duplex. Are you stupid or what?'

'We thought that place belonged to John Brewer,' Charlie said.
The old woman nodded her head. 'Oh, I see. You *are* stupid.
Let me explain some facts of life. Jack is a nickname for John.
Jackie is the diminutive of Jack. Are you both following me here?'

'Yes, ma'am,' we said in unison, both sitting on the cold ground,
our hands on our heads.

'So, as it seems I must repeat myself, what are you yard birds
doing looking in Jackie's window?'

'Just wanted to see if he was home, ma'am,' I said.

'Not answering your knock is usually sufficient for most
people,' she said. She hadn't let go of her two-handed stance
with the revolver. I thought that at her age – somewhere around
one hundred or so – her arms must be getting tired. But it didn't
seem to be the case.

'We're not most people,' I said, trying for a little bravado.
'We're police.'

'Not from around here,' she said. 'According to these badges.
But that's OK. I got the real police coming. We'll let them sort
this out.'

Charlie and I looked at each other. We should have notified
somebody at Oklahoma City PD that we were here. We hadn't
done that. We could be in deep shit. Or just embarrassed to death
sitting here on the ground with our hands over our heads and an
old woman holding a gun on us.

We heard the sirens, then a squad car pulled to a stop in front
of the duplex. Two officers got out, a man and a woman.

'Hey, Miz Teal,' the woman said. 'Got you a couple of live
ones, I see.'

'Hey, Becky, Bruce. These two claim they're law enforcement.'
She kicked the badges on the dirt toward the two uniforms.

'We can explain—' Charlie started.

'Shut up,' the woman said, bending to pick up the badges. She
looked at one, handed it to her partner, looked at the other and
handed that one to him as well. Then she looked at us. 'Did you
report in to anybody at HQ?'

'Ah, not yet,' I said. 'We were headed that way—'

'But stopped here first to do some peeping Tom stuff?' she asked.

'Well, we've got someone we need to question—' Charlie
started.

'Bruce, get on the horn and get a detective down here.' Her partner nodded and headed back to the squad.

'I think you can lower your weapon, Miz Teal,' the female officer said.

'Good. My arms were getting tired.' She lowered her revolver and turned to the officer. 'You got this, Becky? *Judge Judy*'s about to come on. I never miss *Judge Judy* if I can help it.'

'You go on ahead, Miz Teal. We got this.'

We all watched the old woman walk into her side of the duplex, then Officer Becky looked at me and Charlie, both with our hands still on our heads and our butts still on the ground, and began to laugh.

Jean MacDonnell was surprised that she hadn't heard from Milt yet. It was almost time for dinner and she knew he was as excited about eating at that steakhouse as he was about seeing her and John. But where he was at that moment was a mystery.

When the knock came on the door of the hotel suite, she went to it with a reprimand on her lips, only to find Holly and Mrs Pettigrew standing there.

'Mrs Pettigrew!' she exclaimed. 'I'm so glad to see you!' She ushered them in and asked, 'How are you?'

'Well, I shouldn't complain,' she said, settling down on the nearest easy chair. 'I'm alive, at least.'

'Well, thank God,' Jean said.

'More thanks to Him than anyone at that hospital!' she said, making a *tsk, tsk* sound with a pursed mouth.

'I'm so sorry you've had such a rough time,' Jean said. 'Can I get you something? We have juice and a few sodas, but I could make coffee.'

'I only drink decaf,' Mrs Pettigrew said.

'Let me go look.' Turning to Holly, she said, 'Can I get you something?'

'Let me go with you to help,' Holly said and followed Jean into the small kitchen area.

'You OK?' Jean asked in a low voice.

'She means well,' Holly said, her voice also low.

Jean found some decaf coffee in a drawer and said to Mrs Pettigrew, 'Found it! Should just take a minute.'

'Maybe something cold. You got any sweet tea?'

Jean just looked at Holly, one eyebrow raised.

'Let me,' Holly said and went about the fixing of sweet tea while Jean watched, fascinated.

'So,' Jean finally said, 'it's just iced tea with sugar?'

'But the sugar has to go in while the tea's still hot or it won't taste right,' Holly answered.

'Gotja,' Jean said, although her voice told another story.

'Where's Milt?' Holly asked as she took the iced tea to her mother-in-law.

'I wish I knew. He was supposed to be here in time for dinner.'

Jean's son John and Emmett's and Jasmine's daughter Petal took that moment to come running out of the bedroom, still in bathing suits and wet from the huge tub in the adjoining bathroom.

'Hey, guys!' Holly said with a big smile. 'This suite has a swimming pool?'

'No,' Jean said, laughing. 'Just a really big bathtub.'

'You let those two in the bathtub together?' Mrs Pettigrew said, her brows knitted.

'Yes, in their bathing suits,' Jean answered.

'Well, in my day we never!' Mrs Pettigrew said. She made a show of looking around the room. 'And this suite, as you call it. It must cost a fortune in a hotel this fancy. Motel Six is fine with me.' She looked at Holly. 'We should find one of those. You and Dalton can't afford this!'

'The county's paying for it,' Jean said.

Mrs Pettigrew stood up. 'So my taxes are gonna go up, right? This is just plain wrong!'

Jean walked up to the older woman and put one hand on her shoulder. 'The county's paying the equivalent of motel rooms for all of us. I'm paying extra to stay in a decent hotel with decent room service because I want to. And I want us all to be together so I got a suite big enough for all of us.'

Mrs Pettigrew harrumphed then sighed and sat back down. 'I guess you got all that doctor money just lying around. Well, I don't see why you should spend it on the likes of me. Motel Six is just fine by me.'

'But we're already here, Mama,' Holly said. 'And you need to rest.' Turning to Jean, she asked, 'Where's our room?'

Jean led them to the connecting door to the double room. 'Right through here,' she said, wondering how long she'd be able to put up with 'the likes' of Mrs Pettigrew.

The gas station was closed when Emmett drove by. Glancing at his watch, he noticed it was almost seven in the evening. Things mostly shut down in Longbranch around six or so. He called the shop and was lucky to find Anna Alvarez still there.

'Anna, need an address on Lou Anne Evans,' he said.

'How's Jasmine?' she asked.

'Still out like a light.'

'Sounds like you're in your truck,' Anna said.

'Yeah. So what?' Emmett said, a little defensively.

'Nothing. I just thought—'

'That I needed to spend every waking moment at my comatose wife's bedside? Well, there's a killer out there and I need to find out who the hell it is!'

'Fourteen fifteen Cavern Road,' Anna said.

'Thanks,' Emmett said and hung up.

Was he being a bad husband? Or a good cop? He wasn't sure. Maybe a little of both, or neither. Could go either way, but he figured he'd better apologize to Anna the next time he saw her.

Fourteen fifteen Cavern Road was a two-story colonial in a heavily wooded area with no other houses around. Emmett wondered if all the land around it belonged to the Evanses, but decided he didn't really care. There were two cars in the driveway – a ten-year-old Lincoln Town Car and a new Toyota Camry. There was a double door at the front and columns holding up a porch – Tara style. The house was painted white brick with black shutters. He got out of his Land Cruiser, walked up to the front door and rang the doorbell. Tara's theme could be heard inside. No coincidence, that, Emmett thought.

The door opened and Tyler Evans was standing there.

'Hey, Deputy,' he said, somewhat surprised.

'Need to talk to your mama,' Emmett said.

Tyler looked behind him furtively then back to Emmett. 'Maybe not such a good idea. She's in a mood,' Tyler said.

'I don't really care,' Emmett said, stepping over the threshold into the foyer. A big chandelier hung from the ceiling with an antique hall stand to the left and the opening to the living room on the right. Emmett could see lots of French provincial furniture in a room that didn't look a bit lived in.

Lou Anne Evans came out from the back of the house, drying her hands on a dishtowel.

'What the hell do you want?' she said on seeing Emmett.

'Need to talk to you, ma'am,' he said.

'Talk to my lawyer!' she said.

'Fine. Then I'll need to take you back to the sheriff's office and book you. Your lawyer can meet us there.'

'The hell you will!' she said. She sighed. 'Whatever,' she said, and turned and walked back the way she came.

Tyler motioned for Emmett to follow. They both found themselves in a large room – fireplace and family room on one side, breakfast area and kitchen on the other. Lots more lived-in than the front room.

Lou Anne sat down on a bright red sofa. Emmett took a matching armchair across from her while Tyler stayed standing, his arm on the fireplace mantel like somebody in an English drawing-room mystery.

'What do you want?' she demanded.

What Emmett really wanted was to swab her for DNA, but he hadn't thought about going by the office to get a kit. He thought for a moment that he could just ask Mrs Evans for a Q-Tip, but then thought that might be asking too much. Maybe he could ask for the bathroom and steal her toothbrush.

'Ma'am, I need to know where you were yesterday morning and the day before.'

'Didn't somebody already ask us this?' Lou Anne Evans said, looking at her son.

'Yeah, they sure did, Mama,' Tyler said.

'You getting forgetful, Deputy?' the woman asked, staring daggers at Emmett.

'The only alibi you got for yesterday is from your son, and sorry but kinfolk do tend to lie for each other,' Emmett said.

'Are you calling my son a liar?' Lou Anne said, jumping up from the sofa.

'Yes, ma'am,' Emmett said, still sitting.

There was a laugh from the area of the fireplace. 'What are you laughing at?' she yelled at her son.

'Mama, he's right. You were there and all, but even if you weren't, I'da said you were. Same as you woulda said for me.'

She sat back down. 'Well, I was there.'

'I need to get a sample of your DNA,' Emmett said.

Tyler Evans pushed away from the fireplace mantel. 'Now's the time we talk about a lawyer, Mama.' To Emmett, he said, 'Not without a warrant, and I'm gonna have to ask you to leave now, Deputy.'

Emmett stood up, thinking about how he pretty much blew this interview. But since his mind was still more than half on his comatose wife, he wasn't all that surprised.

Anthony drove back to the shop, sick to his stomach. He thought maybe he really should go see a doctor. He hadn't been to one since they moved back to Longbranch and that had been quite a while. The stomach pains started soon after the incident at the Connors' house and had been getting steadily worse after what happened to Maryanne and the baby. And now, just being around the Connors again made him feel like . . .

He pulled over to the side of the road, opened his door and vomited on the pavement below. He saw that there was blood in the vomit. Yeah, he thought, maybe he really should see a doctor. After this was all over. He closed the car door, leaned back in his seat and wiped his mouth with the back of his hand. A doctor might give him something for the pain in his stomach, he thought, but nobody could give him anything for the pain in his soul.

Dalton sat at his desk in the bullpen. He wasn't doing much. Charlie Smith had sent over one of his officers, Mike Reynolds, a guy Dalton had gotten to know at the stand-off at the Longbranch Inn. Mike's girl, now his wife, had been one of the hostages, too, even though she hadn't been one of the guests at that party for Holly. No, she'd actually been a member of the family that had taken everybody hostage, but she hadn't been a real part of it. If it hadn't been for her, they might all still be there, Dalton thought. Her having a baby almost at the scene and all kind of put a damper on her family's shenanigans. So Mike and Dalton had sort of become friends, in as much as they said hi to each other whenever they saw one another, and once even sat together at the Longbranch Inn when they both went in at the same time for lunch. But Mike was out now, cruising the county, giving Dalton and Anthony and Anna the space they needed to take care of the real business of the sheriff's department.

Dalton didn't have a lot of friends outside the sheriff's department. In fact, except for his mama, the sheriff's department was his family. His wife, Holly, of course, and Milt, who he felt was like a father to him. And he saw Jasmine as the sister he never had, which made Emmett his sort of brother-in-law. And Anthony? He was like a little brother. And the thing about Anthony was he never talked down to Dalton like everybody else did. Milt not so much, but Emmett and Jasmine for sure. But not Anthony. Anthony acted like he thought Dalton was just as smart as him. He hated that Anthony's wife and baby had been hurt, hated that as much as he hated that his mama had been hurt. But he didn't know what to do about any of it. Hell, even Milt and Emmett didn't know what to do. Milt was in Oklahoma City now, doing whatever, and Emmett was at his wife's bedside hoping she'd wake up. Anthony was out on a domestic call, but here Dalton was doing nothing.

He looked over at the newbie – Anna Alvarez. Even she was busy, doing what his Holly usually did – working the computer. He studied her for a minute, thinking she was just about as good at that thing as Holly. Just about. Nobody was as good at anything as Holly was. He smiled at the thought and picked up the phone when it rang.

Emmett Hopkins was sick to death of the hospital cafeteria food and had asked Dalton to pick him up some fried chicken and fixings from the Chicken Shack. He was on his third piece of chicken when he heard a small voice.

'Where's Petal?'

Emmett dropped the Styrofoam box from the Chicken Shack on the floor, he was that startled. 'Jasmine? Honey?' he said, pulling his chair closer to the hospital bed. 'Baby?'

'Where's Petal?' Jasmine asked again.

'She's with Jean. Jean took her and Johnny Mac to Oklahoma

City to keep them out of harm's way. They're OK. I talked to her less than an hour ago. She's fine, honey.'

Jasmine touched her head. 'What happened? I've got a headache. And I'm thirsty.'

'You were in a car wreck, honey. Just hold on, I'll get somebody to help.' Emmett grabbed the buzzer to call the nurse. When someone answered, he said, 'She's awake. My wife's awake. We need some water and some aspirin.'

'Be right there,' the disembodied voice said.

Emmett had been trying real hard, sitting in that chair, watching his wife in her coma, not to think about those many years ago when he'd sat in a similar chair in a similar room in this same hospital, waiting for his son to die. Watching his first wife wither away as their son's life faded from the leukemia that ravaged his small body. They were both dead now, his son and his first wife, and he'd finally found some happiness he never suspected he'd find again. And it had been good, this new life with Jasmine and Petal. His beautiful wife and his beautiful daughter. All any man could ask for. But this . . . Sitting here watching her with no signs of the spark that was Jasmine was hell. The same hell he'd lived through before and he thought he'd never have to live through again.

But then that voice. And life was back to normal. Life was back to being beautiful and sunny and happy once more. Jasmine was back and she was thirsty and by damn somebody better be bringing her some water!

Me and Charlie Smith got to the hotel a little after seven and I hoped like hell that my family hadn't eaten without me. I had the coupon for the steakhouse so I knew they wouldn't go there, but I had to be back in Longbranch in the morning and I didn't really want to eat my steak dinner without them. I would, mind you. I just didn't *want* to.

Charlie checked himself into the hotel while I went upstairs to the suite number Jean had given me. One rap on the door and it opened to reveal a bright-eyed Petal Hopkins.

'Aunt Jean!' she yelled as she ran back into the room. 'It's Uncle Milt!'

I followed the child into the suite and was surprised to see Holly and Miz Pettigrew sitting in the living area, sipping sweet tea and watching a rerun of *Jeopardy!*

'Hey, Miz Pettigrew!' I said, walking into the living area. 'How you doing?'

'As well as can be expected,' she said, her tone of voice reminding me of the Eeyore voice Jasmine used to have when she was married to her first husband. I had been hoping never to hear that voice again, but Miz Pettigrew sure had it down pat.

My wife came into the living area, leaning heavily on her one crutch. She looked like she'd had a hard day. I could certainly sympathize. Mine hadn't been that great either.

I kissed her full on the mouth and asked, 'Y'all eaten yet?'

'No, waiting for you.'

I grinned. 'Great. I still have that coupon for the steakhouse.'

'Works for me,' she said, grinning back. 'We can all go. I'll pick up the difference.'

'Miz Doctor Moneybags wants to pay for everything,' Miz Pettigrew said. 'But I think I'll just stay here and have room service send me up some crackers or something.' She sighed. 'You go on ahead, Holly. You and that baby need some nourishment.'

'There's a full room-service menu, Mama,' Holly said. 'We can get something nice to eat and then hop into bed. Maybe watch one of those new movies on demand.'

'I haven't seen a new movie since *Mary Poppins*,' she said. 'They're all just nasty these days. Naked people and dead bodies everywhere. And the language! Lord have mercy!'

'Well, we can just read or—'

'No, now, you go on,' she said, and that Eeyore voice was loud and clear. 'I won't be adding any fancy dinner to Doctor Moneybags' bill. I can do just fine with some sweet tea and some crackers. That's all I need.'

I could see tears forming in Holly's eyes. I know a lot of women cry when they get mad. I didn't know about Holly. Was she sad about the old lady? Mad at her for her bullshit? Or was she just pregnant? Don't tell my wife I said that. She gets mad whenever I insinuate that something might be hormonal.

'Kids, go change your clothes,' Jean said. 'Holly, I really want you to come with us.'

Holly pulled Jean away from the living area and I followed to hear what she was gonna say.

'I can't just leave her here,' Holly said.

''Cause she'll never let you hear the end of it,' I suggested.

Holly sighed. 'Well, yeah. Exactly.'

'Don't play into her neuroses,' Jean said. 'You deserve to get out of here and especially away from her for an hour or two. You've been taking care of her for days. It's time to take care of you and that baby.'

'But—'

'But me no buts,' Jean said, pushing Holly toward the door to the adjoining room she shared with Miz Pettigrew. 'Doctor's orders. Put on something pretty.'

'Let me call Charlie,' I said, heading for the room phone.

'No problem, but let him know he's paying for his own meal,' my wife – Dr Moneybags – said.

The sheriff's department was quiet. Anthony had let the Permeter brothers go since there was nothing to keep them there. Anna had already left for home and he and Dalton sat at their desks, staring at nothing in particular. Dalton had nowhere he needed to be since both his wife and his mother were in Oklahoma City.

Finally Dalton said, 'So it's a woman?'

'That's what Milt said,' Anthony said.

'Who d'you think it is?' Dalton asked.

Anthony shrugged. 'Got no idea. Got a swab from Reba Connors, just to see. But I sorta doubt it.'

'Who else is a woman?' Dalton asked, which made Anthony laugh, it being such a dumb question. Dalton must have realized that because he amended it with, 'I mean, we got any other women suspects?'

'Hum, like Maudeen Sanders' daughter?' Anthony said. He hit a few keys on the computer and said, 'Lynette Sanders. She's going to school in Dallas. SMU.'

'Smu?' Dalton said.

Anthony held back the laugh that came to his throat. He really liked Dalton and didn't want to make him feel stupid. People were always doing that to him and Anthony had vowed early on in his time at the sheriff's department that he never would.

'Southern Methodist University,' he said by way of clarification.
'Oh,' Dalton said. 'I'm a Methodist! I didn't know we had our
own university!'

'Yep. In Dallas,' Anthony told him.

'Can we get someone down there – the police, I mean, to go
swab her and send us the results?'

'I don't know,' Anthony said. 'It's a thought.'

'So there we were,' Charlie said, 'our butts on the cold hard ground,
our hands on top of our heads, our creds in the dirt, and the police
show up!'

My wife was laughing a little too hard. Even my son seemed
to see a great deal of humor in the visual Charlie had created.

'It wasn't that funny,' I said, half to myself. Holly, sitting next
to me, patted my hand but the tears in her eyes this time I recognized. She too was finding this way too funny.

'And the long and short of it,' I said, trying for a little dignity,
'is that we ended up at the main police building apologizing for
not having gotten an escort. Took us hours to do that.'

'Only because we had to listen to the two cops on the scene
describe it to everybody who walked by!' Charlie said and laughed.

'You know, Charlie,' I said, giving him the evil eye, 'I'm gonna
tell this same story to your wife and kids – in all the gory detail.'

'Whoa, shit. Sorry, y'all. I just made that all up!' Charlie said
and laughed some more. The boy was getting on my last nerve.

'So you know that whoever was in Mama's house was a woman?'
Holly said and I nodded.

'Could the DNA belong to any of her bridge partners?'

I hadn't thought of that. That would be a real bummer. 'Would
one of them be using Miz Pettigrew's broom?' I asked.

'I can't see why they would, or why Mama would let them.'
Holly shook her head. 'No, I really can't see that, but we can ask
her when we get back to the hotel, if she's still awake.'

'Oh, she'll still be up,' my wife said ominously.

Holly looked at Jean, started to say something, changed her mind
and bent her head to her food. I had some fun in my mind filling
in all the things she might be thinking. But I couldn't help thinking
Jean had sorta lucked out, what with my mama having passed on
quite a while back. She'd been a wonderful woman, my mama, but

a formidable one. The thought of those two women – my wife and my mama – together made my blood run cold.

'I'll have the ME compare the two dead ladies' DNA with what we got. Rule 'em out for sure,' I said, by way of lightening the situation.

'Good idea,' Jean said.

At the same time, Holly said, 'That should work.'

The steak was everything my sister said it would be, plus a little more. I had a beer to wash it all down and Jean didn't even give it a second look. Not that she disapproves of drinking – she's Irish, after all – but beer has more calories than, say, a glass of white wine, and Jean was all about the calories since my heart attack. We headed back to the hotel around ten, with me carrying Petal who had passed out in her chair at the table and Johnny Mac walking with his mama, holding the hand that wasn't working her crutch. He looked like he was about ready to pass out, too. Charlie Smith said goodbye in the lobby, heading for the bar, while the rest of us caught the elevator to our floor.

Jean was right about Miz Pettigrew. She was up, sitting in front of the TV, watching the Food Network. She muted it when we walked in. 'Land's sake, they make some silly stuff on these shows! Nobody seems to have heard about meat and potatoes!'

'Well, we sure did!' I said, bringing Petal in and placing her on the sofa. 'You missed some good steaks!'

'That's OK,' said Eeyore – I mean, Miz Pettigrew. 'I ate some potato chips out of that cabinet. I left you the money on the counter, Doctor McDonnell.'

'I brought you some leftovers,' Holly said, taking the bag she carried to the large table. 'Some really good rib-eye, potatoes *au gratin* and some asparagus.'

'If I eat this late I'll get nightmares!' Miz Pettigrew said, making that *tsk, tsk* sound. Then she sighed. 'I guess I'll just go to bed and let you young people have your fun.'

'Just a minute, ma'am. I need to ask you a question,' I said.

She stopped and turned toward me, every inch of her a silent scream. 'Well?' she finally said.

'Did any of your bridge players use your broom?'

She stared at me, big-eyed. 'Lord, no!' she said vehemently. 'What kind of a housekeeper do you think I am? You think I'm the kind of woman who needs *help* keeping her house clean? Lord love a duck!'

And with that she was off. Very slowly, way too slowly, while we all watched patiently. Finally she opened the connecting door and shut it behind her, and we all heaved a sigh of relief.

'You were right,' I said to Holly.

'So you never actually saw the guy you came here to see?' my wife asked after we all got seated, Johnny Mac with his head in my lap.

'We'll see him in the morning. The city detective called him and made an appointment for him to come in tomorrow at around nine.'

'Did the detective tell him what this was about?' Holly asked.

I shook my head. 'No, we asked him not to. Want to kind of spring it on him. See how he reacts.'

Both Jean and Holly nodded. Then we had to discuss sleeping arrangements. We had both kids asleep on the sofa. Jean said Petal had been sleeping with her, but I made it pretty plain that I would rather be the one to do that. So Holly volunteered to share her bed with the girl and we left Johnny Mac on the sofa where he'd spent the night before. A pillow and blanket were on the hearth by the fireplace (yeah, this suite had a fireplace, I kid you not!), and I fixed him up then carried Petal into the adjoining room where Miz Pettigrew was already in bed with the lights off. But there was enough light from the suite beyond to show us the way. I got the little girl situated, said goodnight to Holly and headed off to see if my wife was in the mood.

TWELVE

Jean was on vacation and she planned on sleeping in this second full day. But Milt woke her up as he and Charlie were getting ready to leave for their interview at Oklahoma City PD with John Connors' son, and after kissing him goodbye and falling back to sleep, the phone rang.

Still a little groggy, she picked it up and said, 'What?'

'Hey, Jean. Did I wake you?'

'Emmett?' she said, rubbing her eyes. 'Oh, hi. No, of course not.'

He laughed. 'You shouldn't lie.'

'OK, so maybe a little.'

'Guess what?' Emmett said.

'Guessing games this early?'

'Jasmine's awake!'

Jean fell back on her pillow, feeling tears sting her eyes. 'Oh, thank God! How is she?'

'A little shaky but mostly anxious about her baby bird.'

'Let me go see if Petal's awake,' Jean said. 'Hold on.'

She put the phone down, put on her robe, grabbed her crutch and headed into the living room. Petal and John were sitting on the sofa playing video games while Mrs Pettigrew glared at them disapprovingly. Holly was setting out a breakfast that had been delivered, presumably, by room service.

'Petal,' Jean called. 'Someone wants to talk to you on the phone.'

'I'm in the middle of something!' Petal said.

'Now, young lady!' Jean said, but smiled as she said it.

Petal sighed and Jean brought the girl the living-room extension.

'Hello?' Petal said. Then a big smile, a sob, and, 'Mommy!'

Jean motioned for everyone to head out to the balcony and give the girl some privacy.

'It's cold out here!' Mrs Pettigrew said.

'Here, Mama, take my sweater,' Holly said, taking off her cardigan to hand to her mother-in-law.

'No, now you and that baby need it more than me. I just don't see why we have to come outside, but if Miz Doctor says so I guess we jump.'

Jean held her temper. The woman had been through a lot. Lost two of her best friends, been shot at and suffered concussion, stuck in the hospital for days and now forced from her home and stuck with a bunch of people she barely knew. The psychiatrist part of Jean knew this. The human part wanted to kick the old lady in the butt to shut her up.

Petal came to the sliding glass doors of the suite and motioned to Jean. 'Mama wants to talk to you.'

Jean took the phone and pulled the child to her with a hug. 'You OK?' she asked Petal.

'Oh, yeah!' she said. 'I'm great!'

'Let's all go in,' Jean said to the rest and took the phone into the master bedroom.

'Jasmine?' she said once the door was shut.

'Jean, thanks so much—'

'Hush. How are you? How do you feel?'

'Like I've been rode hard and put up wet,' Jasmine said and laughed. 'But I'm alive and conscious and I think that's pretty damn good.'

'No, not pretty damn good, it's wonderful,' Jean said with a smile.

'How's Petal doing?' Jasmine asked.

'She's been worried about you but now she has a big smile on her face. She and John are getting on great, and everything would be hunky-dory except for one thing.'

'What?' Jasmine asked, her voice anxious.

'It would be icing on the cake if Mrs Pettigrew could go back home and leave us here without her.'

Jasmine laughed. 'I've known that woman most of my life. And I understand perfectly.'

'You get some rest, OK? Let me talk to Emmett.'

The phone was handed over and Jean said, 'What do the doctors say?'

'They're looking at a full recovery. She'll be out of commission for a couple of weeks but, once they check her over again, she should be good to go.'

'Excellent,' Jean said. 'Who's in charge?'

'Doctor Mitchell,' Emmett said.

'He's very good,' Jean assured him. 'Keep us posted on both Jasmine and what's happening back home. Any more – you know . . .'

'Accidents?' he suggested.

'Euphemistically put but yeah, accidents.'

'We'll let you know. Take care of my girl.'

'Of course. Like she's my own,' Jean said, said goodbye and hung up. And shot up a prayer of thanks for Jasmine's recovery.

Oklahoma City PD headquarters were a lot fancier than anything in Prophesy County but that was to be expected, I figured. It was a big city and they had a larger tax base than we did. Lots of industry and stuff. My brother-in-law's used-car part stores were the biggest hire in the whole of Prophesy County. Sad, when you think about it. We used to have a company that made lawn furniture but they moved their business overseas; we had a paper products distributor that hired a bunch of people but they went bust. A mattress factory moved in sometime in the nineties but it only lasted a couple of years. People farmed, ranched, fixed vehicles, air conditioners and plumbing and electrics, or owned a store in town and held on by their fingernails. Except for the Longbranch Inn's dining room, we didn't have much to attract tourists, although some of the shops holding on did sell souvenirs and antiques. Mostly, though, we were like a lot of small towns: barely scraping by. Which was one reason I drove my personal car to Oklahoma City rather than take a county vehicle. We were way overdue on upgrades and the budget for fixing the cars we did have was laughable. No county vehicle would have made the miles.

A few people snickered as me and Charlie made our way through the maze of detective cubicles to the interrogation room where we were to meet with Detective Juarez and the man of the moment, John Brewer, formerly John Connors, Jr.

Detective Juarez was a handsome Latino that I pretty much figured the women swooned over, which was evident when the line of female employees – including Officer Becky from the day before – made their way past the plate-glass window that looked into the interrogation room. They certainly weren't looking at John Brewer.

A strong wind would have blown poor John, Jr into the next county, he was that skinny. And his face was pocked from teenage acne, with still a couple of oozing sores visible on his forehead and chin. I could tell he was John Connors' son, though – he had John's hawk-like nose and weak chin. The kid was wearing baggy blue jeans and a blue nylon work shirt with the Walmart logo.

Me and Charlie shook hands with Detective Juarez and nodded at John Brewer.

'Thanks for meeting with us, Mr Brewer,' Charlie said.

We all took seats at the table, me and Charlie opposite Detective Juarez and John Brewer. 'Mr Brewer, we wanted to ask you about your dad,' I said.

'My dad? What about him?'

'Just wondered what your reaction was to him getting his head injury and all,' I said.

Brewer's eyes grew wide. 'Head injury? Oh my God! What happened?' He jumped up from his chair. 'Was it a car wreck? Is he alive? Where is he?'

Charlie and I looked at each other and I began to see where I might have made a mistake. 'Sorry, not your dad, Mr Brewer, but your birth dad, John Connors.'

John Brewer sat down hard on his chair. 'Who? What the hell you talking about?'

Again, me and Charlie exchanged a look. I nodded at Charlie to take the lead. I seemed to be messing it up.

'Ah, Mr Brewer, are you aware that your mother was married before her current husband?'

'No, she wasn't!' John Brewer said, again jumping to his feet. 'Who the hell are you to say shit like that about my mama?'

I glanced at Detective Juarez. His head was down, his hand over his mouth. I think the asshole was trying not to laugh out loud. All I can say is that me and Charlie didn't do a very good job of knocking down the stereotype of the country bumpkin peace officers. No, we did not.

OK, so John Brewer wasn't aware that he was born John Connors, Jr, or that his current dad was his stepdad and his birth dad was the basket case we had in Prophesy County. But, and this was not good, we needed to confirm that. And the only way to confirm that John Brewer was not aware of his parentage was to talk to his mama, who was not going to be happy that we had blundered in and blurted out a secret she'd kept hidden for over twenty years. But, knowing that the DNA proved a woman was responsible, that sort of let off John Brewer, but his mom? Did she give a crap about an ex-husband she hadn't seen in some twenty-odd years? What fun jobs me and Charlie had. I sat there in that interrogation room and counted up the days until I was eligible for retirement. Too damn many.

'Mr Brewer,' I said, 'I'm real sorry you found out about all this like you did. We thought you knew.'

'Knew what? You calling my mama a whore?' he said, his voice loud as he again stood up, his hands fisted.

'Nobody said that, boy,' Charlie said, patting the air. 'You need to calm down. And you need to sit back down right now.'

We waited in silence the minutes it took John Brewer to accomplish those two tasks. Once he was down, Detective Juarez said, 'Jackie, I'm real sorry about the way this all came about. I didn't know what these guys needed to talk to you about. And I sure didn't know Mike isn't your real dad—'

'He *is* my real dad!' John – Jackie – Brewer said.

'You're right. He's the one who raised you so he is your real dad. This other yahoo, well, I'm not sure exactly what these two are after,' Juarez said, leaning back in his chair and staring at us.

Jackie folded his arms over his sunken chest and glared our way.

'We need to talk to your mother,' I said, 'and verify that you didn't know about this.'

'Well, good luck with that. My mama passed two years ago. Breast cancer.'

There went that half-baked theory. 'I'm real sorry,' I said. 'Then maybe your stepdad.'

'He ain't my *step* nothing! He's my dad!'

'Sorry. Yeah, maybe we need to talk to him,' I said.

Juarez coughed like he was choking. 'What?' I demanded, glaring at him.

'Well, now, you might want to reconsider that,' Juarez said.

'And why's that?' I said, still glaring.

Juarez laughed and looked at Jackie Brewer, who grinned back at him. 'I don't know, Mannie,' Jackie said, calling Juarez by a first name we'd never been privy to. 'I think it might be fun to see these two tell my dad I'm not his son!'

Charlie leaned into me and whispered in my ear, 'Something's going on we don't know about.'

'No shit, Sherlock!' I whispered back.

John 'Jackie' Brewer née Connors stood up. 'I'll be happy to take you to see my daddy,' he said, still grinning.

I looked at Detective Juarez. 'You coming?' I asked.

He stood, grinning from ear to ear. 'Wouldn't miss it for the world,' he said.

Sylvia Bradshaw, the new EMT partnered with Jasper Thorne, stared at herself in the mirror, adjusting the red wig that covered her burned and bald scalp. After four major plastic surgeries, her face was still a mess. And her ass was a bit of a mess, too, from them taking so much skin off it to repair the burns she'd suffered to her left cheek, chin and nose. She remembered her younger brother used to call her butt-face when they were kids. She laughed mirthlessly. Well, she really was one now.

The door to the locker opened and Jasper called in, 'You decent?'

'Yeah,' she said, and pulled herself away from the image in the mirror.

'We got a call,' Jasper said.

'Another deputy bite the big one?' Sylvia asked.

'Hope not,' Jasper said, heading out in front of her.

'Whatever,' she said.

Anna Alvarez sat at her computer in the bullpen of the sheriff's office and stared at the stats in front of her. She was just damn glad they weren't making her go out on calls anymore. She was terrified of messing something up so bad they'd start to ask questions. One thing Anna didn't need was questions.

'You find anything more on Maudeen Sanders' kid?' Anthony asked her, setting a hip down on the corner of her desk.

'All I can tell you is she's doing real good at SMU – on the dean's list three semesters in a row.'

'What's she studying?' Anthony asked.

'Liberal arts,' Anna answered.

He laughed. 'Yeah, a degree in that and a dollar still won't get you a cup of coffee.'

'Yeah, but you might be able to get a job as a barista.'

'Good one. I think maybe I should go to Dallas and check her out,' Anthony said.

Anna gave him a look. 'Still having problems at home?'

Anthony straightened up from the desk and moved away. 'No. Everything's great,' he said.

Dalton came in the front door, escorting a very drunk old woman. 'Come on in and sit down, Miz York,' he said to her.

'Whatja got?' Anthony asked as Dalton settled the woman on the bench seat in the foyer and walked toward the counter that separated that area from the bullpen.

'Miz York. Again,' Dalton said and sighed. 'She was peeing on

Mr Staples' roses and he flagged me down as I was coming in.
She's as drunk as Cooter Brown.'

'Wanna put her in a cell to sleep it off?' Anthony asked.

'That's what I was thinking. Milt's done that with guys who're
drunk, and if we don't have any men in the cells it should be OK,
right?'

'Right,' Anthony agreed. 'We're empty now.'

'Good,' Dalton said, and headed for his charge.

'Maybe some coffee?' Anna suggested.

'Good idea,' Dalton said. 'Miz York, we're gonna get a little
coffee in you, then you can go lay down for a spell. How's that
sound?'

'Coffee's bad for you,' the old woman said. 'Got any bourbon?'

Me and Charlie found out what was so funny about us confronting
Jackie Brewer's stepdad. We discovered two things: Michael
Brewer was the pastor of the Family Values Evangelical Church
of the Lord and Savior, and just happened to be the former Mike
the Mighty, Oklahoma heavyweight wrestler of the year from 1972
to 1980. He was big, mean and didn't have much of a sense of
humor. And all that is an understatement. The only thing different
about Pastor Michael Brewer from Mike the Mighty of the seven-
ties was his hair was gray. He still had the handlebar mustache
and the muscular hamhock-sized arms.

I had misgivings. That's another way of saying I was scared
shitless. There were two scenarios, neither one having a good
ending. Number one, Mike the Mighty didn't know Jackie wasn't
his kid, at which point he'd beat the living shit out of anyone who
dared to say it was so; and number two, Mike the Mighty did
know Jackie wasn't his kid but had been keeping that secret close
to his chest for some twenty-odd years. At which point he'd beat
the living shit out of anyone who confessed to telling his kid the
truth.

So I thought I'd make Charlie do it.

He had other ideas.

'What's this all about?' Pastor Brewer said after we'd been
introduced.

We were in the sanctuary of the Family Values Evangelical
Church of the Lord and Savior, which was a storefront in a mostly

defunct strip mall on the outskirts of Oklahoma City. It was pretty much a plain space, no stained glass or fancy pews. Folding chairs were stacked up against the walls and the pulpit sat atop a raised platform of flatbed crates. But Pastor Brewer didn't really need a raised platform. He was pretty much a presence as he just stood there. Six foot five or six, close to three hundred pounds, and not much of it fat, he was definitely formidable.

I noticed Detective Juarez and Jackie Brewer had moved back a bit. Like, maybe a lot. This didn't bode well.

I looked at Charlie, who seemed to be studying the layout of his shoes. Personally, I didn't think they looked that complicated. I had a feeling that if anyone was gonna speak, it was gonna have to be me. I fought my brain for a strategy and came up with: 'Pastor Brewer, are you acquainted with a man in Prophesy County by the name of John Connors?' I asked.

Brewer looked at his stepson, then back at me, then back at Jackie. 'Son, need you to go in my study and fetch me my Bible.'

'You got your Bible in your hand, Daddy,' Jackie said.

'My study Bible,' Pastor Brewer said.

Jackie shrugged, grinned at Detective Juarez and left the sanctuary where we were all standing.

'What's this about?' Brewer asked again.

'Are you aware of the man I just mentioned?' I asked.

He looked behind him to make sure his stepson was out of earshot. 'Yes,' he said.

'Could you tell me your relationship to that man?'

'I got no relationship to that man,' he said. 'But he was my late wife's first husband, if that's what you're after.'

'Was your stepson aware of that?' I asked.

'My *son*,' he said, emphasizing the lack of 'step' in front of the word, 'knows only that I'm his daddy. And that's all he needs to know.'

'Cat's outta the bag, Mike,' Detective Juarez said.

Mike the Mighty's head swung around and he glared at Juarez. 'What?'

Juarez, being the bastard he obviously was, used his head to nod at me and Charlie. 'They told him,' he said.

'Why'd you go and do that?' he said, sounding a lot more like the wrestler than the preacher.

'Sir, I'm real sorry. We've got a situation down in Prophesy County and we needed to know if your son was aware of John Connors or his troubles,' I said.

'Well, I guess he is now!' The man steeled himself, closed his eyes and his mouth moved, I hoped in a prayer of forgiveness. 'What troubles does that evil bastard have?' he finally asked, opening his eyes.

'Nothing that concerns you and yours, obviously,' I said. 'Again, sir, I'm sorry we brought this upon you. We'll be leaving now.'

'You best be doing that,' the preaching wrestler said as we hightailed it out the door of the storefront.

'You need to go to the shop,' Jasmine told her husband. 'God only knows what's happening with just Dalton and Anthony in charge.'

'I'm not leaving you!' Emmett said.

'Please!' she said and laughed. 'Leave me! You're driving me nuts!'

'I'm just trying to help—'

'I know, honey, and you've been doing great. But I need some me time, you know? I've got a lot to think about and some healing to do, and I really can't rest that much with you hovering over me twenty-four-seven!'

'So you just want me to leave?' Emmett asked, his feelings obviously hurt.

Jasmine reached for his hand. 'Only for a little while. But then you come back, you hear?'

'How long?' he asked, his voice a little whiny.

'As long as it takes to see what's going on at the shop and for you to go home and take a shower and change your clothes. Of course, maybe you should do that *before* you go to the shop.'

'You saying I stink?' Emmett asked, lifting one arm to smell his pit. He made a face. 'Never mind.' He leaned down and kissed her. 'Next time you smell me you'll think I bathed in roses.'

'Personally, I like a more manly smell,' Jasmine said, her hand on the back of his neck. 'But this,' she said, scrunching up her nose, 'is just a little *too* manly.'

'I'm outta here,' Emmett said, and slipped out of the room.

He'd been in the hospital so long he wasn't sure if he

remembered where he'd parked. He walked the huge parking lot, hitting the alarm button on his key fob until he heard the beep of his car and saw the flashing lights. He crawled in and wondered if a nap might be in order – either before or after the shower. He'd barely made it inside his house before he discovered that the shower was definitely going to happen *after* a nap. The sofa was the closest spot and he flopped down on it.

Thoughts were flying through his brain – worries about Jasmine, about Petal and about everybody associated with the sheriff's department. He needed to figure out what was going on. It was his duty to figure out what was going on. He really needed to figure out . . .

He woke up two hours later. It was the first time in days he'd slept in a reclining position. The chair he'd been using at the hospital didn't induce sleep. He stretched and laid there for a few minutes, trying to orient himself. Shower. Shop. Hospital. Those were his priorities. But he thought a beer might not be inappropriate – before he brushed his teeth, of course.

An hour later he was back in his car and pulling into the employee parking lot at the sheriff's department. He noted there were only two squad cars in the parking lot. The third one must be out patrolling. That was a good thing, until he remembered that the third one was the one Jasmine had been in when she'd crashed. So no one was out patrolling. Not so good.

He went straight to the bullpen, not even stopping at his office to drop off his jacket. All three deputies were sitting there.

'Why the fuck aren't y'all out on patrol? Anna could hold down the fort, for God's sake!' he shouted.

'Mike Reynolds is patrolling for us,' Anthony said, mentioning the Longbranch police officer. 'Milt and Charlie came up with that plan. I just got back from a domestic out in Bishop and Dalton's been taking care of a drunk we got in lock-up.'

Emmett's breathing slowed and he felt embarrassed. 'Sorry, y'all,' he finally said. 'Things have been tense lately.'

'Don't we know it. We heard that Jasmine's out of her coma,' Anthony said.

'Yeah, yeah, she is. Doing real good,' Emmett said.

'Holly called,' Dalton said by way of explanation. 'Said Petal got to talk to her mama.'

'Yeah,' Emmett said and grinned. 'That did both of my gals a lot of good.'

Anna stood up and approached the counter. She reached across and patted Emmett's sleeve. 'I'm so glad Jasmine's OK.'

'Yeah,' Dalton said.

Anthony grinned and said, 'You betcha.'

Emmett heaved a sigh. 'So, Dalton, who's your drunk in the tank?'

'Miz York,' Dalton said. 'She's sleeping it off.'

'Did you call her daughter?' Emmett asked.

'Yes, sir, and she said to leave her here for all she cared. But then she calmed down and said she'd come by before we closed to get her.'

'I'm sure having a mama like that's a burden,' Emmett said.

'Yes, sir. I'm real lucky,' Dalton said.

Emmett couldn't help remembering what Jean had said to Jasmine and thought luck wasn't the word he'd use. Turning to Anthony, he said, 'Come on back and tell me about the domestic.'

Emmett walked back to his office, Anthony following behind. Once seated, Anthony said, 'Couple by the name of Shawny. He's a lawyer in Bishop, she's a stay-at-home mom. She hit him in the head with a hot iron.'

'Jesus!' Emmett said, taken aback. 'Was she defending herself?'

'Not so the husband mentioned. And according to her, it had something to do with his legal assistant.'

'Is he pressing charges?' Emmett asked.

'No, he kept saying it was an accident. The couple's teenage daughter said her mama did it on purpose but . . .' Anthony shrugged.

'Law says you gotta bring her in,' Emmett said.

'Well, yeah, but the husband kept saying it was an accident and he finally got the daughter to agree.'

'But you don't think it was?'

'Hell, no. She clocked him a good one. Got the burn imprint of that iron right on his left cheek. Iron won't be much good for clothes after that.'

'So? What's your plan?' Emmett asked.

'Keep an eye on her, mostly,' Anthony said. 'And maybe keep an eye on the legal assistant.' He shrugged. 'Tell the truth, Emmett, with what's been going on here I was kinda afraid to spend too much time and energy on it, you know, in case . . .'

'We can't let the county go to hell just cause we got some asshole trying to kill us all,' Emmett said, then laughed. 'Never thought I'd say those words.'

'Yeah, does kinda stretch the imagination, huh?'

'Keep in touch with the husband. Let him know we're keeping an eye and an ear out, OK?'

'Yes, sir,' Anthony said. 'Meanwhile?'

'Talked to Milt. He says John Connors, Jr is a washout. I'm not sure we got anything else.'

'Maudeen Sanders' kid? Lynette. The one down in Dallas?' Anthony said.

'That's a long shot,' Emmett said.

'Yeah, but it's our last shot.'

'Maybe we should call her—' Emmett started.

Anthony interrupted. 'I'd be more than willing to drive down there and interview her in person, Emmett. Really.'

Emmett shook his head. 'Let's wait until Milt gets back. I don't think we got the resources right now for anybody else to be going on a road trip.'

Anthony nodded, trying not to show his disappointment, while Emmett rearranged the files on his desk.

'Wait a minute,' he said, pulling a sheet out of one of the files. 'We looked at just about everybody except Witovec!'

'Who?' Anthony asked.

'Hank Witovec! The asshole who pistol-whipped that gas station attendant during that robbery with Jesse Trevino. Went down hard for it 'cause Jesse rolled on him? Remember?'

'Oh, yeah. I observed that interview with Milt. Trevino's out, right, but isn't that other guy, Witovec, still in prison?'

'Yeah, *he* is, but what about his family?'

'He got family?' Anthony asked.

'I'm looking, I'm looking!' Emmett said, shuffling through the papers in front of him. 'Next of kin his father, Anson Witovec, now deceased. Damn.'

'Anything else?'

'Just a minute. He had a girlfriend who was interviewed at the time of the arrest. Tried to give him an alibi but Trevino sorta messed that up.'

'How long ago was that?'

''Bout four or five years, maybe.'

'So why would she start harassing us now? And why me? I was barely here at the time!'

'Whoever's doing this doesn't seem to have a rhyme or reason for it,' Emmett said. 'Seems whatever happened, she – whoever *she* is – blames the entire department.'

'Which just brings up Reba Connors to my mind,' Anthony said, looking down at his feet.

'Gotta get over it, Anthony. You made a mistake. Nothing intentional in what happened. You got lost,' Emmett said. 'You've done nothing but good before and after that day. The lady needs help, professional help, only the kind of help Jean MacDonnell can give her. But she won't go looking for it and I doubt if Jean walked up to her and offered free counseling that she'd take it. For some reason she must like living with her sadness and hate.'

Anthony took a deep breath and said, 'OK, right. Meanwhile, we got a name for this girlfriend of Witovec's?'

'Nadine Hamm,' Emmett read. 'Works at Wendy's Cut and Curl – at least, she did five years ago.'

Anthony stood up. 'Think I'll go visit Nadine.'

'Works for me,' Emmett said and closed the file.

THIRTEEN

Me and Charlie went by the hotel and had lunch with Jean and the others, then headed on back to Prophesy County. Emmett called me on my cell phone and told me about them looking at Hank Witovec's old girlfriend.

'Nadine Hamm,' I said. 'I remember her. Pretty little thing. Couldn't believe she'd even look at ol' Hank. Looked like a bucket of snakes, that dude. But love's love, right?'

'That's what they tell me,' Emmett said.

'So keep me posted. Haven't seen hide nor hair of that girl since Witovec went up. She may not even be around our parts any more.'

'Just doing what we can do,' Emmett said.

'Don't I know it,' I said, sighed and hung up. Just doing what we can do. That's all me and Charlie were doing in Oklahoma City. But in our case it was a big bag of nothing.

And now that we knew the DNA belonged to a woman, it let out a lot of suspects. Like the Permeter brothers, Jesse Trevino, the two Evans boys and Troy Vaught. Which left Mrs Vaught, who was more than a long shot – kind of a stupid idea – Lou Anne Evans, whose DNA we needed to get, Reba Connors, who never left her home, and Maudeen Sanders' daughter Lynette, who was in Dallas.

I remembered asking Anna to look into Judge Norman's files to see how many cross references we'd get. I called the shop and asked her about it.

'Well, all the ones we already knew about,' Anna said. 'The Permeter brothers, Trevino and Witovec and Mrs Sanders. But that's all that stood out.'

'Shit,' I said, mostly under my breath, but I apologized just in case she heard me.

'Heard it before, Sheriff,' she said.

'Anything else you can do with that damned computer?' I asked.

'Let me go back further into what Holly dug up,' she said. 'Maybe I can cross reference things we haven't considered.'

I sighed. 'Yeah. All we need is more suspects,' I said.

'Sorry, Sheriff. That's all I got.'

'I know,' I said. 'We're just doing what we can do.'

Wendy's Cut & Curl was a four-station salon that did it all: haircuts, perms, color and weaves. It even had two pedicure chairs with little jacuzzis for the feet. Anthony felt a bit odd going in. He'd never been in a white woman's salon. His mama and his wife went to a salon that specialized in African-American hair. He didn't even know, until he saw the sign, that white women did weaves. Everything stopped the minute he walked in. Not a sound. He wasn't sure if it was because of his uniform, his sex, or his race – or maybe a mix of all three.

'Ladies,' he said, doffing his regulation Stetson. 'Can I speak to whoever's in charge?'

A sizable woman in skin-tight ripped jeans, a flowered T-shirt thing showing so much cleavage he was afraid they were gonna fall out and hot-pink cowboy boots stepped away from the first station.

'I'm Wendy. This is my place,' she said. Her hair was an impressive white blonde and several times bigger than the size of her head. Her make-up tended toward blue eyeshadow and hot-pink blush.

'Ma'am, I'm Deputy Anthony Dobbins from the sheriff's department,' he said. 'I'm looking for a young woman who used to work for you about four or five years or so ago. Name of Nadine Hamm.'

Wendy let out an unladylike snort which brought giggles from two of the other stations, stylists and clients.

'Oh, now, why'd you be wanting Nadine?' Wendy asked.

'Sheriff's department business, ma'am,' Anthony said.

Wendy turned back to her client who she'd been combing out and continued with the ratting process. 'Well, Nadine hasn't been around here since she got caught lying for that bastard boyfriend of hers. What was his name, Sandy?'

'Hank,' called the stylist by the third chair.

'Yes, ma'am,' Anthony confirmed. 'Hank Witovec. You happened to know where she went to?'

'Maybe McAlester?' Sandy called from the third station. 'So she could be near ol' Hank.' Sandy shook her head. 'Ugliest man alive but that girl really had it bad for him.'

'She upset about Hank going up?' Anthony asked.

Sandy moved away from her client, coming closer to Anthony. She was younger than Wendy, maybe in her mid- to late-twenties. Her eye make-up was black, as was her lipstick. Her hair was blacker than pitch-black, part shaved, part spiked, and she had tats and piercings in every visible spot. As she was wearing short shorts and a halter top, there was a lot visible. Being early March, Anthony thought it was too cold outside for the outfit, but the inside of the salon was pretty damned hot so he couldn't really blame her.

'Oh, yeah,' she said, answering Anthony's question. 'Me and her were roommates, over at the Tides Apartments, on Fifteenth Street?'

Anthony nodded his agreement that the Tides Apartments were definitely on Fifteenth Street.

'And she was just beside herself. She said Hank told her he didn't do it and, for some stupid reason, she actually believed him. That's why she made up the alibi, but hell, if anybody'd asked me

I'da wrecked the alibi if Hank's partner hadn't. I mean, she said she and Hank spent the night together that night and it was horse-shit. He wasn't there at all and I was home all night. I mean, I liked Nadine all right but I wasn't gonna get myself in trouble for that Hank. She didn't say the lie in court, though, so I guess she didn't break a law?'

'Right,' Anthony said.

'Well, right after he got sentenced she took off in the middle of the night. Still owed me half the rent for that month, too! Bitch.'

'You got no idea where she went?'

Sandy shook her head. 'Naw. But if you find her, remind her she owes me money, OK?' she said and moved back to her client, apologizing as she went.

'Anything else, Deputy?' Wendy asked, smoothing out the hairdo she was working on.

'No, ma'am. I guess that's all.'

'Well, you tell your wife that I've got product in for Afro hair. Spread the word to your people, OK?'

'Yes, ma'am,' Anthony said, 'I'll surely do that.'

The blast came out of nowhere. She was thrown across the room. The heat was unbearable. Her hair was on fire. Her face, oh, God, her face . . .

Sylvia Bradshaw jerked awake. She was sitting in the driver's seat of the ambulance, her partner Jasper Thorne inside the hospital flirting with some nurse. She couldn't believe she fell asleep. Not like her. But the dreams had been waking her up on nights lately. They hadn't done that in a long time. But right now, with all the pressure . . . All the memories were flooding back. Her therapist at the rehab hospital would have said it made sense, that you can't go back to where it all happened without reliving it somewhat. You can't put as much stress on yourself as Sylvia was doing without it coming out somewhere. Like a pressure cooker. That steam's gotta go somewhere.

The automatic doors to the hospital ER opened and Jasper came strutting out. Typical man, Sylvia thought. He figured all that flirting was gonna get him some. And him a married man, too.

*   *   *

I was finally back at the shop, sitting behind my desk, hoping Charlie Smith would keep his mouth shut about the fiasco in Oklahoma City. Somehow I doubted it. The boy found it funny. I mean, yeah, there was some humor there – if it had happened to somebody else. I tried to put Oklahoma City out of my mind as I bent to work on the myriad of forms littering my desk top. Half of them were things Holly would normally take care of, but Holly wasn't here and I wasn't inclined to throw this on Anna. I mean, she was doing all the computer work, which was taking her off patrol. I didn't need to overload the girl, new as she was.

I'd lucked out after Nita had decided to quit. I'd barely started a search when Anna had shown up with her credentials in her hand. Commendations, good reviews, good grades out of the academy – who wouldn't hire her? She said she was tired of dealing with all the drugs on the Texas border and wanted something a little more quiet. Thought Prophesy County would do her just fine. Well, she thought wrong. It hadn't been a good time to join the department – not with some nut job out there trying to pick us off one by one.

I can't say she'd lived up to the hype her paperwork had promised. She seemed a little timid to me. I mean, I don't want my deputies being outright aggressive but they did need to show a little backbone. Ten years ago I woulda put it down to her being of the female persuasion, but then along came Jean, Jasmine, Nita Skitteridge and a half-dozen more women that could and would take me on in a heartbeat. So I've had to change my tune about the so-called weaker sex. No, this was Anna. And it just didn't jibe with her commendations and reviews. But maybe the Laredo police department had different standards. After all, it was Texas, not Oklahoma. As I've always said, in Oklahoma we do things better than in Texas. No matter what *they* say.

Anthony came in the side door and stuck his head in my office. 'Hey, Sheriff? Got a minute?'

'Sure,' I said, glad to be taken away from the forms on my desk. 'What's up?'

'I went to where that Nadine Hamm used to work. Wendy's Cut & Curl?'

'Yeah?'

'They said she left town right after Witovec was sentenced. Her old roommate who works there said she thinks she moved to McAlester to be close to Hank.'

I shook my head. There's no accounting for taste, I thought. Pretty little thing like that following a low-life like Witovec to a prison town.

'Want me to follow up? See if she's in McAlester?' Anthony asked.

'Ah, hell, Anthony. Your guess is as good as mine. I got no idea what the hell's going on around here. I mean, I'm not a hundred percent sure our perp is even a woman. Sure, we got that DNA but we don't know how long that blood was on that broom handle or how many people could have had access to it.'

'The blood was sticky when the police found it, Sheriff. Couldn't have been more than a few hours old, which jibes with the time the house was empty, everybody off to the hospital and all.'

I nodded my head. He was right. The DNA belonged to a woman, and it was highly likely that that woman was our killer. And we did have a plethora of women. Just about as many as men. No matter how much I wanted to stick this on the Permeter brothers, it wasn't them. Unless their mother or Nick's wife could be behind it all. I thought about that for a minute, then considered it to be a stupid idea. Which seemed to be the only kind of ideas I was coming up with lately.

'We still got Maudeen Sanders' daughter,' Anthony said. 'I'd be more than willing to drive down to Dallas and check her out.'

I shook my head. 'If the girl's in Dallas then she's not doing this, right? Maybe we should make some calls to her school, her dorm, roommates, whatever, see if she's been down there all this time.'

Anthony sighed and stood up. I had no idea what bee was in his bonnet. 'Yes, sir, I'll get on that,' he said, sounding dejected, and left my office.

I wondered how things were going at home. Normally, I woulda called Jean and had her stop by and see Anthony's wife, Maryanne, on the pretext of just checking up on her and the baby. But Jean was in Oklahoma City having a lot more fun than I was. Even with Miz Pettigrew there with her. I grinned when I thought about that. My wife *did* have her hands full with that woman, that was for damn sure.

Two phone lines rang at once. I saw one being picked up, presumably by Anna, so I picked the second line up myself.

'Sheriff Kovak,' I said.

'Sheriff, this is Buddy Sheridan over at the pool hall?'

'Yeah, hey, Buddy, how's it hanging?'

'Bad, man, real bad. Sheriff, I sorta got a problem? Like, Joe Permeter's bleeding all over my floor.'

'Why's he doing that?' I asked, rising, I thought, to the occasion.

'Mainly 'cause he's dead?'

'You sure about that?' I asked.

'He doesn't have a face?'

'So how you know it's Joe?' I asked, standing up and grabbing my jacket.

''Cause his pecker's sticking out and it's got that ring in it he's been bragging about? Who else but Joe would have a ring in his pecker?'

I didn't know about the piercing but it didn't surprise me that Joe Permeter would decorate his pecker.

'Don't touch anything, Buddy. I'm on my way.'

'Sheriff?'

'Yeah, Buddy?'

'I sorta already touched lots of stuff,' he said.

I sighed. 'Well, just don't touch anything else,' I said, hung up and headed to my car.

Between the two of them, Anthony and Anna found the Dallas information on Maudeen Sanders' daughter, Lynette. She lived off-campus in a house with five other people. Anna found a list of her classes for the past few days but soon found out that at Lynette's level of schooling the professors didn't exactly take class registration. There was no way to know if she was attending classes or not. There was no landline at the house Lynette shared. Anna speculated that each person had their own cell phone so they didn't need a landline.

'Lots of people don't do landlines anymore,' she informed Anthony.

'Yeah, I know. Me and Maryanne don't have one and I've tried to talk my folks into getting cell phones, but they're too damn stubborn.'

'Yeah, I just use my cell, too. I mean, who needs a landline?'

'Exactly,' Anthony agreed. 'But in this case, it would be nice to be able to talk to some of the other residents of that house. See if Lynette's been missing the past few days.'

Anna tapped a few keys and said, 'We're in luck. Lynette's not on the lease. There's two names on the lease,' she said as she tapped a few more keys, 'another on the electric bill, and, yep, here we go, a fourth on the water bill.'

'So we got names but no cell-phone numbers, right? Any way to look that up?'

'Well, maybe,' Anna said, then looked up and grinned. 'Why don't you go do something useful while I mess around here a little?'

He cocked his head at her. 'You gonna do something illegal?'

'You really want to know?'

Anthony shook his head but added, 'See what you can find on Nadine Hamm while you're at it. She might be in McAlester.' Then he left her to whatever she had in mind.

'We just supposed to sit here and do nothing all day?' Mrs Pettigrew asked the room in general.

Johnny Mac and Petal were at the big table, doing the assignments from school Jean had brought with them. Holly was sitting on the sofa next to her mother-in-law, trying her hand at crocheting. Jean was at the suite's desk with her laptop, catching up on paperwork from her office at the hospital.

Holly put down the crocheting, sighed and said, 'Is there something you want to do, Mama?'

'Yes, ma'am, there surely is!' she said with a little heat in her voice. 'I wanna go home! That's all! I just wanna go home!' And then the old woman burst into tears, jumped up from the sofa faster than Jean ever suspected she could and hightailed it to the room she shared with Holly.

'Mama, she OK?' Johnny Mac asked.

'She'll be fine, honey,' Jean said, looking at Holly.

'I best go in there and check—' Holly started.

'No,' Jean said. 'Let her alone for a little while. I know this has been hard on her, Holly, but it's been hard on all of us, especially you. Having to worry about her *and* your baby. She needs to see that we're all in this together. Maybe some time alone will help that.'

Holly sighed again. 'You don't know Mama,' she said. She stood up. 'It's all well and good, what you're saying, Jean, but Mama's mama and she's not going to change at this late date. And, yes, she's been through a lot. More than the rest of us, really.' And with that, she headed into the adjoining room.

Jean watched her go, one hand on her slightly swollen belly, and hoped all the stress they were all going through wouldn't hurt that baby brewing inside. Deep down, Jean understood where Mrs Pettigrew was coming from. She wanted to go home, too. She wanted her home and her son back in school, and she even missed her sister-in-law Jewel and her husband Harmon. But one thing she was going to insist upon, once they got back, was that she, Jean, was going back in the kitchen. After these few days without Jewel's cooking, actually eating good food, she'd be damned if she was going back to cauliflower surprise.

Jasmine was holding Emmett's arm as they walked the halls of the hospital. The doctor had said one more day then she could go home. And that's all she could think about.

'You go get Petal tomorrow morning, drive back and the two of you can pick me up—' Jasmine started.

'Like hell!' Emmett said. 'When it's time for you to get out, I'm taking you straight to Oklahoma City. You'll be staying in a double room with Petal on the same floor as Jean and them. It's already arranged.'

Jasmine pulled away from her husband. 'Like hell your ownself! I'm not going to Oklahoma City for you or anybody else! And my daughter's coming home!'

'Need I remind you there's somebody out there trying to kill us? And our families? What makes you think she – whoever the hell *she* is – won't try to get you again?'

'I—'

'Stow it! You're going to the city if I have to hog-tie you and carry you up there on my back!'

'Emmett! I'm a trained deputy with a gun! Try hog-tying me and see what the hell happens!'

They stood in the hospital corridor staring at each other, then

Emmett laughed. 'Yeah, you could take me, I know that.' Sobering, he said, 'But you and Petal aren't safe here in town. You gotta go, honey. You're not in shape physically to handle any more of this crazy woman's shenanigans.'

'What about you?' she countered. 'You're in as much danger as I am! You and Milt and Anthony and Anna! Should we all just up and go to the city? Leave the county on its own? And if we did, what's to say she wouldn't wait us out? We'd have to go home sometime. Unless we all sold our houses and moved elsewhere. But then we'd have to split up, change our names—'

'OK, OK!' Emmett said. 'I get your drift. But, honey, you're injured—'

'I'm fine, the doctor said so—'

'He said you're OK to leave the hospital. But I distinctly heard him say you needed lots of bed rest! You gonna do that in your squad car? Which is still in the shop, by the way.'

Sullenly, Jasmine took his arm and proceeded back toward her room. 'Three days. I'll give you and Milt three days to solve this crap, then I'm coming back and taking names, you hear me?'

Emmett grinned. 'Yeah, baby, I hear you.'

I'd hollered at Anthony as I left the shop, telling him I'd radio in. I didn't see any need for back-up since Joe Permeter was already dead. I'm sure the list of people wanting to off Joe Permeter was vast and mostly women – plus maybe a few ex-boyfriends or current husbands. But could it have anything to do with what had been going on? How could it? He wasn't part of the sheriff's department – he was a suspect! Why would she go after a suspect? My mind was going in so many circles I was getting dizzy. So I decided I'd shut it off for a while. I'm remarkably good at doing that.

Buddy's pool hall was a hundred yards from the city limits sign of Longbranch, which put it in county jurisdiction. It was a long, low space, a former strip mall that had gone belly up and which Buddy Sheridan had bought for a song. He'd taken the entire mall, opened it up, put a bar at one end, pool tables on the other and pinball machines and video game consoles in the middle. Buddy Sheridan was quickly becoming one of the richest men in the county. Which was OK. Buddy was a pretty nice guy.

I'd gone to school with Buddy's mother, a homecoming queen, head cheerleader, beautiful – you name it, Donna Sheridan was the 'it' girl of our class. She went with Todd Singleton, the quarterback of the football team, point guard of the basketball team, pitcher for the baseball team, homecoming king and most handsome of our class. Todd got his draft notice before we graduated and was off to Vietnam only months after boot camp and a quick R&R at home. Donna didn't find out she was pregnant until he was overseas. Poor Todd didn't make it more than a month in Nam before he got killed in a raid in Saigon. He never even made it in-country. So Donna was a fallen woman, which is what people thought back in those days, but she ponied up, kept her baby and glared at anybody who looked at her funny when she walked her baby on the streets. Needless to say, Buddy Sheridan is her son. Donna owns a real-estate company and is doing quite well, but has never married. Or maybe that should read 'and' has never married. Nothing to say, these days, that a woman's gotta get married.

Unfortunately Buddy took after his dad in the brains department. Donna was the alpha in that relationship. Buddy dropped out of high school as soon as he was able to, went to work mopping floors at his mom's office, accidentally sold a house when nobody was in the office, got a real good commission, put that into buying the strip mall and the rest, as they say, is history.

Buddy was sitting on the front step outside the entrance to the pool hall, his elbow on his knee and his head resting on one hand. He stood when I pulled into the parking lot, waving at me like I might miss him. He was a big guy, like his daddy, but somehow the beauty of his mama and the handsomeness of his daddy didn't mix well. Buddy wasn't exactly butt-ugly but I guess you could say he was a little less than attractive. His nose was too big, his ears stuck out and, as my daddy used to say, he could eat a corn on the cob through a barbed-wire fence, he was that buck-toothed.

I got out and went to shake his hand. 'Hey, Buddy, sorry about all this.'

'Oh, yeah, me, too. Joe worked for me?'

'That's what I heard. Bartender, right?'

'Yeah. And he cleaned up some nights when I had to get home early. Last night was one of those nights, ya know?'

'Right. So he stayed after you left?'

'Right,' Buddy said, expelling a breath, like he'd been saving it up.

'Anybody else stay late?' I asked.

'Well, now, I don't know. I got a couple of waitresses. I think Mindy Hayes was on last night. Want me to call her?'

I patted him on the arm. 'That's OK, Buddy. I'll get her address and go ask her about that.' I sighed. 'Might as well go inside now.'

Buddy Sheridan made a face. 'Sheriff, it's real bad.'

I patted him on the arm again and followed him inside.

This was Anna's thing. This was what she was born to do. This was what she was best at. Trolling the Web, sneaking in here, there, everywhere. She'd been doing it since she was thirteen years old. And it had almost caught up with her. Almost. It had taken a tragedy to get her out of it. But she didn't want to think about that. She wanted to find what she could on Lynette Sanders' housemates and track down her alibi, if there was one. Anna really didn't care where Lynette was or wasn't, but this was what she was supposed to be doing now, and she'd play along as long as she could.

While the computer was doing its thing on Lynette, Anna decided to start a search on Nadine Hamm. It didn't take long. Nadine Hamm was now living in Bishop, right here in Prophesy County. She printed out the paperwork and ran to find Anthony.

Well, there was a man's body lying on the floor of the pool hall, close to the bar, pants down around his knees and a decorated pecker laying flaccid against the thigh. I turned my back to the pecker, reached into the back pocket of the jeans and found a wallet. No doubt about it, the faceless body belonged to the late Joe Permeter.

My cell phone rang. The read-out said it was the shop so I walked away from the body and answered it.

'Kovak,' I said.

'Sheriff, it's Anthony. Anna found Nadine Hamm!'

'Well, that's nice. She in McAlester?' I asked.

'No, sir. Right here in the county. Up in Bishop.'

I thought about that. So Nadine was back, if she'd ever really left. There were some highfaluting hair salons up in Bishop, being that it was the town where all the rich folk of the county lived. Maybe she just got her a better job than the one at Wendy's Cut & Curl. Which didn't rule out the fact that she was still pissed about old Hank and had been doing all this. But she wasn't tall enough, I told myself. The girl couldn't be more than five foot three or four. But if she stood up on her tiptoes, tried to make us think it was a man . . . It could be her. Who knew? Maybe she had a daddy who taught her how to shoot and cut brake lines and mess with alarm systems. Anything was possible.

'You wanna take a ride to Bishop?' I asked Anthony.

'Yes, sir!' he said, a little eager to get going.

'OK, you do that. And get back to me.'

He hung up without saying goodbye. Then I thought, Nadine Hamm. Pretty little thing. But maybe she was nuts. I mean, after all, she was in love with Hank Witovec and who, except a crazy person, would fall for him?

So I walked back to the body of Joe Permeter and sighed. I really needed another dead body like I needed a ring in my pecker.

Anthony put on the siren as he left the shop, headed through Longbranch on the highway to Bishop. He shut it off once he got to the town so he could hear Siri tell him where to go to find Nadine Hamm's address. When he found it, his mouth dropped open.

It was a big house, even by Bishop standards. Maybe the biggest in a town full of big houses. And it was on a lot of land. Maybe ten acres, unlike most of the houses in Bishop, which were either on an acre or less or snug up against each other like there wasn't enough room to spread out.

It was in a Tudor style, with wings and fancy windows and a portico that led to a four-car garage in the back, in the same Tudor style of the house. Anthony got out of his squad car and walked up to the front door, which was a mammoth thing made out of what looked like super-thick oak with wrought-iron handles and a wrought-iron pull cord. So he pulled it. A gong sounded inside the house. When the door opened a man in a suit stood there.

'May I help you, sir?' he said.

Oh, jeez, Anthony thought. It's a frigging butler! 'Ah, yes, I'm looking for a woman by the name of Nadine Hamm?'

'May I say who's calling, sir?' the frigging butler asked.

Anthony straightened his shoulders. 'Deputy Dobbins from the Prophesy County Sheriff's Department.'

The man nodded and opened the door wider. Taking off his Stetson, Anthony stepped into a foyer that was about half the size of his whole house.

'I'll let madam know you're here,' the man said. He didn't have an English accent. Anthony was disappointed by that.

He stood there for a long moment, checking out the place. The chandelier above his head was about the size of his wife's car. The flooring was white marble with a gray streak running hither and yon. He touched a wall to see if he was right, and sure enough it was covered in fabric, not wallpaper. And the fabric felt like silk, although a lot of things felt like silk to Anthony. There were bits and pieces of French-looking antiques placed here and there and, all in all, Anthony figured his yearly salary wouldn't cover a month's mortgage on this place.

The butler came back. 'Madam will see you,' he said and turned toward a closed door about three closed doors down from where Anthony stood. Anthony followed.

The butler opened the door, stepped aside and nodded Anthony in. A woman was standing by a roaring fireplace. She was not what Anthony had been led to expect. She was blonde, the honey blonde that nature intended, with large blue eyes, full lips, a slightly upturned nose and a perfect body. She was dressed conservatively in a straight medium-blue dress that reached her knees and had a scoop neck that only showed what Anthony thought were perfect collarbones with sleeves that went a little below her elbows. There was a tennis bracelet on one wrist, the diamonds bigger than any he'd seen on such a bracelet himself, and the ring on her left hand looked to Anthony like the Hope diamond. He admitted to himself that he could be mistaken.

'Hi!' the woman said and smiled brightly, her perfect teeth perfectly white. 'I'm Nadine Osterman. Formerly Hamm. How can I help you?'

'Ah,' Anthony started, realizing that wasn't a good beginning.

Nadine's smile softened. 'Why don't we both sit down, Deputy?' she said.

He waited for her to pick a white-and-gold brocade chair, then sat gingerly down on the sky-blue, high-backed sofa across from her.

'My husband's all right, isn't he?' she asked, a frown marring her perfect face.

'As far as I know, ma'am,' Anthony said. 'I didn't know you were married, actually, ma'am.' He cleared his throat. 'I'm here about Hank Witovec.'

Nadine's eyes grew big. 'What's he done now?' she asked.

'Nothing that I know of, ma'am,' he said, then chided himself for his behavior. He was almost shucking and jiving in front of this woman, something he'd never done in his life. What *was* his problem? he wondered. 'The thing is, ma'am,' he started again, 'we've been having some trouble at the sheriff's office that seems to be connected to someone we put away. And we're just checking up on the family members and loved ones of some of those perps. I mean perpetrators, ma'am.'

'Am I or my family in danger, Deputy?' she asked, clasping her hands in front of her.

'Oh no, ma'am. Seems to be the other way around. We think a family member or loved one of somebody we put away might be wanting to take a little revenge.'

'Oh!' she said, her face lighting up. 'And you think if I was stupid enough to go with Hank Witovec and even try to give him a phony alibi, I might be stupid enough to want revenge for you taking away my big old baby?' She laughed.

Anthony cringed. He was pretty sure this woman had nothing to do with what was going on. 'Well, ma'am, we're checking up on a lot of people.'

'I'm sure you are!' she said, seeming delighted. She shook her head and her face got serious. 'Yes, at one time I was very stupid. So stupid I almost landed myself in jail for lying for that no good son of a bitch. I was so upset I left Longbranch in the middle of the night and went home to Tulsa.' She smiled. 'Got a job at a fancy men's salon, which is where I met Henry, my husband. He moved his company to Bishop and so, of course, we moved too. Henry and I have two little girls. They're both upstairs with the nanny right now. Would you like to meet them?'

'Sure, yes, ma'am, that would be nice. I've got a baby girl myself. Three months old.'

'How wonderful!' she said and clapped her hands together.

'But, ma'am, I gotta ask you about your whereabouts for a couple of time periods,' he said.

'Oh, of course! But if it helps, Henry and I and the girls just got back from a cruise two days ago. We were gone three weeks. Does that cover your time period?'

Anthony sighed. 'Yes, ma'am, it surely does.'

Nadine Osterman stood up. 'So let's hop upstairs so you can meet the girls! They'll just love your uniform!'

I got the ball rolling with the ME's office, then called in the incident to Emmett.

'What the hell?' he said when I told him.

'My sentiments exactly,' I said.

'You think this ties in with all this other crap?'

I sighed. 'How could it? I mean, what could one have to do with the other?'

'Damned if I know,' Emmett said.

'Look, I'm going to go notify the family and then check out the last person I know that might have seen ol' Joe. Anyway, can you head back to the shop?'

'I'm on my way,' he said and we disconnected.

The one thing – OK, one of many things – I didn't want to do at that very moment was go tell Nick Permeter and his mama that baby brother Joe was lying in a pool of his own blood on the floor of the pool hall. Five'd get you ten Nick was gonna blame it on the sheriff's department, maybe even yours truly.

I waited until the ME got there, took down all the particulars I could get out of Buddy Sheridan, then headed to my squad car and off to the Permeter farm. Life sometimes sucks great big river rocks, know what I mean?

FOURTEEN

'Dalton, you think you can get away for a day?' Holly asked her husband over the phone.

'I don't know, babe. We still got all this going on, with that crazy woman and all, but we ain't doing much. How come you want me to get away?'

'It's Mama—'

Dalton sat up straight in his chair, panic giving him perfect posture. 'Is she OK? What happened?'

'She's OK, honey, really,' Holly said. 'It's just that she's so depressed. She wants so bad to go home, but we both know she can't, not yet. But I think if she saw you, maybe . . .'

'Maybe it would make her happy?' Dalton suggested.

Holly smiled. 'Exactly.'

'Let me talk to Milt. Maybe I can leave now and be there 'fore it gets dark.'

'Call me back and let me know.'

'Don't say nothing to Mama until I let you know,' Dalton said.

'I won't,' Holly said, made her goodbyes and hung up.

Mrs Pettigrew had been lying down for over an hour. Holly had checked a couple of times to make sure she was still alive, and had come back into the living room of the suite satisfied each time. But Holly knew enough psychology to know that excessive sleep was one of the signs of depression.

Sitting down next to Jean on the sofa, she asked, 'Do you think Mama is situationally depressed or chronically depressed?'

Jean looked at her. 'I'm not sure,' she said. 'That's a good question, though. Before all this happened, was she moody?'

Holly thought about it for a moment, then said, 'I'd have to say yes. But Dalton swears that's just her way. Which I guess means she's always been moody.'

'That doesn't rule out chronic depression,' Jean said.

'So you think she should go on anti-depressants?'

'That would be up to her family doctor, Holly. I can't diagnose her unless she's my patient and,' Jean laughed slightly, 'with her current outlook regarding yours truly, I'd say the chances of her ever being my patient are slim to never going to happen.'

Holly nodded. 'Yeah, Mama does seem to want to blame you for just about everything.'

'Maybe subconsciously she knows I can handle it.'

'Maybe,' Holly agreed. 'You think she really blames me but doesn't want to take it out on me because of the baby?'

'Why would she blame you? You've had nothing to do with any of this.'

'Neither have you,' Holly said.

'True,' Jean said. She patted Holly's shoulder. 'Who knows what's in her mind? The best we can do is try to be there for her, make her as comfortable as we can.'

Holly sighed long and hard. 'Yeah. I guess.'

'Not much of an answer, huh?'

Holly reached over and hugged Jean. 'No, not much,' she said.

I'd personally never been out to the Permeter farm and hoped I'd never have to do it again. It wasn't the nicest farm in the county, that was for damn sure. Grass was high wherever there weren't cows to eat it; fences were knocked down in places and patched with one or two strips of barbed wire. The house needed a paint job, as did the barn and most of the outbuildings. Seems the last time any of it was painted was when there was a sale on half cans of multiple paint colors: the house was a dismal white, the barn a faded red, one outbuilding was a peeling green and another was a color not seen in nature. Somebody must have been looking out of the window, 'cause Nick Permeter came out of the front door of the house and stood on the slanted porch waiting for me before I even stopped the engine of the squad car.

When I did get out, he shouted from the porch, 'What now? You come to arrest me for peeing out back of my barn?'

'Need to talk to you and your mama inside the house, Nick.'

'You got a warrant? That's the only way you're getting inside my house!' he yelled. 'And you ain't never talking to Mama!'

'Nick, I got bad news your mama needs to hear. Her and you both,' I said.

He stared at me. He must have seen something in my face that told him it was real bad because he nodded, turned and opened the front door, holding it for me as I came up the steps of the porch.

The house smelled musty – moldy, even – with an overlay of cooked cabbage. The linoleum on the floor was cracked and missing in places and the walls were old, unpainted shiplap.

Nick called out 'Mama,' as we came in and an older woman came out of the kitchen, followed by a younger one. 'Betty, you see to dinner. Mama, come on in the living room.'

I followed him in and waited for Miz Permeter to take a seat. There were plenty of options. The medium-sized room was stuffed with two sofas, a love seat, two lounge chairs and an overstuffed chair with an ottoman. The old lady took one of the lounge chairs. Nick took the other one while I opted for the chair with the ottoman.

'Ma'am, Nick, I'm real sorry to tell y'all . . . Buddy Sheridan opened up the pool hall a little while ago and he found Joe. He'd been shot. I'm really sorry.'

'He in the hospital?' the mama asked.

'No, ma'am. I'm afraid he didn't make it. The ME has the body now—'

Nick jumped up from the lounge chair. 'You're saying Joe's dead?' he demanded.

'Yes, sir, that's what I'm saying. I'm really sorry.'

Nick was silent for a moment, as was his mama. Then she began to wail, and at the same time Nick charged me. The chair I was sitting in flew over backwards and I found myself sprawled on my back with Nick Permeter's hands around my throat. I had the wherewithal to draw my weapon and stick it in his nose. The grip on my throat lessened as I shoved the weapon harder up his nose. Finally he let go and I got up, holstering my gun.

'You might wanna see to your mama,' I said, noticing my voice sounded a little croaky.

'Who did it?' Nick demanded. 'You shoot him?'

'No, I didn't, Nick. But I'm gonna find out who did and we'll make 'em pay.'

'Not if I find him first!' Nick said and hightailed it out the front door.

By that time, the other Miz Permeter, Nick's wife Betty, was in the living room, taking care of mama. I decided it was a good time for me to take my leave.

Emmett got back to the shop and sat in his office, thinking things over. Joe Permeter, one of their more deserving yet least likely suspects, was dead. Why? he wondered. Could it have anything to do with what had been going on? How could it? Why would it? When his cell phone rang, he saw from the read-out that it was Milt.

'Yeah?' Emmett said.

'I made the notification to the Permeters. And now I need to rest my brain. I got the address for the last person to see Joe. Mindy Hayes. Lives in town, over at the Shanghai La. Apartment 204. Already called Charlie and told him we'd be interviewing her. You up for it?'

'On my way,' Emmett said and hung up.

He knew the Shanghai La all right. When he'd been police chief of Longbranch he'd seen a lot of action at the old Shanghai La apartments. Mostly dope, fist fights, domestics and a couple of assaults, one sexual. The place had been built in the eighties and he doubted if any repairs had been done since then. It looked like a good wind could blow it down. He wasn't sure how it had stayed standing here in tornado alley. He pulled up to the front entrance and walked in. They were garden apartments built in more or less a square. The front had two apartments on each side with rickety staircases going up on the left and on the right. In the middle of the square was the pool. Or what had been the pool. It was empty now, and as Emmett climbed the steps he could see into it. The space was filled with trash, including a couple of lawn chairs and what appeared to be a dead poodle. He decided not to investigate that.

He found apartment two-oh-four a little down from the stairway and rapped on the front door as there was no bell to be found. It took two more raps before the door opened to reveal a bleary-eyed young woman clutching a terry-cloth robe around her ample body.

'What?' she demanded.

'Mindy Hayes?' Emmett asked.

'I don't want any trouble,' she said, and started to slam the door.

Emmett stuck his cowboy boot in the space quickly before she could shut it all the way. 'Ma'am, I'm a deputy sheriff and this is sheriff's business.' He showed her his badge.

She loosened the door from his boot and looked at him with bloodshot eyes. 'I haven't done nothing!' she said.

'No, ma'am. I'm not here about anything you did. I just need to ask you some questions. Mind if I come in?'

'I ain't dressed!' she said.

'I'll wait out here if you want,' Emmett said.

She sighed. 'Oh, hell. Come on in. I'm up now.'

She turned her back on Emmett and walked inside. Emmett recognized the furnishings from when the Shanghai La had been his beat. It was the only place in town with furnished apartments, and this furniture looked exactly like the furniture he'd seen back in the day, just a lot more beat up and seedy. Mindy flopped down on a semi-broken sofa so Emmett pulled a chair from the dinette set that took up most of the space in the living room.

'Whatja want?' Mindy asked.

She looked to Emmett to be staring thirty in the eye. Her red hair didn't look natural and it stuck up in all sorts of nasty ways. Her bare feet were dirty and the terry-cloth robe could use some bleach.

'Ma'am,' he started, 'may I ask what time you left work last night?'

'Huh?' She'd been leaning back against the sofa but pulled herself forward and scowled. 'Is Buddy saying I stole something? 'Cause I never!'

'No, ma'am. It's nothing like that. Remember what time you left?'

She leaned back and shrugged. 'Usual time. 'Bout two-thirty, thereabouts.'

'Was Joe Permeter there when you left?'

She laughed. 'Oh, yeah. He was cleaning up supposedly but still trying to get me to go to his house with him. I told him once was enough for me.'

'So when you left he was still there cleaning up?' Emmett said.

'Ain't that what I just said?'

'Was there anyone else around?' Emmett asked.

'No, the place was closed. Everybody was gone. I was the only waitress working last night. Just me and Joe pretending to be a bartender, but that boy can't even make a mojito. You call that a bartender?'

'When you left did you see anyone outside? Any extra cars? Anything like that?'

She shook her head. 'Didn't notice. Wasn't really looking. I had a date so I was anxious to get out of there.' She cocked her head. 'Why you asking all these questions? The place get robbed or what?'

'No, ma'am,' Emmett said, then, seeing how Milt had already notified the next of kin, and what with Buddy Sheridan having found the body, and Buddy more than likely telling his mom, who would tell everyone she worked with and even people coming to buy a house, he decided to go ahead and tell her. 'Joe Permeter was shot dead last night at the pool hall.'

She made a loud noise then cupped her hands around her mouth and nose, like some women do. Finally she lowered her hands and asked, 'Did they shoot him in the johnson?'

'Ma'am?'

'Well, if they shot him in his privates then you could be sure it was a woman.'

'No, ma'am, he was shot in the face,' Emmett said.

Mindy frowned. 'Well, that's a shame. For all his assholicness, Joe had a real pretty face.'

Seeing that not much more was forthcoming from the last person, other than the killer, to see Joe Permeter alive, Emmett took his leave and headed back to the shop. He figured he'd call Milt when he got there and let him know about another dead end. He turned into the parking lot just as the front of the building exploded.

I was still on my way back to the shop from the Permeter farm when Emmett called me on my cell and told me about the explosion.

'Anybody hurt?' I asked, reaching for my siren and turning it on.

'I don't know! I don't know!' Emmett shouted. 'I'm trying to get in now!'

'You call the fire department?' I asked.

'Jesus, Milt. Of course!' he said, and hung up in my ear.

By the time I got to the shop, there were two fire trucks and an ambulance in front of the building. Since the whole county only has two fire trucks I was scared witless. Add the ambulance to that and I was not thinking as straight as I might have been.

I rushed up to the front doors but the fire chief caught my arm. 'Can't go in this way, Milt,' he said. Pointing, he said, 'Go in your side door.'

'Anybody hurt?' I asked.

He shook his head. 'Minor cuts and burns.'

I heaved a sigh of relief, thanked him and headed around the building to the employee entrance. Once inside, I coughed a little at the smoke still lingering in the air then glanced in my office to see if it was still standing. It was – and it was crowded. Dalton, Anthony, Anna and Emmett were crammed inside.

'What the hell happened?' I asked.

Everybody started talking at once and I said, 'Anthony! You say.'

'Yes, sir. We were all back in the bullpen, writing up reports, and Anna here was on the computer doing stuff, when the front doors just blew in! I mean, it was crazy! They just blew in like nothing! Then the big bang and we all hit the floor.'

'No fire?' I asked.

'No, sir. Just the explosion.'

'What does the fire chief say?' I asked Emmett.

'Looks like a bomb,' he said.

I sank down in one of my visitors' chairs as Emmett was busy occupying my desk chair. 'When is this shit going to stop?' I asked the room in general. There was no quick answer.

So there were plastic sheets on the front of the sheriff's office that matched the plastic sheets on the back of the sheriff's house. There was something sorta poetic about that, I thought. The deputies were back in the bullpen and Emmett was sitting in one of my visitors' chairs while I was righteously back in my paid-for-it-myself black leather swivel chair.

'What now?' Emmett asked.

I had no idea. As the ultimate authority figure in this particular building, I had nothing to say. My mind was blank. Basically, I had nothing.

Before I could embarrass myself by answering, Dalton stuck his head in the doorway of my office.

'Milt, I know this is probably a bad time but I promised Holly I'd ask. Mama's real depressed like and Holly thinks me going up there could help a bit. What do you think?'

I looked at Emmett and he said, 'And while he's on his way he can pick up Jasmine and take her with him.'

'Sounds like a plan,' I said. As plans go, at least it was one.

Dalton took off and Emmett used my phone to call Jasmine to tell her to pack. I could hear his end of the conversation.

'Hey, honey, Dalton's going to the city to see his mama. I asked him to stop by and pick you up, so start pack—'

Then, 'Ah, well, no, and you gotta go—'

Followed by, 'Listen here—'

Finally, 'Somebody blew up the station, Jasmine. Whoever this bitch is she's not letting up so you're going and I'll hog-tie—'

I heard the last line. 'So shoot me. Start packing.' And he hung up.

'That Jasmine,' I said, grinning.

'Don't even!' Emmett said. He sighed. 'I think she'll go. If not for her own safe-keeping then at least to see Petal.'

I nodded. 'Mothers are like that.'

'So now what?'

I sighed. 'Nick Permeter took off right after I told him about Joe. Says he's out to kill whoever did it. Doubt he'll have any better luck than we've been having but we need to find him. You know his truck?'

'Yeah,' Emmett admitted.

'Well, go look for it. He's out there wanting blood for his brother. And we can't have that.'

'Why me?' Emmett all but whined.

'Why not you?'

He pushed himself up from the chair. 'I knew, eventually, one of these days, coming to work for you was gonna bite me in the butt,' he said.

'Cry me a river,' I said.

'So what do I do if I find him?'

'Shoot him?' I shook my head. 'Probably not. Use your best judgment.'

'OK, so I can shoot him,' Emmett said and left my office.

I got back to the forms on my deck and the accumulated mail that had been piling up since all this started going down. I noted one envelope on the bottom of the pile, old enough to have been put there by Holly, not Anna, from the Laredo, Texas police department. I'd sent off for confirmation and a recommendation only a couple of days after hiring Anna but it had been over a month. I grabbed the envelope and tore it open. What I found inside was a game changer.

Emmett called to tell me he hadn't found Nick Permeter. All I said was, 'Get over here now,' and hung up.

I looked once again at the letter I'd received over a week ago from the Laredo PD. I had to bounce this off someone, and Emmett had always been a good catch. I didn't want to go off half-cocked. This was too important. Too many things were riding on my next move. Although every part of my being was twitching, ready to storm out of my office to the bullpen. Ready to end this crap once and for all.

It took Emmett ten long minutes to pull into the parking lot, open the side door and sit his butt down in my chair.

'Close the door,' I said.

He reached behind him and shoved it closed.

'What the hell's got your panties in a twist?' he asked.

I handed him the letter. He read it, looked at me then re-read it. Then looked at me again.

'What the hell—'

'You thinking what I'm thinking?' I asked.

The letter read: 'Dear Sheriff Kovak, I regret to inform you that Laredo police officer Anna Alvarez was killed in the line of duty on December the twelfth last year. She was an exemplary officer and our loss is both professional and personal. I have no idea who you have in your county claiming to be Anna Alvarez, but if she is stating that she is the former Anna Alvarez from the Laredo PD, then she is committing some type of fraud. I wish you luck in your pursuit of this person. Sincerely, Douglas Knight, Deputy Police Chief, Laredo, Texas.'

I called Anthony in the office, made him shut the door behind him and handed him the letter.

Anthony's mouth had dropped open as he began reading and slammed shut when he finished. 'What the hell?' he said.

'That's not Anna Alvarez,' I said, nodding my head toward the bullpen.

'OK,' Anthony said. 'Then who the hell is she?'

'That's the sixty-four-thousand-dollar question,' Emmett said.

We all looked at the closed door of my office, as if we could see through it to the bullpen.

'You think *she's* doing this?' Anthony asked, his voice almost squeaking.

'Seems likely,' I said. 'Although she's not tall enough to leave that note.' My gut was killing me. Mainly because I wasn't screaming, cursing, or running out there and cuffing 'Anna Alvarez.'

'We gotta play this right, Milt,' Emmett said. 'We got no proof. We've got to get some before we show our hand—'

There was a knock on the door and Anna – or whoever the hell she was – stuck her head through the door. 'Sheriff, I think I found something!'

She looked from one to the other of us as there was no quick response. 'Something wrong?' she asked.

'No, nothing,' I said, trying a smile that felt more like a grimace. 'Whatja got?'

'Well,' she said, 'I was doing what you'd asked me to do, going through the stuff Holly found and comparing it to Judge Norman's cases, and I came across something.'

'And what would that be?' I asked, wondering what bullshit she was getting ready to spit out.

'Ah, here, Anna, take my seat,' Anthony said, standing up and going toward the doorway, I guess for a quick getaway if necessary. The coward.

Anna sat down. 'There's this one case that stood out. There was this guy that got blown up in a meth lab—'

'Yeah. I remember that. But he died. No next of kin,' I said.

'Yes, sir, but the entire department was at that raid. And there was one other person there that night. The guy – his name was Earl Jessup – had his girlfriend there. Eden Brown. She got burned real bad so the judge only sentenced her to a couple of years, and those she spent in the burns ward at the Warrior Correctional Center in Taft. But I'm thinking maybe—'

Anthony said, 'Dalton told me Jasper Thorne's new partner has burns scars all over her face. He saw her when they took those ladies from the bridge club to the hospital.'

I looked at Emmett, then at Anthony. 'How new is she?' I asked.

'Want me to check on the computer?' Anna asked.

'Yeah, quick,' I said, almost forgetting I was fixing to cuff her.

She was back in less than five minutes. 'The hospital's employee records show she was employed three weeks ago.'

'How'd you get in the hospital employee records?' Emmett asked. 'Aren't those, you know, private?'

'Never mind,' I said. 'That's not important. What's important is finding out who she is. Anybody know her name?'

'Sylvia Bradshaw,' Anna said.

'I take it you're one of those hacker people, right, Anna, or whatever your name is? The jig's up, but I need you so don't move. Get into the women's prison's database and see if we can get a picture of that burn victim . . . Eden?'

'Brown. Yes, sir. And I don't know what you're talking—'

'Whatever,' I said, dismissing her. 'Just do your job while you still have it.'

Anthony was sitting at his desk, trying hard not to look at 'Anna Alvarez.' He couldn't believe it. That she could cut his wife's brake lines, shoot out Dalton's tire . . . Then he remembered. That day at the shooting range. He and Anna and Dalton trying to requalify. Dalton did good, Anthony did OK and Anna did shitty. He and Dalton had agreed to fudge the results. Just a little. How could someone who was that bad a shot shoot a tire out? Not to mention shoot through a moving car's window and almost kill the driver, like she had with Jasmine? Answer was she couldn't. Unless she'd been pretending at the range. But why would she do that? A bad score could have lost her this job, which she seemed to need in order to perpetrate her evil plans. Besides, she'd been with him when Jasmine was shot off the road, and maybe when Dalton's tire had been blown. They had no idea when Maryanne's brake lines had been cut, or the judge's, for that matter.

Anthony stood up to head to Milt's office but Anna stopped him. 'Would you give this to Milt? And tell Holly the rest of it's there – all she has to do is look for it.'

'Yeah, sure,' Anthony said, distracted by his own mission.

Once in Milt's office, he handed him the paper Anna had given him. 'What's this?' Milt asked. Anthony shrugged.

'Eden Brown,' Milt said. 'She looked like that ambulance driver?'

'I don't know, but it's gotta be her, not Anna,' Anthony said. 'I know you're gonna be pissed off about this, Sheriff, but when me and Dalton were at the range a couple of weeks ago with Anna, she didn't qualify. Me and Dalton sorta helped her score along a little bit.'

Milt stood up. 'Why the hell'd you do that?' he demanded.

'Not the point, sir,' Anthony said, and when Milt started to argue that statement, he interrupted. 'The point is, Sheriff, if she's such a bad shot she couldn't qualify at the range without help, how the hell did she shoot out Dalton's tire or Jasmine's window? Both of those cars were moving at the time.'

Milt sat back down and looked at Emmett. Emmett looked at Anthony.

Milt stood up again and walked to the door of his office, the others following behind as he headed into the bullpen. Anna Alvarez was gone, along with all her belongings.

Sylvia Bradshaw drove the ambulance to a call out in the country. She was still itchy from the night before. That damned bartender. She'd just been sitting there at the bar of the pool hall, doing some tequila shots, minding her own business. Then she hears him, talking to some other douche bag, saying how maybe she – meaning Sylvia – should have stayed home. Why'd she want to come in a place like this? Think anybody would want to pick *her* up? Then he said he wouldn't fuck her with a ten-foot dick. Who the hell was he to say that about her? Who did he think he was? Some no-good bartender! And she sat there, getting madder and madder, the heat building up, burning her face all over again. Goddamn man! That's what they all were. But this one was the worst. This one . . . Who the hell did he think he was?

Sylvia always kept her rifle in the trunk of her car. She'd never been a Boy Scout but she believed in their motto: be prepared. Sylvia was always prepared for this particular eventuality. She sat in her car until the bar closed and she saw the waitress leave. And she waited some more. Then, seeing no one else around, she took her rifle and went inside the pool hall. He'd been standing there, leaning on the push broom, a beer bottle to his mouth. He'd seen her and turned.

'We're closed,' was all he'd said.

'That's it?' she'd asked. 'You got nothing else to say to me?'

'What?' Joe had asked, frowning.

'You had a lot to say a while ago. Talking about me.'

Light had seemed to dawn as he simultaneously heard her words and saw the rifle she held to her side.

'Hey, lady, I don't know what you're talking about. That other guy—'

'Bullshit,' she'd said. 'You think you're pretty awesome, don't you?'

'Look, you need to leave—'

'Take down your pants.'

'What the fuck? Honey, no way!'

She'd lifted the rifle and pointed it at him, shouting, 'Take off your goddamn pants!'

Joe, who always went commando, had undone his belt and unfastened his jeans, letting them fall to his knees.

Sylvia had seen the ring in his penis and begun to laugh. 'You're real proud of that thing, aren't you, boy?'

'Look, lady—'

'I don't know whether to shoot you in the dick or in the face,' Sylvia had said, quietly studying on the subject. 'Which do you suggest?' she'd asked him.

Joe had turned his body like he was going to run but he hadn't been able to take his eyes off the woman with the gun.

'OK, the face,' she'd said and fired.

All that time in the burns unit had taught Sylvia Bradshaw a thing or two about first aid – enough to bluff her way into this job. This perfect job. It was all she'd thought about lying there, suffering through one operation after another – killing the bastards who'd ruined her life. Lots of time off to do what needed to be done but also keep her tuned into what was going on in the sheriff's department. She was pretty pissed she hadn't killed even one of them yet, but she still had time. Nobody knew or suspected.

Now, driving the ambulance out to the country, she kept looking at Jasper Thorne, the lying, cheating bastard. She was beginning to think it wasn't enough to take out her vengeance on just the sheriff's department. Hell, if the EMTs had been faster getting her to the hospital after the meth lab blew up, she might not have lost her baby. They'd all ruined her life. All of them. That stupid raid. If they hadn't come in sirens blazing, guns drawn, Earl wouldn't have goofed up so bad that he blew up the place. They made him nervous, with their sirens and all. And she'd crawled out of that hell hole on her belly, her face, her head, so much of her on fire. The pain was more than a person should have to bear. And this asshole, Jasper, with a wife and kids at home, inside the hospital making plans to screw some nurse. God, men! She thought. They're such assholes. Earl was an asshole. Saying they could strike it rich with the meth. Hell, he hadn't sold one batch before he blew himself up and ruined her for life. And killed their baby. Sylvia's hands tightened on the steering wheel. If Earl wasn't already dead, she'd make him so.

The radio squawked and Jasper picked it up. 'Ambulance three,' he said into the mic. The response came out garbled but even Sylvia had been around long enough to understand what the operator was saying. 'Return to base. Ambulance one will take your call. Return to base immediately. Over.'

'Will do,' Jasper said into the mic, looked at Sylvia and shrugged. 'Over and out,' he said. To Sylvia, he said, 'Wonder what that's about?'

'Don't know,' she said but she had an inkling of an idea. Maybe the jig was up. Maybe they knew.

Jasper reached for the siren switch and turned it to the off position. There was blessed silence. 'Somebody's ass is in a sling, I just hope it's not mine,' Jasper said.

'You done anything bad lately?' Sylvia asked him.

'Me? Hell, I'm clean as the driven snow,' Jasper said.

'No, you're not.'

He laughed. 'What you talking about? I ain't done nothing to get my ass in trouble.'

'You were trying to screw that nurse.'

'Huh? What nurse?'

'Lolly, Lanie, whatever the hell her name is.'

'Lotty? Girl, she's my sister-in-law! We always tease. She's not my type. Besides which, my woman's got a short leash on this boy. I don't stray. No sir-re-bob.'

'Liar!' Sylvia shouted.

Jasper looked at her, stunned. He said, 'No, Sylvia, I ain't lying. The girl's my wife's little sister. She's got a boyfriend. A fireman in Tulsa. Hell, he's so fit he'd make mincemeat outta me if I tried anything with Lotty. Your man messin' around on you, girl? Is that where this is coming from?'

'You're all liars, every one of you!' she screamed, her foot pressing down harder and harder on the accelerator. The ambulance was reaching its top speed and still she pressed harder.

'Girl, you need to slow this bus down, you hear?' Jasper said, holding on tight to his door and glad he had on his seat belt but wishing this old bus had air bags. 'You gonna wreck this thing!'

'And maybe you'll die!' she screamed. 'Nobody else did! I tried and tried and all I got was two old ladies who weren't anybody's kin! Y'all killed my baby! Turnabout's fair play, isn't that what they say? Well, I'm turning about!'

With the ambulance at top speed, Sylvia Bradshaw, formerly Eden Brown, turned the steering wheel ninety degrees and slammed on the brakes. The ambulance began to roll.

FIFTEEN

I came to the art of policing late in life, after a stint in the Air Force and then more years than I care to remember as a used-car salesman for my ex-brother-in-law. I was in my mid-thirties when I decided I'd had enough of that and, with the encouragement of the long-time sheriff of Prophesy County, Elberry Blankenship, I went to the police academy and came back to town to become a fully-fledged deputy. Dalton Pettigrew and Jasmine (then) Bodine, both in their early twenties, were already on the job. I'm just saying all this because for the twenty-odd years I've been with the department, those two were always there. We've had others come and go but Dalton and Jasmine were fixtures. So it sorta came as not so much a surprise, not even a disappointment, but more a sweet sadness when Jasmine told me that after her medical leave was up she wouldn't be coming back. She wanted to be a stay-at-home mom, a wife who cooked, room mother at Petal's school, all those things she couldn't do working full time and not knowing what her hours were going to be on a given day. I understood. The thought of being a stay-at-home dad was appealing to me.

So it was gonna be just me and Dalton, and Anthony, of course. But so many people were gone now. Sheriff Blankenship, who I replaced, old Mike Neeley, who moved off years ago to Dallas and Nita Skitteridge, Anthony's cousin, who'd taken the road Jasmine was on last year. And, although Holly kept saying she was coming back after her maternity leave, who knew whether she really would. It's hard to leave a newborn, even if it is with its grandma. And of course, we'd lost Anna.

Anna Alvarez had disappeared. We'd sent out ads to replace Nita Skitteridge as far away as Dallas and Houston – maybe she'd seen one. And where better to hide than in a small county like ours? Nobody could find her, though I must admit, after I got more info out of Laredo, I really didn't try very hard. Seems the real Anna Alvarez did die in the line of duty down there on the border of Mexico. Happenstance being what it is, she happened to die the same week her twin sister, April Alvarez, was indicted for computer fraud, which is another way of saying she hacked into some places she wasn't supposed to hack into. If Holly decided to stay home with her baby, I might put a little more juice into finding Anna – or April, or whatever. She'd have to change her name again but she was real good on the computer. Just saying.

Holly followed up on the trails Anna/April had left for her on the computer. Some interesting points were that Eden Brown was raised on a farm in west Texas, the oldest of three girls, and the one her daddy designated as the boy. She did all the grunt work, fixing farm equipment and such, and was her daddy's partner on hunting and fishing trips, which sorta took care of the cut brake lines and the good shot part of the scenario. Holly was also able to find out enough on Eden Brown's whereabouts for the crucial times to send her back to jail for a good long time. Brown pled guilty to keep the death penalty off the table, but she wouldn't be seeing daylight – at least not in my lifetime.

I called Bob Huntley, Judge Norman's bailiff, to let him know the outcome. 'Eden Brown,' he said. 'I remember her. Real bad burns. Lost a baby. But Dave let her off easy – three years in a burns ward. A better burns ward than she'd have gotten on her own dime, that's for damn sure!'

But Eden Brown had admitted that she came out of rehab intent on killing Judge Norman. He was the one who let the sheriff's department off scot-free; the one who sent her to prison. But after she'd killed him, she knew it wasn't enough.

The DNA swab had proved to be Eden Brown's. When asked, she said she'd spilt some of the flour Miz Pettigrew had on the counter and used the broom to brush it up. Since she had very little feeling left in her hands and face due to the burns, she never even noticed she'd been pricked by a splinter.

'Hey, Sheriff, I told your deputy to give me five minutes alone with whoever killed Dave, but seeing as how I've never hit a woman in my life, I don't really want to start now.'

'I hear you,' I said. 'She won't be out for a long, long time.'

'Guess that's the best I can hope for.'

'One other thing, Mr Huntley—'

'Call me Bob.'

'Milt. Anyway, you know John and Reba Connors?'

'Yeah, I do,' he said, his voice a real cautious monotone.

'Could you look into it and see if they're getting disability from the county? I mean, the man's seriously brain damaged and Reba, well, Reba is pretty much a basket case.'

'I'll look into it, Milt. I guess I didn't realize how serious it was.'

'Yeah, it's pretty damned serious.'

'I'll get on that right away. Dave was real fond of Reba, as was I. She was a good woman.'

'Sorry about your loss, Mr Huntley. Let me know if there's anything the department can ever do for you,' I said.

'Does that include traffic tickets?'

Feeling it was just a joke, I laughed and hung up.

Jasper Thorne had two broken ribs and a broken wrist, all of which only kept him in the hospital overnight. He was home the next day with his wife taking good care of him and demanding of the hospital that his next partner be male. Why she thought a man would be less likely to want to kill Jasper was beyond me. Hell, just looking at him made me want to kill him half the time.

We found Nick Permeter and his pick-up truck close to my house,

the pick-up half in the creek that flowed down Mountain Falls. He
was drunk as a skunk and, try as he might, Anthony couldn't find a
weapon on him. Instead of putting his ass back in jail, I told Anthony
just to take him home to his women. The least we could do.

The vacationers in Oklahoma City all came back, and I wouldn't
say that Miz Pettigrew was the happiest one to see her home. My
wife said she thought about kissing our hardwood floors. And then
she did something I'd been hoping she'd do for the last several
months: she kicked my sister out of the kitchen. I knew Jean was
gonna keep me on a diet but it was better than the one I'd been
on with Jewel's cooking – mainly not eating anything.

The only person who seemed reluctant to come home was my
son. At first I thought it was because he was gonna have to go
back to school. But when he asked me, 'Daddy, when did you
know you loved Mama?' I changed my mind. I showed him a
picture of Eden Brown, aka Sylvia Bradshaw, and asked him if
this was who he'd seen at the window the night of the ice storm.

'Oh,' he said, looking at it. 'Ah, I shouldn't have said that.'

'Said what, son?' I asked.

'That it looked like a monster, or somebody wearing a monster
mask. I mean,' he said, taking a deep breath, 'this lady can't help
it that she's got those scars, Dad.'

'You're right about that, son, and I'm proud of you for those
thoughts, but the one thing she could help was not trying to kill
everybody in sight.'

'Why'd she do it, Daddy?' he asked, still looking at the picture
of Eden Brown.

'Well, son, I think she just went a little crazy. With all the
physical pain from the burns and all the surgeries she had to have,
and then the mental pain because she lost the baby she was carrying,
I guess she just went a little nuts.'

He looked up at me with those big eyes so like his mother's
that they sometimes give me a shiver. 'I'm real sorry all that
happened to her, Dad, but why'd she think it was y'alls fault?'

'It was a raid. We'd heard about that new meth lab and we were
doing a real crackdown on those start-up labs back then, trying to
nip it all in the bud, so the whole department was out there. Lights
and sirens. Guy just got spooked, I guess, and zigged when he
shoulda zagged. The whole trailer went up with that lady inside.'

He shook his head and handed me back the picture of Eden Brown. 'I'm not so sure I wanna go into law enforcement, Dad,' he said. 'I think maybe I'll be a doctor, like Mom.'

'That's not a half-bad idea,' I said, ruffling his hair and thinking that retirement I'd been looking at would have to wait a couple more decades.

And I talked to both my wife and Anthony about him getting some sessions with her to talk about all that had happened to him since he'd moved back to Prophesy County – the whole mess with the Connors and his wife and baby being hurt by our nut job. Anthony was reluctant at first, but when I said I really didn't want to make it a condition of keeping his job, he relented. I was able to get the county to pay for it, not telling them which deputy it was, just saying that maybe all of 'em needed a little counseling after what they'd been through. They agreed to one at a time.

And so it goes. One day at a time in our little town. Some days are golden and some are bat shit crazy, but it keeps us on our toes.

Lightning Source UK Ltd.
Milton Keynes UK
UKOW04f0606210118
316484UK00002B/7/P